THE
SERIES

LUST

CARMEN ROSALES

PREFACE

The sons of Kenyan just take what they want and who they want. The combination of their wealth, influence, and hostility makes them a serious threat.

When it comes to getting his hands on Gia, Dravin will literally do anything. He's after her, but he has a secret that no one outside the Order knows about. What will Gia do when she finds out? Give in to her desires, or be the sacrifice?

Jess is fleeing from a dark past. Her inner demons may be dark, but they all have names.

When she runs into members of the Order, they tried to break her but they didn't realize she was already broken.

Reid and Valen are both dangerous, sinful, and enjoy a challenge. They begin to feed on Jess's lust for desire.

After one taste, they can't stop.

Gia and her roommate Jess have realized they are Prey in a dangerous game of seduction.

There is only one way out: play the game or change the rules.

ALSO BY CARMEN ROSALES

Delilah Croww

Whispers in the Dark

Circle of Freaks

Lovers Fate

Erotic Quill Publishing, LLC
3020 NE 41st Terrace STE 9 #243
Homestead, Fl. 33033

www.carmenrosales.com

ABOUT THE AUTHOR

Dear Reader,

The triggers include depression, death, suicide, acts of violence, and acts of bullying. All sex is for the enjoyment of all characters involved. This series touches themes that might be triggering for some readers.

If you or know anyone you know that is suffering from mental health and needs help. Please call National Suicide Prevention Lifeline.

PROLOGUE

GIA

"WHAT'S WRONG?" Jess asks me. We are back at the dorm after a full day of classes.

"I need to talk to you. I need to talk to someone, but I don't know who to talk to."

Jess gets up and gives me a hug, wrapping her arms around me. "What's wrong, Gia? Tell me. Did something happen? Did someone hurt you?"

"Yes, to the first and no to the second," I sniff.

"What's wrong?"

My eyes close and tears escape running down my cheeks. "I'm pregnant," I blurt into her shirt, making a wet spot.

"What?"

I raise my head and sniff. "I'm pregnant."

"Shit," she mutters.

She sits down on the edge of her bed and holds her curls tight on top of her head. "Yeah, I get it. Double fuck." She lifts her legs, sits crisscross, and pats the bed so I can sit beside her.

I sit and rub my face with my forearm. "What am I going to do?"

"First off, are you sure? These things can be false positives, you know."

I pull the paper out of my coat pocket and hold it up. It is from the clinic.

"Blood doesn't lie. I started the pill, but I was too late. I wanted to give myself time but didn't think, and now I'm done."

"Done? No way. You have the hottest guy on campus who is crazy in love with you. He's a little off and intimidating but rich as fuck, and you have his kid growing inside you. It's a win-win in my book."

"Yeah, you forget that he is one of the sons of the Order."

"Yeah. I get it, but—"

I interrupt her. "It means I have to marry him and he controls my life. If he wants to cheat on me, he can, and I can't do shit about it. He can do whatever he wants. I would be his slave, and I wouldn't have a choice. They have everything at their disposal. Even if I move to Greece to escape them, I'm sure they have a member there, too. They're like the fucking Illuminati."

"That's a myth, by the way."

I raise my hands and place them on my head. "Yeah, but these people aren't, Jess."

She lowers my hands and places them on my lap. I wipe my face with a tissue she picks up from the tissue box. I sniff and take a deep breath to calm my nerves down. I've been feeling emotional and crappy. I have mood swings, and the smell of certain colognes makes me gag—except Dravin's. His scent calms me down, if anything. It is like the child growing inside me recognizes him and knows.

"You need to tell him, Gia. He needs to know."

"I know, but I'm afraid."

"Don't be. He will be happy."

"Except I have the feeling the others won't be. Like Veronica."

Jess snorts. "I'll handle that bitch. Trust me. She has bigger things to worry about."

"How's that?"

"That's another story."

There is a knock at our door, and I try to quickly compose myself while she opens it. When she opens the door wider to see who is standing there, I sigh in relief. It's Reid.

"Hi," he greets Jess. Then he peers in the door and sees me. I give him a watery smile. "Hey, partner."

His eyes narrow because he sees me crying. "Tell me," he says in a stern tone.

"It's nothing."

He points and looks at Jess. "Tell me," he repeats.

"She's pregnant," Jess blurts.

I lie flat on the bed with a thud. "Thanks a lot, blabbermouth. Now he's going to run back to the fort and tell the puppet master."

Reid walks over and looks down at me with a knowing grin. There is something different about the way he is staring at me. My heart beats wildly, like when a cat catches a mouse or a tiger pins down a gazelle. He tilts his head and gazes down at my stomach, then picks up the paper I have clutched in my hand and reads it. His eyes scan through the test results. He chuckles like in a horror movie, and Jess looks at him like, *What the fuck?*

His dark eyes meet mine, and he says, "Welcome to the Order."

CHAPTER ONE

GIA

I'M en route to Dravin's house. When Reid found out I was pregnant, he made me feel very uneasy. The emotion that crossed his face as he saw me crying sent shivers down my spine—the kind of shivers you feel when watching a scary movie, and you can imagine what the starring characters are going through.

Reid walked closer, watching my tear-stained cheeks, and then he smiled sinisterly and gave me the expression of a man hiding a secret about the future. Like a predator that hasn't shown its true colors, and it's too late to walk away after you're caught in a cage.

So, I assume they all take their Prey seriously. Dravin explained to me the ways in which the Order exerts its influence to achieve its goals. The basics of it all, yet I know there is more. He was just brushing the surface.

When I open the door to leave the building, a blast of icy air rushes in, and I wrap my winter coat more tightly about me. Temperatures are dropping, and the thought of my unborn child causes tears of unease to form in the back of my eyes. Where have I gone wrong? You'd think a guy like Dravin would try his hardest to prevent me from falling pregnant so soon. I know it's also my fault for not taking the proper precautions, even if he is what I want for my future. You can't help yourself when you fall in love. It blinds you when you're trapped in the feeling. That person is all you think about. He becomes the first thing you think about when you wake up and the last person you think about when you fall asleep. They become everything. They consume every waking moment. He consumes every waking moment.

To this day, I still remember what Dravin's dad had to say

about raising a child that belonged to Dravin, but I didn't think he meant right now. When he said, "after graduation," I assumed he meant somewhere in the far future.

To be honest, at first, I thought a guy like Dravin would lose interest in a girl like me. I love the flowers, the letters, and the sex. What girl wouldn't? Obviously, from the attention he gets around here, I'm not the only one who would have fallen for him or has fallen for him.

I'm scrolling through my phone to order a ride-share when I hear the rumble of a motorcycle getting closer. I look up, and it's a black-and-red sports bike coming toward me, the exhaust causing a small cloud of smoke against the cold air. The rider is wearing all-black gear, including the helmet and visor. My heart begins to race as the rider revs the engine.

I raise my shoulders at the piercing sound as it assaults my ears. The leaves that have fallen from the trees are scattered around from the force of air emitted from the exhaust. The biker is riding on the walkway, not caring if it leads into the building.

After a few seconds, the rider cuts the engine and I take a step back, not knowing who is riding the powerful bike. Rather than going back inside the building to safety, I stand there frozen, not moving. Wondering whose face is under the helmet. His body is completely covered, not giving anything away, and I can't help but be curious.

After careful inspection, I found that the bike resembles a professional racing motorcycle—the kind you see on TV in Europe. Since the rider's face is obscured by the helmet, I have no idea who he is, but based on the sartorial choice of jacket and trousers, which are tailored to fit over wide shoulders and powerful thighs, it is obvious that the rider is male.

I take a deep breath and try to shift away from where I am staring at the unknown rider, but my legs are immobilized. I ignore the chill in the air as I watch the guy place his feet on each side of the motorcycle between his knees, then remove his gloves. As I release my breath and gaze down at the tattoos on his knuckles, I recognize the tattoos across the skin of his hands when he pulls the last covered finger. *Dravin.*

"What are you doing here? I was just about to go to your house."

He takes off his helmet, his hair tousled, but he doesn't care. In fact, he probably wouldn't care if it were sticking up in a funny manner. Dravin always looks amazing, no matter what he wears or how he wears it. Some people are just lucky that way.

He looks directly at me, and his attitude is gloomy and impenetrable. An odd feeling snakes up my spine. There are times he acts differently around me. He is quiet, reserved, like he is watching me, studying me. I'm not always sure he's the one who's been sending me letters and flowers. It's as if he were two distinct people in one package. He baffles me. As much as he piques my interest, he terrifies me. Sometimes.

"Are you sure about that?" he asks.

I nod. "Yeah, where else would I be headed to?"

He holds his helmet and gives me a side grin and chuckles, folding his arms over the gas tank of the bike and turning his head in my direction.

"What's so funny? I need to talk to you. It's important."

I want to snap at him, but I know it won't help him listen to what I have to say any better. It's unclear how he'll react to the news. How angry will he be? Disappointed? Tell me to go fuck myself. Be happy.

"What do you need to tell me that you're running off at sundown alone looking for me at my house without calling anyone to take you?" he scolds.

"What I have to tell you cannot wait," I retort.

The trembling spreads to my hands, and I release a puff of air through pursed lips, mimicking the appearance of smoke.

My hands keep trembling, and he picks up on it. A tense shiver can fool him into thinking it's the weather outside, but the truth is that I'm rather anxious.

What's the best way for me to break the news that I'm expecting? I did the math and won't start showing until after graduation, which is why I really don't want anyone to know about it.

Because it would officially initiate me into the Order, I had no intention of informing him until at least a month later. In case I miscarry. I read that first-time pregnancies could result in miscarriages.

Initially, I was hesitant to be with him because he belonged to the Order, but then I remembered the baby. It's too late. I'm too late to make that kind of decision—not because of the baby, but because I love him. I'm in love with him. There is only one way to move, and that is forward… with him.

"Get on," he says in a stern tone.

"What?" I ask, shaking my head. He can't be serious. I have never been on a motorcycle before. I shouldn't because of my condition, but it's not like I can blurt it out right here, right now.

"You heard me. Come here." He waves at me with his helmet so that I can step closer.

When I walk up, his eyes roam over my jacket. "Zip that up, and let me place the helmet over your head," he instructs.

"I don't know how to ride, and I don't think I should," I say instead. I can't tell him right now, in front of the dorm hall.

Watching him on his motorcycle reminded me of the day I first arrived at Kenyan and saw him for the first time. He was holding a helmet while pointing me in the right direction. It was apparent he rode a motorcycle, but the helmet he was holding at the time was different.

After I zip up my winter jacket like he instructed, he places the helmet over my head and fastens the chin strap. The helmet is a bit loose, but he fixes the problem and opens the visor so I can see his eyes: one light and one dark.

He motions with his fingers to the right side of the bike. "You see the pegs?"

I nod, breathing in the scent of his cologne coming from the pads inside the helmet. His voice sounds muffled because of the helmet padding against my ear, and I take a deep breath and listen to his instructions. You would think it would smell of sweat, but it smells of ocean breeze and him.

"You place one foot on each side and you wrap your hands around my waist and do not let go," He instructs. "Make sure you keep your hands on tight, alright?"

"Okay," I say, loud enough so my voice doesn't sound muffled.

Once he puts his gloves back on and fires the engine, revving the gas, the sound is more bearable with the helmet on. I place my right foot on the peg and hold on to his shoulder, swinging my leg over the back seat until I'm fully seated.

He slides his leather gloved hands over my fingers that are locked over his leather jacket at his waist.

He caresses them, and I like the feeling of being this close to him wrapped around his body. My spine is tingling with anxious anticipation when he turns the key in the ignition and starts up the bike.

As soon as I hear the click of the clutch, I brace myself since he is shifting gears on the motorcycle. Shortly after he sets foot on the road, I open my eyes and see the road underneath us, like the massive belt of a running machine.

The asphalt on the road is going at a breakneck pace. He's not reckless, but traveling 50 mph on a motorbike is different from doing so in a vehicle. Every one of your senses is amplified, and you feel every gust of wind and bump on the road. The only things that count are your emotions and the events occurring around you at the moment. I can simultaneously hear the machine whirring between my legs and feel the firmness of his muscles as I lean against his back. As if there is no separation between us. Danger right below but safe above having him in my arms.

After ten minutes, I glance to my left and see that we are no longer on the street where Dravin lives. He takes a corner into a street I'm not familiar with, but I can see immediately that the homes there are grander and more spacious. Partially obscured by tall gates and high walls.

A greater sense of foreboding as we pass each gate. These residences are more like estates, complete with massive gates and tall hedges on all sides.

Trees moan and swing as they shed their leaves. My jacket isn't protecting me from the wind's icy sting, and I don't feel Dravin tensing up or shivering in the chilly wind. Therefore, his suit must be designed for this kind of weather.

I'm relieved when the black iron gate swings open toward him as he slows down. He waits until there is enough room for the bike to pass through without having to wait for it to completely open. The sting of the chill is quickly getting to me.

A dark-gray stone walk leads to double doors of a house that gleams gold from their windows. The outside wall sconces give forth the same warm light as the inside ones, but they are powered not by bulbs but by fire. To my right are six black garage doors.

After the left garage door is entirely open, there are seven more bikes in a row, different brands and models, their beautiful paint jobs glistening beneath the glow of the garage lights.

He taps my leg, which I take to be a signal to get off, and then he extends his arm out, palm up, to help me maintain my balance as I swing my leg over.

Once I am on solid ground, he drives the bike forward and parks it inside, moving the kickstand with the heel of his boot. My eyes look around the massive house, taking it all in.

Once the engine is switched off, the stillness engulfs me. The silence mixed with a small ringing in my ears from the loud bike. He walks over to where he left me standing, the sound of his boots over the cobblestone driveway, watching me fumbling with the chin strap.

His gloves are removed, and his warm fingers glide over mine, and he undoes the strap. He squeezes his fingers over my freezing hands and his lips curl down into a grimace.

He quickly lifts the helmet off my head, and my hands fly to pat down the strands that stick up. I run my fingers over the long tresses of my hair, noticing they are slightly knotted from the ride over, but not too bad.

I'm about to ask him whose house this is, when his voice floats back over from placing his helmet on a shelf in the garage. "Let's get you inside. It's getting too cold out here."

"Where are we?" I ask.

He looks around, and his countenance is unsure. For some reason, I can't quite place it. Something seems odd with his attitude. In some ways, it is him, but in others, it isn't. To me, he still looks the same. He has the same gait but a very different demeanor.

The Dravin standing before me is not the Dravin I know; he seems possessed. In my opinion, this is not the same Dravin I fell in love with. This is a rare side of him I've only seen a few times, but trying to get to know him better, I didn't give it much thought. I constructed the reason for his actions in my mind as him coming to grips with the evil that lurks within him. There is clearly something sinister inside him, if I had any doubts before. Something about him appears threatening. Dangerous.

Looking at his brighter left eye, I see that the right one is as dark as a storm at sea. It reminds me of the moment before a thunderstorm breaks out when the first black clouds roll in and the lightning strikes the water. Illuminating the dark depths.

He leans in toward me, his gaze fixed on mine. "You said you were on your way to my house." He points to the entrance. "This is my house."

Incredulity makes me raise an eyebrow. *What the fuck?*

My throat clears and my chin goes up. "You know the house I was talking about. Stop attempting to screw with my mind; I have no idea how many homes you have. You should have said something if you're in a grumpy mood; then I wouldn't have gone with you when I could have gone back to my room."

His face breaks out in a broad smile. I feel him come closer until his lips are almost brushing mine. He examines my top lip before moving on to the rest of my face and then my jacket.

He's on the cusp now of bringing our lips together; I need only to sway a centimeter for our lips to connect. Damn him. He makes me weak. When I'm with him, I totally lose my sense of reason.

"You know what I meant, Dravin," I whisper.

The tip of his tongue peeks out of his mouth. He tilts his head like he is going to devour my lips in a single kiss, but he doesn't. "You're right. I am in a mood, but it has to do with me not being inside of you. I want you on my bed with your legs spread out while I decide which way I'm going to fuck you with my tongue and then how I'm going to feed my dick to your pussy."

The movement of his thumb causes my chest to rise and fall. My thighs clench, trying to catch the drip of my arousal as it slides down my thighs while the cool air fans the heat breaking out all over my skin.

His thumb pulls my bottom lip, exposing my teeth. "Such a pretty mouth. There is nothing I want more than to keep you in my bed."

"I am in your bed. I practically live in your bed."

I'm more in his bed at his house than my own dorm room. Sometimes, I miss Jess, but then Dravin is inside me, filling me. Making me forget that I'm in college and that it's my senior year. It's like my future doesn't exist. Only the present. When I'm with Dravin, nothing else matters except us.

"This is my father's house."

He brought me here. Why?

"Why?" I ask.

He knows that I'm asking why he brought me to his parents' house.

His thumb slides across my bottom lip. "Why not?" he counters.

I shiver with eagerness. He brought me here to sleep with him in his bed at this house, but I didn't come with him to have sex. I came to tell him that I'm pregnant.

CHAPTER TWO

JESS

SHORTLY AFTER GIA LEFT, Reid was texting on his phone, possibly alerting Dravin that she was on her way. From the moment we met, Gia has been one of my closest friends. In truth, my only friend.

I'm from a boring tiny town in Ohio where the only exciting event is the football game. It's uncommon for girls who live on the outskirts of town in trailers to have any close friends. Well, the good kind. The type of friends that don't get into trouble.

Living in a trailer park, those types of friends don't exist. Why? They've earned a bad reputation as people who aren't deserving of reverence. Unless you have money. Then everyone is your friend.

The child who lives in a trailer with her single mother receives little notice from the outside world. Most people automatically assume that someone who lives in a trailer park is either a drug user themselves or the child of someone who is. Once that child grows up, it doesn't mean they won't look at you differently or feel sorry for you. It just means you're just part of the cycle, and it starts all over again.

"Are you coming later?" Reid asks as he looks at my night-stand, acting like he is interested in anything I keep there.

He turns his head to the side, watching me as I sit on the bed cross-legged like a lion, ready to pounce.

When he asks whether I plan to drop by later, he means for sex. Sorry to be the bearer of bad news, but the answer is no. I had sex with Reid twice and once with Valen, all in the same room, albeit never at the same time.

I have my limits. My reasons for wanting it, but then I have my guilt. The only way I am able to cope with it is to separate emotion from sex.

It was a hard lesson to learn, but after high school and what I went through with the boy I had a crush on since eighth grade, I'm viewed as less than worthy.

Listening to Gia and what she had to say about the secret society called the Order and what Dravin told her, I was intrigued but also scared.

They consider us outsiders. *Prey*. Gia has nothing to worry about because she has the attention of one of the sons of Kenyan, and he will destroy anyone who touches her or breathes the wrong way in her direction.

She has people who care about her in her corner, including me. Reid and Valen are obviously close to Dravin, and they take care of who they consider to be their own. And right now, that includes Gia.

As for me, these people can try to break me, but they haven't figured out I'm already fucked up and broken. Sex is just a way for me to forget what they did to me back home.

What falling for a guy without thinking can cost you, but he showed me what I meant to him. How they all saw me. How everyone that finds out where I came from will see me. They will judge me. They will hurt me. They will try to destroy me. And now, prey on me.

I notice Reid pretending to be interested in going through my stuff. It's as if you're pretending to be interested in what you're looking at by caressing it and stroking it again, but your attention is elsewhere. My favorite string bracelet, which he is caressing without realizing it, is usually hidden from view.

It was the first friendship bracelet I made, hoping to find a friend when I was twelve. I had enough materials to make two, but no takers. I was planning to give one to Gia since we have stuck together and we get along.

I watch him as he holds and stretches it and I reach out to

snatch it from his grasp before he ruins it. After I tell him that I'm not interested in his offer. Who knows how he will react? I'm not afraid of Reid or anyone who goes to Kenyan. I've already met with evil. I know how it deceives. How it dances.

How it takes.

How it feeds.

"I don't think that is a good idea."

His eyes flock to mine like two dark orbs pinning me to my bed. He tilts his head, raising his brows in surprise. I don't think anyone has denied Reid before.

"Why?" he asks.

I lick my lips nervously, turning the black string of the bracelet with my fingers. Rubbing it with the pads of my thumbs. The silence, beginning to stretch like an invisible band between us, is ready to snap.

"I'm not going to have sex with you. I'm not interested in complicating things."

His nostrils flare and he yanks the bracelet from my fingers, making me flinch. When I try to reach for it, he leans close until our eyes are on the same level. When I think he is going to give me back the bracelet, his lip curls in a menacing smile.

My heart sinks when he lifts the bracelet with one hand and takes his fingers from his other and pulls it, snapping it in half. I blink back at the sudden rise of tears.

His look is stern and unyielding. The two pieces of thread fall from his fingers like something filthy you want to get off your hands. I hold back the wrath that is boiling to the surface of my skin, ready to spill from my mouth. I know to him it's trivial—a stupid piece of string made by a twelve-year-old.

It isn't the kind you find in a store or even in a market. But to me, it means more. Like a diamond tennis bracelet. Something I feel proud of because I made it. Something no one could take away from me.

He leans close. His tone is deep and ominous. "You're right. Come to think of it. Garret was right. You are a bad lay."

He leaves the room without turning around to look back. I feel like he's trying to cut me in two with his words. To hurt me. But all they do is remind me that he isn't different from the rest. He sees me as nothing.

Unworthy.

Easy to destroy.

It's what they all think of me. I'm just used to it.

CHAPTER THREE

GIA

I FOLLOW him through the door of his parents' home. A place he has never taken me aback, until now. I find it odd that he hasn't taken me here before. The times I have met up with him or slept over, it is always at his house one block over.

My intention was to tell him at his house where we would have privacy. Away from prying ears, like his father or any other staff, they must have been working here because there is no way they do not have any staff on hand. This place is enormous. Like an old museum. There is elaborately carved wood paneling on half of the walls. High windows. As I peer through the thick scarlet drapes, I take note of the five ornate chandeliers that hang low from the ceiling, each emitting a warm glow like candles that make it clear that the Bedfords are fond of low lighting. There's a spooky air of darkness and silence about it.

A piano sits to the right of the main window, which looks out over the front lawn and the enormous fountain guarded by a gargoyle. Gee, not only would it be a fun addition to your Halloween decorations, but it also gives off an air of eerie presence. It's as though vampires have made their home here—something out of a vampire and werewolves novel. The house smells like wood, expensive carpet, and rich bergamot.

Dravin ascends the grand staircase, which is carpeted in the middle by a red runner and has dark wood steps on the sides. The railings are of the same color with gargoyles on the ends. I'm thankful he makes it easy for me to keep up by going at a slower clip.

Once we reach the landing, there is a long hallway that splits to the left and right, creating two separate wings. At the end, there is a large stained-glass window with a distinct symbol similar to the one on campus. It appears centuries old and is not something you can easily do. He walks past three doors on each side, with lighted sconces in between each room casting a glow.

He finally stops in front of a huge solid wood door and turns the antique handle, swinging the wood door open with a slight creaking sound. He walks in, removing his jacket and I take two steps forward and follow him inside.

This room is very different than his own personal home. It has a king-size bed, but its decor is more classic and even ancient. When he walks in, and I come in a little closer, I can see that the shelves on each side of the wooden desk are stacked with books. The books look like they have been here for quite some time. Like they are first editions and not copies you buy in a local bookstore. Some have leather binding and cream paper that have seen count-less hands smoothing the pages. I had no idea he was a reader or even enjoyed books. From our one-on-one conversations, I assumed he was primarily interested in computers.

As he takes off his jacket and lays it on the bed, removing his tee, I take a deep breath, watching the motion of his body. The rippling effect in his abdominal muscles, resembling the powerful strength of an animal in action, makes me aware of him.

He faces me shirtless, staring at me while I do the same to him, but my eyes are everywhere except his face. Memorizing every dip and groove of his muscles under taught skin, the countless lines and shading of his tattoos.

"I want to talk," I say.

His expression is severe, not in fury but in desire. He has given me this look before, right before he asks me to come to bed so he can touch me. Kiss me. Fuck me.

"Later," he quips.

"It's important," I counter.

"I know, but right now, there is something more important I must do first."

My eyes dart to the left and then to the right looking around his room. The intricate dark wallpaper, the dark wood floors with red carpet under the imposing wood bed with satin sheets.

Unfamiliar.

Cold.

Distant.

His passionate eyes connect with mine, and he strides forward intently like a predator. I take a few steps back until I feel the cold, hard wall near the doorway behind me.

"What are you doing?" I ask nervously.

He would never harm me, yet the expression in his eyes is different. Calculating. When his nose brushes up against my cheek, I get a whiff of his scent. A hint of leather and motorcycle in his cologne. Manly. Intoxicating.

His lips graze the flesh on my lower cheek, jaw, and neck until he reaches the place directly beneath my ear that prompts all my nerve endings to rise on alert. Goose bumps spread on my skin like an avalanche effect, causing my bra to feel tight over my breasts. He reaches and unzips my jacket with skillful fingers, pulling it over my shoulders without taking his lips from my skin.

My heart is pounding in my chest. My lower belly flutters and I don't know if it's because I subconsciously know there is a baby growing inside me or if it's him causing havoc over my body.

He pins me against the wall and slips my jacket down my arms. Having him so near causes a thumping and a lulling in my chest in a rhythm I can't control. It's intense, and my core starts to pool in need, awakening all my senses.

"Do you remember, Gia? Our first time," he rasps.

I close my eyes, remembering the day I sought him out. Mad at him for ignoring me. Mad at him because he was talking to another girl who wasn't me. I ran into his arms and let him have me in front of the fireplace.

I nod and whisper, "Yes. I remember."

When his lips brush the skin just below my right ear, I gasp and maybe even whimper. I feel a tightening in my thighs, consumed by everything, his very presence, from the scent of wood in his room to the tenderness of his kisses to the graze of his teeth on my skin, is entirely seductive.

"You remember how full you were when I was pounding your pretty pussy? How much I loved it when you told me to go deeper, breaking that pussy in."

Oh god. When I close my eyes, I can still feel the sensation of him fucking me so hard that day, I let out a low groan. It only hurt for a few seconds and then he made it feel good right after. He never talks about that day in front of the fireplace. Maybe it's because of the way he acted after. It was both so good and so fucked up.

"Yes," I whisper, wanting him inside me again.

"Did you like it, baby? Do you want me inside you again?"

"I need to tell you something," I say on a moan, trying to tell him what I came to say, but I want him. I want him inside me.

"You can tell me after you spread your legs for me. I want you in my bed." He leans into me, pinning me. His lips hovering over mine. He wraps his hand over my neck. His thumb pressing over my pulse. "In this bed. I don't want to take you soft," he rasps. "I don't want to take you hard."

Fuck. He slides two fingers inside my pants, feeling my wet slit with the pads of his fingers. I moan, arching my back and rubbing myself on them in want. In need.

"I want to take you deep. Deep inside you, so you can remember me."

"I do remember you," I say on a whimper, getting confused. "Always."

He hooks one finger inside my wet folds and captures my lips with his and I'm lost. My purpose all but forgotten and the only thing that is left is the need to feel him inside me. He kisses me deep, stroking his tongue inside my mouth, taking all my breaths, exploring my need for him. Consuming me all over again. We break apart. We come together. Over and over, but it's not enough.

When he finally pulls away, our foreheads are still pressed together, and our breaths are mixed like we're breathing the same air. "I need to be inside you, Gia," he says on a breathless whisper.

He stands back and watches as I take off my shirt, pants, and shoes until I'm left wearing just my lace underwear. Rather than just undoing his pants, he takes off every piece of clothing till he stands nude in front of me. When my eyes flick to his cock, it's standing at attention to the point of leaking. A drop of precum crests on the tip, almost dripping on the wood floor. My tongue snakes out on my lower lip, wanting to be the one to taste the drop of his cum.

Dropping to my knees, I look up while my hand wraps around his thick shaft. I stroke him from root to tip so the bead of cum lands on my fingers, coating my hand to use it as a balm so I can stroke him.

He spreads his hand on the wall to hold himself while he watches me lick my lips and take him inside my mouth on a moan. I have never given him a blow job because I didn't know how, but I secretly watched porn online. When the moment was right, I wanted to pleasure him like he does to me when we are alone in his room.

He groans when I take him deeper, savoring the sweet, salty taste of him. "Jesus."

His other hand slides behind the back of my head while I take him as deep as I can go. His thumb caresses my jaw as tears begin to pool from my eyes.

His lips part, but his bottom lip is pinched between his teeth. "Such a pretty mouth."

Dravin's cock is thick and long and has a slight curve that I love. His piercings roll on my tongue as I slide back and forth, feeling the metal and smooth skin.

The salty taste of him on my tongue explodes as he grunts, fucking my mouth. "Yeah, baby. Just like that. Take it."

I gasp when he speeds up, going deeper with each thrust in my mouth. My eyes dart up and tears stream down my face with each thrust.

His eyes meet mine, as his bottom lip is still snagged between his teeth. The look of pleasure across his face spurs me on, moving faster, but he pulls out right before he comes.

My tongue licks my lips and his eyes darken. He lifts me gently so I can stand, and then he carries me like a bride to the bed. "I need to be inside you," he growls.

My arms wrap around his neck, my cheek resting on his chest, and I breathe him in. He lays me down on the thick, deep-red comforter, pulling the corner so all that is left is the cool red satin sheet.

He lays me gently like a sacred offering, settling between my legs so that my thighs are spread wide. He flicks his finger over the lace of my panties, twirling the fabric and tugging it tight over my skin and ripping it clean off.

He stares at my sex, licking his lips. "Is this for me?" he asks.

I nod, wanting to reach my arms out so I can touch the muscles on his abs and chest. His eyes flick over me slowly until they land on my face. He moves forward, placing the palm of his hand to hold himself up on the mattress while he spreads my dark, long hair over his pillows.

"I love your dark hair over my red sheets and pillows. It's beautiful."

My lips lift in a smile at the compliment. He fists his cock and reaches over to the nightstand and pulls the drawer to grab a condom. I frown because three days ago he didn't use one. What changed? He doesn't know that I'm pregnant but either way, a condom at this point is pointless. I didn't even have time to start birth control after going to the doctor, but he wanted me not to take them.

He doesn't let me ponder it further. He slides the condom on and slides inside me fast, deep as he can go, and I gasp, holding his shoulders like I'm trying to catch my breath.

He closes his eyes and stills inside me. "You're so tight."

I tilt my head up on the pillow and slide my hands down his arms. When his eyes open, I stare, lost inside their depths at the feel of him inside of me. Filling me. Full of him.

"You're so big," I say on a breathless whisper.

He grins. "Say that again."

I smile and he hovers over me, his lips over mine, waiting for me to repeat the words. "You're so big," I repeat.

He slides out and then goes deeper, taking my lips between his and plunging his tongue in my mouth, twirling it with mine.

He fucks my mouth with his tongue at the same time his cock plunges deep inside of me, making my orgasm climb. The slaps of our skin echo inside his room while I moan and he groans with each thrust.

He breaks the kiss and looks down at where we are joined. The shaft of his cock rubbing on my clit as he moves in and out. He goes in deeper like he promised. So deep I feel like I'm going to break apart.

"Dravin," I gasp.

He grips my hips and fucks me in a rhythm. The wet sounds we make as his cock drives into me fill the room, like wet slaps on wet skin. I lift my hips off the mattress and he meets me with every thrust. My tits bounce with every stroke, with every pounding assault, until my orgasm reaches its peak, and I scream his name.

"Dravin! I'm coming."

"I know," he says. His cock swells and with one last thrust, he slams into me, spilling inside the condom. "This pussy is mine, too."

My eyebrows rise in confusion. "What?"

What does he mean? He isn't making sense. He slides out of me and ties the condom and moves off the bed to dispose of it, walking through double doors leading to what must be the bathroom. I sit up on the bed and pull the sheet over my breasts, waiting for him to come back in the room.

He strides toward me as he reenters the room, confident with his cock firmly up in the air.

He kneels on the side of the bed and pulls the sheet away from my body. "Don't cover up from me. I want to see you. All of you. Every time I come for you, you spread those pretty thighs for me. Understood?"

I flinch at his cold tone. Why is he acting this way with me? What have I done? I hear my phone go off. He looks down at my jacket, where my phone's ringtone is relentlessly vibrating with the sound. A series of text messages follow, one right after another.

The back of his skull snaps up. The quirk of his brow rises in mock surprise. "Hmm. I wonder who that could be?" He slides off the bed and walks over.

"Give me my phone, Dravin," I snap in a hard tone.

The abrupt change in his attitude toward me has irritated and upset me. Everything about the situation since he picked me up in front of the dorm building has been off. There seems to be a shift. Taking me to his father's home, having sex in this room. His tone just now. The things he's said.

At first, I shrugged it off at him being in one of his moods and then me trying to tell him that I'm pregnant. I would never deny him. If he needs me, then I'm there. I love him. I love the child growing inside of me. He does get moody sometimes, but this is over the top. A cold fear begins to crawl up my spine. He finds my phone yet makes no move to give it to me.

"Give me my phone," I demand.

He tilts his head, and his smile makes my stomach drop. "No. I want to see who keeps blowing up your phone."

He begins to scroll through it, and anger at him invading my privacy has me scrambling off the bed and charging over to where he stands, not caring that I'm naked.

I reach for my phone, and he lifts it away from my grasp and sticks his other arm out to hold me back. I huff and move to the side, reaching out, but it's useless. He is taller and stronger. He slides his thumb, scrolling through the messages with a wicked smile.

"What the hell, Dravin!" I shout.

He lowers his hand and gives me the phone. I take it and see what has him smiling at me like the cat that got the cream. I scroll through the messages and look at him with a frown.

The messages are from him.

> Dravin: Hey, where are you? I was at your dorm and Jess said you left for my house.
>
> Dravin: Raven?
>
> Dravin: Why aren't you answering me? I keep calling you.
>
> Dravin: I'm home and you're not here.
>
> Dravin: Are you ok? Call me back. Text me. I need to know that you are ok. Please, Raven. I'm worried.

I look up, completely at a loss for words. Confused. My hands shake because I don't know what is going on. Is this a dream? Am I hallucinating? Is he crazy?

He walks over to his jacket, slides his phone out and places his phone to his ear. He watches me as he talks to whomever he calls. "I have your little bird," he says, licking his lips. "I must say. She tastes just as good as the first time I popped her little cherry. You did good."

He smiles at me and then hangs up, ending the call and throwing the phone on the bed.

CHAPTER FOUR

GIA

INHALING DEEPLY, I approach him, my nostrils flaring. "Is this some kind of sick joke?"

There's a hardness to his gaze, and I feel a mixture of anger and helplessness at my inability to make sense of the situation. Something is wrong, but I can't figure out what.

"Get back on the bed," he says sternly.

"Fuck you," I seethe.

"Then get on the bed, and I'll show you how to fuck." He leans closer. "How to really fuck. You like it when I fuck you dirty. I can see it on your face and in the way your pussy takes my cock. Nice and deep. Your pretty nipples, begging me to flick my tongue over them while I break you in."

As he approaches, I back up. Tears burn the backs of my eyes like acid, making me feel cornered and defenseless.

He lowers his voice. "I bet your pussy is begging for it right now. The want and need leaking from that tight cunt down your thighs. Whatever happens in the next five minutes, just remember, I will always be here to lick your sin."

I'm scared and so turned on. He slides his fingers between my thighs and I whimper when he feels my cum leaking.

He drops to his knees and I turn my head as he nuzzles his face on my pussy, sucking and licking the cum that has dripped down my thighs.

"Hmm. Like I said, dirty. Just how I like it."

On instinct, my hand slaps him, hard, across his face, but he just laughs. My hand stings in pain at how hard I slapped him, but he only chuckles.

"Get off me."

"I'm not on you."

He stands and his face is dripping with my cum sliding down his chin. He rushes toward me before I have a chance to move away and rubs it on my face. The smell of me smeared on my neck and cheek. Bastard.

He laughs. "Like I said, I'll always be here to lick your sin. To taste you. To fuck you."

The door to his room opens with a slam, and my head turns to see who entered, and my knees give out. They buckle, but he keeps me from falling, lifting and carrying me to the bed.

I scoot up until I reach the headboard, gripping the sheet to cover my body and take deep breaths in shock. In fear.

I point at the two men in front of me with a shaking finger.

He stands and the look of rage that crosses his face mirrors the other. "What have you done!"

"T-there are two of you," I stammer, and blinding hot tears slide down my face as I try to gulp in air.

I sniff, closing and opening my eyes, hoping it's a trick of the light or my mind. Maybe I'm crazy. I close my eyes and then open them again, but it's still the same. Two men identical in every way are standing in front of me. They're twins.

"Dravin?"

"Yes," they both say at the same time.

My hand slides over my hair, trying to find something to touch. It's real. They're twins. Oh my god. I have slept with both of them. Realization dawns. I'm pregnant, and I don't know which one is the father. They lied.

I look up with tears sliding down my face and they are both standing at the foot of the bed.

"I'm pregnant," I blurt.

One of them smiles and then the other. The Dravin I had just sex with gets dressed. You would think the other would be upset, but he isn't. This must be normal for them. They sleep with the same women. I bet they don't even know there are two of them. I wonder who else knows besides his father. All I know is that they all lied to me.

I watch them, trying to find a way to tell them apart, but I can't. They're the same. The tattoos. Eyes. Hair. They even dress the same, but they can act differently. I just saw how the one I just slept with treated me. Different.

I don't know which one is the father, but the first thing that came to my mind was to tell them the result of their sick, twisted game. I'm pregnant. It's all I know right now.

"I'm sorry, Raven."

My eyes pop open, and I speak to the Dravin, who just came in. "I'm not your fucking Raven. Don't you dare call me that. You lied. Both of you. I just… want to get out of here."

"I'm afraid that isn't possible. If you are pregnant, which I'm assuming you really are and found out recently, you belong to us now. I know we lied to you, but you need to understand some things. Rule—"

I interrupt him, fueled by a rage that I can't control. "I don't give a fuck about your twisted sick rules. You can't make me do shit. I feel disgusted and used. I hate you. This isn't love or want. This is sick and twisted and—"

"You will learn to accept it," Dravin interrupts.

"You will learn to accept us because there is not one without the other. We are both the same physically in every way. We both have the same name but spelled differently. One with an *i* and one with an *e* before the last letter in our first name. The baby isn't mine," the other twin adds.

My head begins spinning, piecing things together. So, Dravin is the father. The other one isn't. How would he know?

I throw my hands up and the sheet falls to my waist before I realize it's too late. Shit. I'm so mad.

Both of their eyes land on my breasts. I try to cover myself and they both try to look away. I know they have both seen me naked and made me come more than once, but still.

"And I'm supposed to accept this. I'm supposed to swallow the fact that you two lied to me while fucking me. What now? You pimp me out?"

Both of them whip their heads at me in sync, and it's as if they are clones. They have the same face, tattoos, even their cocks are pierced the same way. There is no way to know which one is which.

Draven pinches his nose, and I can easily see what I just said annoys him. Well, that's too fucking bad. They are both assholes.

Draven lifts his head and is the first one to speak. He places his arm on Dravin. "I'll tell her. It's better if it comes from me."

"Please. Spit it out. How bad could it get? I'm pregnant by a man who shares me with his twin brother for fun."

Dravin winces and his expression looks torn, but that's too bad. He could have been honest with me. They are both crazy, and the one I just slept with is probably even crazier by the way he talked to me a few minutes ago.

"You will marry my older brother. He gets to marry, and I don't. It disrupts the Order because we are one of the three founding families. It's been one of the rules since the beginning. There could only be one to carry it out. I don't marry, but I get other perks."

I cross my hands protectively. "Like what?" I say sarcastically.

"You. I also get you. You will have all of our children. Only you. You get to have us both. Married to one but not to the other. Unless one of us dies. If one of us dies, you have to marry the other. Either way, you get us both."

I shake my head. "That's sick. Why would you share me? What would you tell our children?"

"It isn't. It's what we both have agreed on since we were old enough to understand. Our children will understand there is only one mother. One woman."

"But if I'm married, I have no right to expect you to be faithful."

I can't believe I'm even arguing about this. I'm going insane. Have them both?

"True. But it won't be that way. We both want you." He looks down at my stomach. "Obviously, we do. We can't wait to see you swollen with our babies. No one on the outside who isn't part of the Order would know which one is with you. It's all within the Order. No one will question anything, or they will die," Draven says.

I laugh sarcastically and point my finger between both of them. "So what? I bed-hop?" I shrug my shoulders and raise my chin. "I make a schedule so you can come to my bed at night? Is there a way I can tell you two apart?"

I swallow nervously when Draven walks forward on the side of the bed to my right and Dravin to my left. My heart starts to beat faster, wondering what they are going to show me. If there is a way, how can both of them be so alike in every way? There isn't a piercing or tattoo on one that isn't on the other. If there is, I haven't noticed.

I'm sitting naked under the sheet in the middle of the bed, and for the first time with Dravin, I'm scared. They both see me tense and one brother gazes at the other.

"Don't be scared," Dravin says.

I lower my head, and my fists squeeze the sheet. I need to get out of here, leave, and think. This is all too much.

Tears fall down my cheeks like a faucet that keeps dripping and there is no way to fix it. "I want to leave," I say softly.

"Don't leave," Draven says.

I look to my right at the face I thought was his brother's. "It was you, wasn't it? The first time."

I know it was him and not Dravin. There is a way to tell them apart, and it's when you let them fuck you. They treat their woman differently in bed. When they touch you—it's different. One is pure sex, and the other is pure lust. One twin is darker than the other. Dirtier than the other.

"Yes," he says, not denying it.

He looks at his brother on the other side of the bed. "I had you first, and I took your innocence. I should have stopped you that day, but that isn't who I am. I couldn't say no because I was going to have you either way."

My eyes dart to his face, pure anger rising. He is so sure of himself.

"At the time, and even today, you might have had me. But I mistook you for your brother. Every moan and scream was for him and never for you," I seethe.

Draven flinches and hardens his jaw at my words, like the slap in the face I gave him earlier, but I can tell that my words cut him deep.

My head whips to Dravin and I swallow the bile of anger coming on from my stomach from his lies and betrayal.

"Don't cry," he says.

How can I not? He's a liar, and I fell for it—all of it. I swallowed the bet with Veronica and the other stuff, but this is my life. I still have a choice, and I'm making it.

"I'm not marrying you. I don't want anything from you."

He shakes his head. "You don't know what you're saying."

I snort, wiping my face. I sniff and lift my head, looking up at the wood paneling on the ceiling in a room that I thought was his and I laugh at my stupidity. Jess warned me. She fucking warned me. I believed all the bullshit he spilled. The flowers. The letters. It was all a trap. His father's words suddenly haunt me. *Breed.*

My eyes settle on him as he tries to reach for me and I move out of his grasp. "You touch me, and I'll scream," I warn him.

His hand falls and the expression that crosses his face is full of remorse.

"I don't want to be with you. Either of you. I want to be left alone. Please, let me get my clothes so I can go home."

"You can't tell anyone you're pregnant," Dravin says.

I laugh sarcastically. "Do you think after what I just learned I would want to tell anyone my baby is from you? I hate you both."

Draven leans close to the bed. "You can't run from us, Gianna. You belong to us, and you will always belong to us."

I shake my head. "I have a choice, and I'm making it. My choice is to be alone. You two have had your fun. Now go fuck around and prey on some other girl who falls for your shit."

Dravin storms off, leaving the room and slamming the door on his way out. Draven turns his head, gazing at me, his eyes roaming all over my body, sending a shiver up my spine.

"He cares about you, and he is happy when he is with you. Don't take that away from him."

"Is he happy knowing that ten minutes ago, your cock was inside me? Does that make him happy? Does it make him happy that he trapped me and lied to me?"

"He will do anything to have you. If it makes me happy, then yes. As long as it's me and no one else. No one touches you except us." His eyes darken, and I see the evil that lurks inside him. "No one, Gia. I'm the one that gets his hands dirty if someone touches you. Your moans and screams are for us."

"You mean you kill them," I retort.

"If it comes to that, then yes. But for you, I'll do worse. My brother has to carry out the Bedford name as the head of the Order. I'm just the backup. It is why I can't marry anyone unless I have to marry you. I can sleep with whoever I want, and I don't have the responsibility that will fall upon my brother when the time comes. I just have to make sure I stand in for him when needed."

"How long?"

He knows I mean,h*ow long have you been doing this?* He walks over and collects my clothes sans panties from the floor. My panties are on the bed, torn to pieces. I grab my bra, pants, and sweater. I reach to grab the shredded fabric off the bed, but he is quicker and snatches them from the bed. I fall on my back, looking up at the ceiling.

He leans over the bed in my line of vision, holding the fabric in front of me but out of reach. "These are mine."

"They're torn."

He tilts his head. "And?"

"They're trash."

He gives me a side grin. "Not to me," he remarks, stuffing them in his pocket.

"You get off on your victim's panties?"

"Who said I have victims? Not of the female variety. Do you know how many girls would kill to be where you are right now?"

I continue to dress, sliding my pants up my thighs, making sure they are on correctly. My eyes find his when I slide my sweater over my head and glide my fingers through my hair. Cocky much?

"Let me guess, hundreds," I mock, scooting off his big bed. "I must have been number four hundred and ninety-nine."

My feet land on the carpet on the side of the bed and I make my way to place my feet inside my shoes, grabbing the jacket, needing to get the hell out of there.

When I grab my phone, he chuckles. "Funny. Actually, six hundred and twenty-two."

Great, I have a number. I guess I set myself up for that one. I turn to leave, but he grabs my wrist, tugging me to him.

Clenching my teeth, I lift my chin. "Let me go, Draven."

"I will, but I need to ask you something. My brother hates himself right now, but he will get over it, or maybe he won't. He can be moody."

"I don't care how he feels. He is a liar, and so are you," I say through gritted teeth. "Like I said, you had your fun. I have a responsibility to plan for and choices to make."

"Like what? You don't have to worry about anything for the rest of your life. You will want for nothing."

"How about love, trust, honesty?"

He pulls me tighter, and I cringe. He bends his head close with a tic in his jaw. "You don't have to fear me. The only thing you have to worry about is when I come for you. And I will come for you, Gianna. I will take pleasure in your body and I will make sure you like it. Where I come from and in the real world, what you're asking for are complicated emotions that don't exist. What does exist is sex, lust, lies, betrayal, and greed. My brother and I are guilty of all of that. I know you're upset, and I get it. But don't think you have power because you carry a Bedford in your belly because you don't." He lowers his voice above a whisper and my legs begin to tremble. "I know Reid, Valen, and Jess know about your pregnancy. I know everything. What you say and when. So be careful, and don't piss me off."

I lift my chin. "Or what?" I challenge.

He bares his teeth. "I will make sure you hurt. There are other types of pain, Gianna. I would never physically hurt you, but make no mistake, I will make you hurt."

"Fuck you."

"I already did, and now I'm losing my patience. I need you to leave. Six hundred and twenty-three is waiting to take me down her throat."

"You're disgusting."

"No, I'm telling you to get the fuck out. I'm done with you. I want a woman who knows what she is doing in bed. I'm wondering how the hell my brother got you pregnant. I figured he would have taught you a few things by now. You need to learn how to pleasure a man and the way things are going, I need someone else to meet my needs."

My lower lip trembles. I don't know why, but his words sting. They shouldn't, but they do. My eyes swim with tears that I refuse to let fall. I rub my lips together to not break in front of him and silently nod, stepping back.

I grip my phone in my hand and scroll to the app, ordering an Uber to pick me up outside his gate.

I was floating in a cloud, thinking that the news of my pregnancy would be my biggest worry. I thought he was Dravin when he came on his motorcycle, but he knew. They all knew. I thought the looks I was receiving from people who are part of the Order were because I had Dravin's attention, but it was bigger than that. This is over. Whatever we had—is over. They broke me. He broke me. They deceived me. I'm trapped.

CHAPTER FIVE

JESS

I HEAR our dorm room door swing open and Gia comes inside crying. Fear claws inside my belly. Something happened.

"What happened?"

In my arms, she sniffs and cries. I hold her close, rocking her gently back and forth, exactly like my mother used to do for me when I was a victim of bullying at school and had to come home to lick my wounds. Holding her close and without speaking to her, I move her black hair off her face.

After twenty minutes of rocking her slowly while seated on my bed, I whisper, "Shh. It's okay, Gia. Tell me when you are ready. Tell me what happened. What did he do?"

I know this has to do with Dravin. I don't want to push her, but she shouldn't be crying this way. She's pregnant.

She wipes her face and takes a deep breath, her sobs racking her body. When she sees the tears streaking my cheeks, she bursts into sobs and tells me everything.

After she's done, I take a moment to ultimately make sense of what she is telling me.

"There's two of them?" I pause. "Motherfuckers."

She nods, grabbing a tissue from her nightstand and blowing her nose. "Yeah, I know. I've been sleeping with identical twin brothers."

"There is no way of telling them apart?"

She shakes her head. "There is only one way."

I raise my brows, trying to figure it out myself. I don't even know if I've seen the other one.

Intrigued about the whole thing, I ask, "How?"

"When they have sex. It's different. The way they treat you."

I point at her as realization dawns. "Your first time. It was with the evil fucked-up one?"

That's what we dubbed Draven with an *E*. The evil twin or, rather, the crazier one. But in all honesty, they're both fucked up.

"Yes. Thinking about it, when I was feeling like a used whore, I remember that there were two times he used a condom."

"When was the second time?"

She looks up and then averts her eyes. "Today." When she found out, she thought it was Dravin with the me being—hypothetically, the nicer one.

I raise my hand, indicating she doesn't have to give me details. "Gotcha."

She tells me everything he said to her, and I sigh, running my fingers through my hair, squeezing tight on the strands to get a grip on my anger for her and releasing my hair that I straightened with my flat iron.

"Fuck them. Just finish your senior year. You won't even be showing until you graduate, anyway. You can find a good job, and I will help you. I always wanted to learn how to be a mom. I would be honored to be Auntie Jess."

She laughs through her tears, trying to wipe her red nose with another tissue. "Auntie Jess. I like it," she says with a smile.

"You don't need them. Forget about them. We will keep quiet and no one has to know. You don't have to marry anyone. Hey, and about screwing both of them, at least they look alike, and you can't forget their names."

We both stare at each other for a second and burst out laughing. Making light of a fucked-up situation.

"Thank you."

"For what?"

She angles her head and balls the soiled tissue with another one as she tosses it in the trash. "For making me feel better. For being my friend. I don't know how you could make light of all this."

I think about the things I have gone through back home and the only different thing is that she thought it was one brother when it was the other, but at least it was consensual.

She wasn't forced at the last minute and they didn't hurt her. Maybe emotionally, but not physically. These guys enjoy playing mind games and are maybe capable of killing people. Definitely on another level of fucked up, but they aren't rapists, and they don't beat up women. Not from what I have seen; they just like to screw around.

The only thing that is really messed up is that Gia is pregnant and after knowing what she knows, I don't think she is sold on the idea. I know I wouldn't be either bringing a kid into their world.

Look at Dravin and his twin brother. Then I think about Reid and Valen. Let's not go so far, being that Veronica is on a whole other level of fucked up.

"Because that is your power," I tell her, resting my head on the palm of my hand with my elbow on the bed. "If you show indifference, it drives people crazy because they see that they couldn't break you. Even if you care, don't show it because they feed off it. They feed off the fear of emotion. It will be hard at first, but then, like everything else, it will become normal. In their world, hurting people and not caring about how it made them feel is normal to them. If you let it eat you up, it will destroy you."

"It hurts," she says softly, closing her eyes.

"I never said it didn't, but you can't let them see that it hurts. Because if you do, if you let them see the part of you that is damaged, that's when they ruin you."

"What do we do now?"

I told her about Reid and Valen and how Reid asked me to go to Dravin's to sleep with him, which probably included Valen.

I turned him down, and he broke my bracelet. I slipped when I showed emotion when I saw he touched it.

He saw that it meant something to me. And when I said something that hurt his pride, denying him what he wanted, he broke it because he knew it would hurt me in some way. But what he didn't realize was that I had made another one—one he didn't know existed.

"We keep our distance and graduate. They keep secrets and have gotten what they wanted, so they will soon tire of our indifference and move on to the other Prey." I make silent quotations and meet her eyes across the room while we face each other. "They say they don't care, right? That they get what they want and who they want."

She nods.

"Then neither will we. We won't give a shit because we get to choose. We just have to make sure it's not part of the Order to survive."

CHAPTER SIX

DRAVEN

"YOU COULD HAVE WAITED until I was ready to tell her," my brother snarls.

He walks in front of the fireplace in his living room like a caged animal, walking back and forth in front of the fire. The glow in the background illuminates the walls, casting a shadow of his features like my own when I'm upset. I could have waited until he told her, but I couldn't resist when I saw her waiting outside her dorm room, scrolling through her phone. I sometimes pass by her dorm to see if I can get a glimpse of her. It probably makes me a stalker, but I can't help it. She's gorgeous. Her face, the softness of her skin, her tight pussy when I stretch her open, filling her.

When I saw her alone, the only thing I could think of was the urge to take her for a little while. To have her all to myself. It was the same feeling I felt when she came barging into Dravin's house when I was there because my father was fucking the housekeeper on the dining room table.

I couldn't stomach seeing his bare ass as he pumped in the girl spread-eagled on the wooden table while she faked her moans. What girls will do to snag a rich guy.

When Gia came and saw me, of course, she didn't know it was me or that Dravin had an identical twin. She came at me with a furious expression, nervously questioning my actions at the swim meet. It was me that she saw talking to Warren's sister.

My brother needed me to fuck with Warren's head. What better way than to have his sister choke on my cock? Since Warren is a member of the Order, they know we're twins, but she thought she'd scored the older twin. The one destined to be a star. The collegiate athlete and star swimmer. One of the three sons to take over the Order. I'm not jealous of my brother. I could have attended Kenyan, but I'm better at dealing with things my way.

She kept waving at me, and I brushed her off. I was there to help my big brother make a point, not entertain his current interest.

I thought the way she kept rambling when she showed up unannounced was funny. I found it amusing, but I also noticed the curve of her ass and the bow of her pretty mouth.

When she paused before walking out of the front door and then ran back into my arms, I couldn't resist her. I wanted to know what she tasted like. I wanted to know what was so special about her. Why my brother was so taken with her. I wanted a taste of her sweet pussy. I also wondered what it would be like to fuck her, knowing my brother was interested even though, deep down, he couldn't get mad at me.

Besides, if she chose him, I would have a taste of her anyway, or I would have pursued her to get it. It was too easy and I didn't stop her. She was willing and I wanted her. Was it wrong? Maybe.

When I asked if she was a virgin and she said yes, I couldn't resist. I wanted to be her first. Her soft kisses, soft skin, and her legs wrapped around me. I wanted her like my next breath, and I knew at that exact moment that I would do anything to have her.

To be her first was a bonus. My brother was falling for a girl no other man had ever touched and the simple fact lit something inside me that I recognized as possession. If she married my brother, then I would be the man who took the most precious thing from her. Something he could never have. Her innocence. Now, she knows it was me, and the asshole in me loves the fact that she would never forget me even though she thought I was him.

"It's done," I quip.

He stops and glares at me. "It's done," he mocks. "Do you know what you have done? She won't even look at me."

I roll my eyes, waving my hand from where I'm seated on the white cream couch. "She'll get over it. She's pregnant. Where would she go?"

He shakes his head at me like I'm an idiot. "You don't know her like I do."

I snort. "I know her the same way you do."

He pauses and angles his head. "Oh yeah? You think you know Gia. Why? Because you fucked her when she thought it was me?"

My teeth grind together at his jab. He knows what she said bothered me. We both knew she would never want me if she knew the truth before I slept with her.

But maybe that's why I did it. I was jealous when I saw the way she smiled at me, thinking I was him. The way her body responded when she let me take her how I wanted. The way her eyes filled with desire when she had my cock in her mouth. Her soft lips wrapped around the shaft of my dick.

I was jealous, and I wanted her to know it was me and not him that could make her come. That I could make her dripping wet just as much, if not more. When she blurted that she was pregnant, I looked at her flat stomach and secretly wished the child that was growing in there was mine because I put it there. I couldn't wait until she had my brother's child. So I could fill her with mine.

I lied to her, telling her I needed her to leave because I was going to fuck someone else. That she was inexperienced and couldn't satisfy me. I wanted to hurt her like she hurt me and took the coward's way out like a pussy.

I lay my head back on the oversized pillows, letting the jab slide. Arguing about Gia was not getting us anywhere. I was already getting a headache listening to him babble.

Compared to my brother Dravin, I'm colder. Unemotional. Except with her. She didn't deserve what we did, but my father wanted it that way. It was to ensure my brother got what he wanted. He wanted her even if he wasn't wholly in love with her. He was infatuated with her. I think it was more the fact that she didn't give in to anyone but him. When they sat me down and told me his decision, I didn't argue because I secretly wanted her. I wanted to be able to fuck her when I wanted and how I wanted. With her willing, of course.

I take a deep breath and give him a possible solution to his funk. It will also rectify this little ache I have for her. There is only one way to diminish her little power over us.

"She isn't going anywhere, Dravin. Go fuck some other chick and get your mind off of it like you always do."

My phone vibrates and I slide it from my front jeans pocket and open the message to see it's from Reid.

> Reid: Hey, Bedford. Party over at Jeremy's. Members only. Bring Dravin. I think he would like his dick stroked.

I slide my phone in my pocket and my eyes dart to my brother, watching the flames of the fire, lost in his thoughts. "Party at Jeremy's. Members only. Let's go."

He grips his phone, watching me get up as I stand and grab my jacket. "Didn't she say she didn't want you or me? She made a choice. Now, let's show her that her choices have consequences. She knows the rules. What's done is done. We can't go back in time."

His eyes, just like my own, find mine and he nods. "Fine. You're right. I can't lose my head over her or anyone. But I'm still pissed off at you."

Reaching the door and pulling it open with my keys and phone in hand, I turn to him, following me. "You'll get over it when the next chick is on her knees worshiping your cock like you're a god."

I just hope it works for the both of us.

CHAPTER SEVEN

GIA

I'M IN ECONOMICS CLASS, and my eyes sting from crying all weekend. I'm all emotional behind closed doors, but I have to keep a straight face. Whispers from girls have been following me everywhere as they cup their hands over their mouths, giggling like we're back in high school.

I don't know what I missed, but I think it's because they haven't seen me lately with Dravin or the other one when he makes an appearance. Jess and I spent the night researching the mysterious twin, Draven.

We found out that he doesn't even attend Kenyan. He probably shows up when his brother doesn't feel like coming to class or when he has something to do.

The members of the Order look the other way if they realize it's Draven instead of his brother, but I think they just can't tell them apart. You really can't. His parents thought this out very well or maybe his father. All their lives, they have been raised to be alike. To serve a purpose. They live like clones of each other. Disguising themselves as the same person. The same name but spelled differently. The same tattoos, piercings, hairstyle. They probably have the same habits, and they even dress the same. Not exactly, but the same style.

It's why I couldn't pick up on it, even if I suspected.

My stomach clenches, and I'm not sure if it's because I'm pregnant or the giggles and smirks directed my way while the professor lectures. I'm scanning all the people seated in the class below me since the classroom has stadium-style seating, which allows a good view of people scrolling through their phones and messaging each other.

My phone vibrates against the desk in front of me, and a message from an unknown number comes through. I unlock my phone and see that there is a video message.

When I pick up my phone, I lower it in my lap, making sure the volume is all the way down in case there is audio that can be heard. I look up and make sure the professor's back is turned as he writes on the board and read the text on the bottom of the blurred cover photo of the video before I press play.

Anonymous: That was quick. She must have been a bad lay. It was too good to be true anyway. You know how Dravin is once he gets his fill. Poor girl. She probably thought she was special or some shit. I wonder what poem he will write about for the next girl. Or maybe it was his twin brother? #Prey #doublethefun

After reading the words, I frown. My stomach clenches, and my hands begin to get clammy at what I might find. My thumb hovers over the screen, and then I finally press play.

I purse my lips and let out a shaky breath. I watch, and my eyes quickly fill with tears at seeing two young women sitting on Dravin and Draven's laps, making out with their hands all over them. I feel the tears cresting to fall down my cheeks. They go down on their knees and start sucking them off from all sides while the twins grab each girl by the back of their heads as they watch their lips wrap around their cocks. Not wanting to witness this further, I stop the video, knowing it would just make me feel sick. Bastards.

Another text from Jess comes through.

Jess: If you get a video via text, please don't open it.

Too late. I know Jess was trying to warn me so I wouldn't have to see it. At least I know why they are whispering and giggling. My nose burns on the inside, trying to keep the tears from running down. I'm trying to hold in the need to sniff so no one notices that I'm about to cry. If they hear it, they will know I saw it, and the whispers and stares won't stop. It's better they assume I saw it and don't care. We're broken up.

I send her back a text and notice my fingers are now shaking.

> Gia: Thanks, but it's too late. I already did. I saw it.

> Jess: I'm so sorry, Gia. But remember, no emotion. That's what they want. It's what they need.

Determined to not let it get to me, I put my phone away and ignore the stares. When class ends, I gather my things, fumbling nervously, but I manage. I think about what they did, knowing it would get back to me. It's fucked up, but I figure you should expect fucked-up things from fucked-up people. It's up to me to not let it get to me. I should have known better, but sometimes you have to own the shit you get yourself into. Life isn't a fairy tale you make up in your head or read in a book.

Things happen.

People use you.

They try to break you. But one thing I have learned is that's the nature of the beast. Evil doesn't die. It morphs throughout time.

CHAPTER EIGHT

GIA

AFTER A WEEK OF HELL, during which I avoided everything and everyone associated with Dravin, I visited his mother's grave at the cemetery off-campus and laid a solitary red rose over her grave. I wanted to escape from my dorm room and find somewhere quiet where no one would stare or make faces at me. I can only imagine what Jess went through before I arrived.

As the sun dips below the horizon, the sky takes on a warm orange hue against the deepening clouds. Surprisingly, I have not heard from Dravin. I expected his brother to give me the silent treatment, but not Dravin. Reid and Valen are avoiding me, but it isn't like we hang out all the time, and we aren't friends. It just feels weird because they don't talk to me like before. No funny comments or nods when they see me in the quad or cafeteria. It is like nothing happened, and we have never met. Dravin avoids me. No more black roses or letters. No text messages wondering where I went after class or if I wanted to spend the night with him at his house. He hasn't asked how I'm feeling.

When I checked with the professor, he said Reid turned in the assignment and that nothing further was required before winter break since it's the end of the semester. The only person I can talk to is Jess. Aside from going to class or the library, she assures me she has no problem staying in the room with me.

It's embarrassing that I'd rather stay in my room and mope than face them at Babylon or around campus after class. Whenever possible, I stay away from the cafeteria and other crowded areas on campus. I'm not really that hungry anyway and the smell of certain foods makes me feel queasy. I know I've lost weight, but I have read that it can be expected in the first trimester. I've been putting off going to the doctor because it is still early. I will after winter break since most doctors are on vacation for the holidays.

My mother has called me a few times to see how I'm doing. I don't tell her that I'm pregnant, but her words from Thanksgiving dinner ring true when I think about what she said about Dravin. I hate lying to her about my situation, but she would never understand.

However, I did tell her that Dravin and I broke up. I told her we just got ahead of ourselves and wanted to go in different directions. I felt mature in telling her that, but in truth, it is a lot more complicated than that.

"Hi," I say, sitting down with my back against the tombstone, my legs crossed over the other.

My shiny boots glitter like a compact mirror against the setting sun, knowing that any minute, the old bell from the church will ring, indicating that it's six in the evening.

"Funny how I thought I was talking to you about one son, but honestly, your other son appeared once or twice. Maybe more than that. It must have been difficult raising two boys that way. I think you're very brave. I'm not sure of your situation or how you must have felt, but that must have been...hard." I look down and my fingers begin to pick the weeds around the marble, tearing out the ugly strands and pulling up specks of dirt over my black leggings. "I'm pregnant," I whisper softly, a tear sliding down my cheeks. "I thought you should know."

After five minutes of crying, my tears begin to dry up after the bell rings. The leaves blow in the wind. Earthy scents mingle with the chill as night falls. The sky changes colors to a darker hue. The warmth of the sun disappears and the cold begins to set in. Pulling myself up by the tombstone's edge, I wipe the dirt from my hands and leggings. As I stand by the grave and look down, I say my last goodbyes.

When I'm almost to the left entrance, I hesitate. I don't know how I know, but it's Dravin. I can feel his presence. I can feel the shift of energy around me. The danger but safety radiates off of him, like meeting an apex predator and not knowing if he will attack or let you go. I know it's him because this is a place where we have met before. A place where we have shared moments. Moments that were confusing, but they were ours. A place we know if we wait long enough, we will find each other.

He walks closer out of the shadows cast by the pillar against the setting of the sun. His eyes follow my footsteps as I walk through the gate. There are no smiles or words to be said. Only uncertainty. I pass by him with my head bowed and his hands reach out to grip my wrist like a hot iron searing my skin.

His fingers feel like butterflies brushing over my skin. My eyes gently go up to meet his. As he gently raises my chin with his finger, a tear escapes my eye, and I turn my head away from him. All I see are the memories of the lies, the hurt, the betrayal, and the video. How quickly he could move on and forget about me.

"I'm sorry, Gia. Whatever you decide to do. Whatever your decision is, I'll accept it. I'm not going to make you suffer anymore because of me and what I did to you." He looks at his mother's grave for a few seconds. Then his eyes meet mine. "I want you to live your life away from here after you graduate. I'm going to stay away from you, and I'll make sure you have everything you need. My brother will do the same. You're free, Gia. Anything you or the baby need, all you have to do is ask me, and it will be provided."

I snort, wiping my nose and face with the sleeve of my jacket. "That's the solution to everything, isn't it? Throwing money at it so it will go away." I snatch my wrist out of his grasp and his eyes darken.

The Dravin I fell in love with is gone, and in his place is this monster they all fear on campus. The hard lines of his jaw tighten as he grinds his teeth. "It's all I can do right now. I'm trying to make it right."

I nod sarcastically. "Okay. Anything else?"

He moves closer, his lip curling as he lowers his voice. "Yeah, there is one last thing. Don't visit my mother's grave anymore. You're not a Bedford. If you're feeling bad or need anything, you call me, but that's it. And stay away from my brother. It's your only warning."

I shrink back from his words. I try to convince myself that this is for the best. He has no use for me, and the Order has no interest in me if I don't agree to their rules. Now that I'm pregnant, he wants me out of his life and he probably regrets it, but there's nothing he can do about it. Because I can only do things on his or their terms. I knew deep down that he would come to his senses. He doesn't love me. He never did. It was all based on lust.

"Why did you lie? Why did you not tell me you had an identical brother and that I might mistake him for you.?"

He steps back and looks over my shoulder as though considering what to say next. After a few seconds, his gaze shifts to mine and in a harsh tone, he says, "I don't have to explain myself to you. This is what is best for you—for me. You're not cut out for this life. I have to fulfill my family's obligations. Things you would never understand. The only responsibility I have concerning you is the child you carry. I made a mistake, and for that, I'm sorry, Gia. My crush on you clouded my judgment, and I foolishly believed that you were the one for me. I was wrong."

His words feel like poison burning in the pit of my stomach. My heart begins to fold in on itself, mixing with the poison drifting inside of me, killing the beat in my heart that was just for him.

As the temperature outside drops, he tucks his hands under his jacket, and I take it all in. The words, the pain, the lies, and the heartbreak.

I read somewhere that your first love is the love that teaches you the most. It's not when you give your heart away; it's the moment they do something to crush your heart. It's in those moments that the learning really begins. In a split second, it occurs. It's their way of showing you what you mean to them. In my case,

I mean nothing. I was considered a little more than a pawn in a bigger game—a bigger plan.

At first, I just wanted to know what it was like for a moment to be with someone like him. Then, I wanted more. I wanted to know what it would feel like to fall in love with someone like him—the good-looking bad boy on campus who noticed me.

I didn't think.

I fell in love.

I fell pregnant.

And it was all a game.

The only thing that is real is that he doesn't feel the same way I do. The pain of his words, mixed with the all-consuming love I have for him, slowly builds into hate.

Tears well up in my eyes, but I won't cry in front of him. I'll save that for when I'm alone. He fucked me, knowing I'd fucked his brother, knowing I could fall pregnant, and said nothing. They played me and now I'm the sacrifice. If he doesn't want me now, what happens when I give birth to his child? What happens to me? What happens to our child?

My hands ball into fists under the sleeves of my jacket. My back is to the gate, but before I sidestep around him, I want just one doubt in my mind answered.

"What happens when I have the baby? What will happen to me and them when they're born? When you take a wife and have to produce heirs? You could at least have the decency to tell me what I should expect."

His jaw hardens a fraction, but then he relaxes and scratches his chin, looking down at my front, landing on my stomach and then rising slowly. "It's not uncommon to have children and not be married, Gia. I will take a wife and have children with someone worthy of being my wife. One that accepts everything. That child will bear my name and continue my family's legacy. As for you and our child, you will be taken care of and provided for, but the baby cannot have my last name. He or she will not be a Bedford."

He walks closer, and my eyes blur as tears begin to crest on my lashes. His face becomes blurry, like a mirage in a dream, but this is real. He is the ruthless monster they say he is. I tense at his expression, hard and cold, aimed directly at me. I never thought he would be like this after everything, crushing me. He leans forward and lowers his voice. "And neither will you."

My hand lifts, brushing the back of my neck as the meaning of his words slice me wide open and I feel the metal that is hanging from my neck. The necklace he gave me had the raven on it. It begins to burn and weigh heavily against my skin and my chest. I lift my other hand and swiftly unclasp the lock.

From where he is standing, he must think I'm fixing my hair, but one thing I do have left is my pride. I can't beat him by not showing emotion from his words, but I'll learn. He can knock me to my knees, but my strength will bring me back up and every time he is near me, I'll remember how I fell.

My fingers grip the necklace as it slides away from my neck like a heavy brick in my hand. His forehead pinches for a moment and his mouth parts like he is about to say something but stays motionless.

My arm reaches out, the raven dangling under my fist. "You can have this back, along with my feelings, my love, my shame, and my tears. Maybe you can give it to the bitches you fuck, the vulture you are, waiting to catch your next Prey."

I walk closer and open my hand, releasing it to the ground. He watches silently, his breaths coming in and out. The puff of air from the cold is visible from the glow of the lamp by the church.

I lower my voice as he stares at the diamond-encrusted raven on the ground, "Or better yet, maybe you could share it with your brother, and both of you can choke on it. I don't want you to take care of me, I don't want you near me, and I don't need anything from you. I'm dead to you. Once I graduate, I'll leave here, and you never have to see or hear from me again."

I step back and turn, walking back to my dorm room, not

caring if he picks up the necklace or if he is watching me. All I hear is the sound of my feet on the concrete pavement mixed with the groaning of the trees as they sway from the wind like they're whispering secrets. He doesn't call me back or stop me. I may be a pawn in everyone's eyes. However, there is one thing I learned from playing chess with an elderly man when I used to volunteer at a group home back in Wisconsin. He once told me *a well-placed pawn is more powerful than a king.*

CHAPTER NINE

DRAVEN

I'M SITTING in my dad's study, checking through his company's books. In the meantime, while my brother has been away at school and busy with his cybersecurity shit, I'm living in his house. I've been assisting my father with his international acquisitions and business dealings. I seem to have an uncanny ability to locate things, as well as a sixth sense for choosing the best course of action. I seem to have been endowed with a sixth instinct for recognizing a bluff and calling it.

Someday, my brother will join in, but he works in technology and I interact with international leaders behind the scenes. You can't believe everything you see on TV. Families who founded nations are the ones who have the most influence and money, and they are the ones who control the government. Secret hands feed the investors who fund governments, politicians, and the world's largest enterprises. As a matter of fact, we're one of them. There is no one we don't have in our pocket and no one we can't place there if we need to.

My phone buzzes on top of the antique wooden desk that has been in my family for centuries. I look to see it is a text from my brother.

> Dravin: It's done.

> Draven: It's for the best.

> Dravin: Not for me.

> Draven: We can't force her into this life. Look what happened to mom. She didn't take to it very well.

My mother committed suicide, and it was Dravin who found her in a pool of blood in the tub. She was battling depression and my father didn't help. He didn't care about my mother after she had us. It was like there was no use for her. She did what he wanted. She produced an heir, but in her case, she produced identical twins.

Dravin: That was different, and you know it.

Draven: You're right, it was, and this is a lot for someone like her. She's innocent, and we've fucked with her enough. The only thing we can do now is protect her. Her not accepting all of this makes her not only a pawn but a target.

> Dravin: I hurt her. I said things to her I can't take back.

> Draven: So did I. Remember, I had her first.

> Dravin: She wasn't yours to take.

> Draven: That's what you get when you play with your food.

> Dravin: She fell in love with me, not you, asshole.

We keep going at it about her. About who would get her first, but I won. Well, sort of. She hates us both. More me than him. She fell in love with my brother, and maybe that is what set me off; I wanted it to be me. It didn't matter how I felt about her. I wanted her poems, her whispers, and the fire that burned in her eyes when I slid inside her to be for me too. She may have fallen in love with him, but I want her more than anyone. He's worried that he hurt her. He had her love, and what hurt me the most was that I never stood a chance. I also wanted a chance, but I didn't get it, and now I never will.

Draven: Stop rubbing it in, asshole. She hates us both. All we can do is protect her and play the part. No one can find out she is pregnant.

Dravin: I made sure Reid and Valen will keep an eye on her roommate Jess. In case they try to get to Gia through her.

Reid and Valen are the other heirs belonging to the founding families of Kenyan. Most people think there are three, but there are really four. I'm plan *B*. I'm the hidden piece, the ace card up the Bedford sleeve. I'm the insurance policy in case my brother fails or is killed. The irony is that I'm my father's favorite, and Dravin was my mother's.

My mother took more to Dravin when she was alive. She had difficulty agreeing to my father's demands and how he raised us. It was fucked up growing up. I had to watch my mother spiral while my father forced us to live our lives like two clones. Everything we did had to be the same. We were even taught to talk and walk alike. Because I was born seconds after, I can't marry. I can have children if I want, but my father never told my mother it had to be from the future Mrs. Bedford. My brother's wife. Why? Because the Order dictated it since we were the first family and because I wasn't supposed to be born. It's better than death, my mother would say when I found out. Your father and I wouldn't allow it if it came to that.

My mother would talk about a woman who would come into our lives like a Raven. The Raven will accept it and learn to love you both, she would say. I didn't believe her like my brother Dravin did. I thought it was all bullshit, and now there is a Raven, but she only fell in love with one and not the other. The other being me. She also didn't accept.

Some people think the president is the first family, but not in our world. In our world, you're born into it. Like the Queen of England, only one can rule. The rest of the members are the monarchy. There is no election when it comes to the founding families, only bloodlines. Bloodlines that control the world. The rest is a smoke screen. A cover to show the world and make them think they have a right, a voice, but in truth, the Order is the right, and we are the voice. Money makes the world go round, and there is nothing truer than it being the root of all evil.

My phone rings, snapping me out of my thoughts. I pick up my phone and see that it's Veronica. I roll my eyes and answer.

"What?" I snap.

Veronica only wants one thing, my dick, or fuck with someone and ruin them. Her little obsession with Warren was a blessing in disguise, but her crazy ass scared him off.

"Is that any way to treat one of the best fucks you ever had in your life?"

"I hardly remember. I have had many."

"You're such an asshole, Bedford. I thought Dravin was a prick, but you are a whole bag of dicks all on your own."

"My dick isn't interested in you, so what do you want?"

I can hear her tapping in the background. She does that when she isn't getting the reaction she hoped. I fucked her three years ago and it was the biggest mistake. She wanted my brother too, but he couldn't stand her, and I didn't blame him. She takes things too far and wants to be the master in control, only when she doesn't get her way, she snaps.

Veronica is beautiful but demented all at the same time. My brother calls her Marsha fucking Brady because that is who she wants to be like, but to me, she is more like the chick from the movie *Fatal Attraction*.

If her father only knew his little Marsha likes to play for the other team. She's addicted to sex and likes to mix her food too, eating everything in one bowl at the same time.

"I thought you should know. Your little stunt at the party has sent a message to the vultures." She chuckles. "This is going to be so much fun. I heard she found out about your little lie, but to me, that means your brother has a dick as big as yours."

"Of course, that is all you think about, Veronica. Are you finished?"

"No, but I want to warn you," she purrs and then lowers her voice. "They all want her now."

I lean back in my father's office chair and look out the window at the perfectly manicured lawn sprinkled with snow from last night, wondering what Gia is doing right now. "So, what's changed?"

"And here I thought you were the smart twin that figures shit out before the rest. She must hate you now, so—you two are out of the game. You two are like the extra game pieces not used. The ones you place back in the box."

My left eye twitches from the anger snaking up my neck like a rash, making the vein on my temple throb. If anyone touches her, Order or no Order, I'll kill them. The only one allowed to touch a hair on her head is my twin brother, and only if she allows it.

Veronica is attempting to provoke me and get under my skin since Gianna has achieved what no one else has: the undivided attention of the Bedford twins. The rumor that we've stopped wanting her has reached her ears, and she wants to know whether it's true.

One thing she doesn't know is that a Bedford is growing inside her, and she won't be easily swayed into falling for anyone else. There is only one other man she has slept with while pregnant, and that man is me, even if I know deep down she wouldn't have done it had she known. It's fucked up. It's dark and twisted, but that's how I am: dark. And I love the taste of sin. Her body is my sacramental bread, and the taste of her pussy is like fine wine. Gianna belongs to Dravin, but she is also mine. Even if she thinks we don't want her.

Taking a deep breath, not wanting to let her hear my annoyance, I calm myself and warn her, "Be careful, Veronica. You wouldn't want me to tell Daddy and everyone else the truth about your little sexcapades and addiction to cock and pussy." I hear her intake of breath over the phone, but I keep going. "Don't worry about your little Warren. We made sure she won't be interested, but if you think you can toy with her, you can go ahead and try. But, I assure you. You will be disappointed."

"Are you threatening me, Bedford?"

I grip my phone, holding myself back. "No. I'm warning you. You can try, but I guarantee you will not like the outcome. She isn't like the others that have come through here, but of course, you already knew that with the way we loved the taste of her."

"If she was so great, then why throw her back into the pit?"

I chuckle, playing it off. "Because all good things come to an end. You know how it goes. We get bored and we all move on."

I have to make it seem we don't care because if you show interest in something or, in this case, someone, people will do anything to get it. They will do just about anything just to have her, even if they will discard her like damaged goods when they're done with her after she signs an NDA. All Prey have to sign one once they graduate. If they violate it, they die.

CHAPTER TEN

JESS

WHAT AN ASSHOLE. Gia told me about her last encounter with Dravin, what he said to her, and how she handled it. She stands at the end of her bed, zipping up her suitcase, ready to leave for winter break even though it is still two weeks away. She is going with her mom instead of her dad back to an apartment her mother rented in Wisconsin.

"Forget about him. Like I said, I'm here if you need any help."

She turns her head and gives me a small smile. "Thank you, Jess. That means a lot. I'm not sure how I'm going to tell my mom. She will be forced to tell my dad, and then my dad will want to kill Dravin. Dravin will respond by telling my dad off, and it will be a mess. What if he threatens my dad?"

I take a deep breath, realizing how hard this must be for her. It's not only a difficult thing to go back home and tell your church-going mother that your ex-billionaire boyfriend knocked you up but wants to keep you a secret and doesn't want to acknowledge his own kid has to be the biggest blow of all.

If it wasn't for who Dravin is and his crazier twin brother, I would want to wring his neck myself, but we both know what he is capable of. It's better to lie low and learn from your mistakes. Play along until you reach the other side like a maze. You learn where not to go every time you hit a dead end until you finally reach the way out.

"Where are you headed?" she asks.

"I need to visit my mom. I didn't go during Thanksgiving break."

"Where did you go, if you don't mind me asking?"

I chew on the corner of my lip, embarrassed and feeling guilty about not going back to spend it with my mom, but I didn't want to face anyone back home. I wasn't ready. I didn't want to risk seeing people from back home. People I'm trying to run away from. My mother doesn't know what happened to me because what was the point of telling her what they did to me? No one is going to listen to a single mom from the trailer park who they think is a drug addict or alcoholic.

Especially about a daughter no one gives a shit about except her. I love my mother too much to put her through that. Ultimately, it won't change what they did or the nightmares. The only way I have been able to cope is to find pleasure in sex like a Band-Aid to a bleeding wound.

"I stayed here."

She gives me a doleful expression. "I'm not going to ask why because you have your reasons, and I don't want to pry unless you want to tell me, but you could have gone with me. I know I should've asked. I'm sorry."

I wave my hand. "Don't be sorry. I'm used to not showing up anyway. It's just me and my mom, and she usually works at the diner to make extra money, but she called and asked me to come this year." I shrug, looking at her. "I think she's afraid I'll run off and forget about her. She sounded sad over the phone."

"That must have been hard."

I nod, nudging my chin toward her. "Not as hard as what you're going through right now with Dravin. To be honest, I want to kill him for doing this to you."

She lets out a slow, shaky breath and looks down at her nails, which have chipped black nail polish that was once glossy and perfect. "I have to move on and forget about him. I know it will be hard, but it's something I have to do. I was stupid and didn't think. My lack of experience with guys is most likely to blame. I wasn't ready for someone like Dravin."

"No one is ready for someone like Dravin."

My heart clenches for her as a tear rolls down her cheek. "I should have been on the pill and not fallen for his lies. I thought it was real when I went to his father's house and his brother was there. He's a real piece of work," she says on a nervous laugh.

I give her a wry smile that turns into a smirk and try to cheer her up. "So, how was it?"

Her eyes lift to mine. "How was what?"

"Draven with an *E*," I say, emphasizing the *E* so that she understands which brother I'm asking about. "Who's better?"

She lifts her face up to the ceiling and snickers. "I can't believe you just asked me that."

I quirk a brow, waiting silently for her answer. She slides her fingers in her hair until they are close to the roots and closes her eyes. "He's…" She trails off.

I get more comfortable on the bed as she tries to open up about how she felt about him, not knowing another brother looked and acted exactly the same. I have a feeling that the members of the Order aren't so sure which one is which half the time.

Holding my head with my hand as I lie down on the mattress, I ask, "How is he? Better? Worse?"

Her eyes find mine, and she says something I didn't expect. "That's the thing. That is the only way I could tell them apart. I couldn't at first, but now that I know, that's the difference. He's dirtier and crazier, and he has this way of making you accept the way he treats you. His brother is passionate and all-consuming, but this one is the dirty version. The one that makes every dirty fantasy you ever thought of come true. The one God warns you about when you think of lust and temptation. It's hard to understand because Dravin is like that, but his twin is crazier on a whole other level of fucked up. If the Dravin I fell for is Samael from the Bible, then his brother Draven is Lucifer himself. He is dark and the very definition of sin. You can see it when you look at him, but at the same time, he comes off as the one that is sent to kill the devil himself."

"He was that good, huh?" I tease.

She smiles. "In a different way. Yeah. He is the one that you don't feel guilty about for acting out the dirtiest things that have crossed your mind because he isn't the one that you marry or introduce to your parents because you are afraid of what they might say. He's the one that you hide under your bed. The one that no one expects to be hidden in your closet. Now, his brother is the one you give your heart and soul to, and the other is the one you give your body to. But if he wants your heart or any part of you, his brother wouldn't object to letting him share that part. You can't belong to one and not the other. My problem is that it goes against everything I was brought up on. Like keeping a deep secret from everyone, but you don't really want to."

"Wow," I say, looking at her and shaking my head. "I wouldn't know how to handle that. I get it. It's fucked up, but deliciously so. To have them both."

She nods and says, "It's dangerous, Jess. It's the scariest feeling that all this time I thought it was one man while he knew the other was filling in for him. Physically, the same in every way. They talk and feel the same, but once he touches you, you lose yourself. There was no way I would have figured it out unless they told me, and it wasn't the Dravin that I fell in love with that did. It was him. The brother that didn't flinch when he found out that he was fucking his pregnant brother's girl. He liked it, Jess. It was nothing to him. To both of them. Where does love fit in all that?"

I avert my gaze because I can't answer her. After the want comes the need. After the need comes the lust for desire. After the desire comes love, then betrayal and heartbreak, followed by shame. I've lived that feeling every day since that night before graduation. How a guy can use your love and dirty it in the cruelest way. To prey on it and then try to defile and destroy you like you're nothing.

"There is nothing I can say but to go with what you feel, Gia. We all have our demons. You just have to do what feels right. What works to keep them at bay so you can function. Your head must feel like a war zone right now, but you will find a way to fight it. To make sense of it." I shrug. "It's all I can say. It's all I know when shit is so fucked up."

"What do you mean?"

"Feel, Gia. Go with what feels right and fuck everyone else. Don't let them mess with you. Learn how to take and only give to those who deserve it."

She needs to stop worrying about everyone else and worry about herself. I have learned that through pain, the only thing that is left is the ashes of what consumed you. Every waking moment you spend worrying about the demons that plague you at night is consumed with anger, shame, regret, and, most of all, the ones you know that caused it. They roam free while you are chained in the darkness of the hell they created.

CHAPTER ELEVEN

DRAVEN

IT'S the last week of classes before winter break. I stand in the dark corridor and watch Gia walk out of her class. The door swings open as college students file out, making their way down the hallway. I notice some girls my brother and I have fucked give her knowing smirks while she looks down, scrolling through her phone. She is probably used to it by now.

Does it bother me? No.

Should I care? No.

Why? Because it's not about me but about Dravin, and the evil asshole in me wants her to secretly pay for shunning him. Denying him is the same as denying me. The only difference in this situation is that she's pregnant with my brother's kid when the entire purpose was for her to have our children.

It sounds fucked up in normal society, but we are not from a normal society. We are born and bred in a fucked up world, part of an evil organization that controls the world. The rules don't apply to us. We must do what is necessary to continue our legacy and our purpose. Gia was part of that purpose until she wasn't. With money comes sacrifices, not that Gianna was a sacrifice. She was a gift. A gift she took away. She felt like a Christmas gift on Christmas morning, all wrapped up in pretty paper with a shiny bow with your name on it, hoping that when you opened it, it was what you secretly wished for and finally would taste victory. But when you opened it, tearing off the paper, all you got was an empty box and a piece of paper telling you better off next time because you cheated and lied.

She has no idea I'm watching—more like stalking her, but who cares? I care about her, just like Dravin does. It's a foreign concept to me, but with her, it just isn't. It makes sense. Everything with this girl does. We dirtied her and involved her in our world, but we couldn't resist. I couldn't resist. We want her. I want her. As the saying goes, the more someone resists, the more you want them.

Her dark hair is like a curtain of silk parted in the middle just the way I like, so I can see her beautiful face and perfect brows when I'm inside her, and she is looking up at me like I'm her God, and she is praying for me to take her to heaven. But the only place I know is the way to hell. The burning flames I create when you cross the gate of the underworld. The underworld of sex, lust, and every dirty fucking fantasy a cock and pussy can make. Heaven is for white picket fences, husbands mowing the grass on Sundays after boring vanilla sex, and wives taking their kids to play dates with other moms from the PTA.

Not me.

Not us.

Not the Bedford men.

We create our own heaven in hell. A place where no one can touch what we consider ours. In this case, we want her. We want to wake up in heaven and fuck her on the breakfast table while the eggs Benedict are served on our plates.

Our lawn is immaculate because there is no way we would waste a Sunday cutting shit that will grow back anyway and just pay someone else to do it when we would rather eat our girl's pussy after her third orgasm. On. The. Fucking. Table. She is our breakfast, lunch, dinner, and dessert. Our kids are being bathed, dressed, and fed in the West Wing because mommy needs her breakfast too, and sausage is always on the menu.

She walks by me, and I take a step back so she can't see me. She'll probably mistake me for my brother, anyway. I'm stalking her because she needs to eat, and we have not seen her in the cafeteria or the little café across campus. It's too cold to walk, and she doesn't take an Uber anywhere and has chosen to eat from vending machines on campus.

I noticed the last time she was spread on my bed, and I was fucking her when she thought I was my twin. She looked thinner, but I would not point it out when thoughts in my brain were left on hold because my dick had better plans. Now that the bomb dropped, and we know it's because she is pregnant, Dravin and I decided that even though he broke it off with her for safety reasons and the fact that she can't handle what is really required for her to be with him, that we would keep an eye on her without her knowing. We take turns most of the time.

We have heard nothing on campus except our phones blowing up from the female population attending Kenyan, supposedly finding God by confessing in the church from the Order wanting to fuck, and the snarky comments about Gia not making the cut with Dravin. At least we know, with her condition, she won't be heading to any of the frat parties to get shit-faced or find a rebound fuck when she is pregnant. The typical shit women do when trying to get over the guy who lied to them and now told them they were a mistake.

The campus door opens as she pushes the metal bar, and I follow her, ignoring the knowing glances and flirtatious stares aimed my way by Jessica and Audrey. Two girls I fucked before Gia arrived. Their fathers are older members of the Order and are plausible options in marrying within to control and keep the alliances going. After Gia, they are nothing in my eyes.

Her dark hair, I remember and prefer to be on my bed sprawled out against my red sheet, whips in the breeze. The bite in the air against my exposed skin.

She stops, and so do I. The smell of the cold mixed with the electricity between us. She senses me the same way I feel her in a room or any place within proximity.

I step forward, hoping to smell her fruity scent, but she turns around, eyes narrowing as they take me in, roaming over my clothes, hoping because praying is worthless. Praying would be on my hands and knees, wanting her to choose to be a Mrs.

Bedford and belong to me. To us. Asking God for one woman to belong to two men that are brothers. Her heart she can give to my brother. But she has to be willing. Hope is all that I have left. I can take the rest, but I want something more meaningful: her soul.

"Why are you following me?"

I walk up to her, looking down into her beautiful eyes, her glossy lips parted. Her cheeks were pink from the cold. The need to just take her lips in mine, eating at me. I have to slide my hands in the front pocket of my jeans to avoid taking her face in my hands and devouring her right there and fuck with what she wants.

"I'm here to take you to eat."

"I'm not hungry."

My eyes dart to her waist, knowing that her breakfast was a multigrain bar. Getting annoyed with her isn't what I want, so I try a different approach.

"We need to ensure you are eating, and we haven't seen you in the cafeteria lately."

She gives a look of annoyance. "On top of telling me I was a mistake and throwing me under the bed like a secret, you don't want anyone to know you're following me? You don't even go here. Keeping tabs on what I eat and where I am. Creepy much."

I grin. She knows which Bedford she is speaking to. Smart girl.

"How do you know I'm not your ex-boyfriend?"

She shakes her head. "As much as it was fun for you to trick me into thinking I was fucking one of you, I am not that stupid. The Bedford that attends Kenyan was wearing something different fifteen minutes ago when he purposely ignored my existence and gave two shits what I ate while chatting up a blonde in the hallway. Unless he likes to change his clothes for every class or has special powers, I'm guessing you are Draven, who lives in the haunted mansion."

I give her a wide grin and a quirk of my eyebrow. "Haunted mansion? It's really not haunted. It's old and historical, but not haunted." She gives me a cute eye roll. You need to eat, and I want to take you."

She lets out a puff of air from those lips I want to reacquaint with my cock. "Fine."

I open the passenger door to my Audi RS7, ensuring the heated seats and heater are on. She slides in after I take her bag and place it in the back seat. I make my way to the driver's seat and slide in, powering up the car.

"Where are you taking me?"

"A diner out of town?"

She stiffens, and my stomach clenches because, knowing my brother, he would take her to the same diner our mother would take us. She took Dravin there more than she did me because I was always with my father. I was the chosen wild card he loved to have close to him like a sidekick.

As I drive toward the diner, the sun shines in the clear blue sky. He took her to the diner, which just won't do. If she went with him, then she would go with me. It shouldn't matter, but her problem is more with Dravin than with me. Yeah, I should have told her she was fucking me and that I was her boyfriend's twin creeping between her sheets disguised as her boyfriend, but I'm not the good guy. I'm the villain. And the villain takes what he wants.

I catch her watching me from the corner of my eye, and she is probably trying to figure out how we look so alike or trying to tell us apart. No one can. The only person who could was my mother. My father could tell based on my brother's hateful behavior because of how my father treated her after she gave birth to the Bedford heirs. And now she is dead.

"You can't."

"I can't what. What are you talking about?"

"You're trying to tell us apart. I'm trying to save you the trouble and the stares that will make me think you want something else."

She snorts. "Trust me. I don't want something else. I already had enough, and I have proof. You can't blame me for trying to tell you two apart. Like a normal person, I like to know who I'm talking to."

I pull into the diner's parking lot, place the car in park, and turn to face her. "Does it matter if I'm him or me? When you didn't know I existed, could you tell?"

She presses the button to turn off the heater and the seats, and I smile inwardly because that means she is flustered, and I'm getting to her. I want her to tell me what she thinks of me; I also lied to her, just like Dravin did, about us being identical, but I want to know. I need to know.

She moistens her lips with the tip of her tongue and my cock twitches. I don't know how to keep my hands to myself much longer. She is right there, and my cock is right here. The space between us is killing me. Pure. Fucking. Torture.

She is my warmth in the winter, my blanket on lonely nights when I feel cold and now there is nothing but cold sheets and meaningless dreams. She was the one who could fill those dreams.

I'm her first, and who doesn't love to be first? I will always be the one she will remember now that she knows the truth.

"I could. I could tell there was something off when it was you. Because when it was you, you took. You didn't ask. You weren't soft. You didn't whisper sweet words in my ear." I roll my eyes. "You were distant, but now I know why. I was just a conquest for you. A curiosity. An itch you wanted to scratch. Now I'm the rash you want to get rid of."

If she only knew that wasn't the case. If she only knew that if I was the one she loved and told me I love you, those would be the days I lived and the days she didn't, like right now, those would be the days I died. A slow, painful death. But she is right about me not being soft. I didn't whisper in her ear things guys whisper to the woman they are falling in love with. Because at the time, I wasn't in love with her, and now, I don't know if I am or not. I just know I can't stay away from her. I don't know what love is. I have never experienced the emotion like Dravin has with her. I never saw it with my parents. I never had those feelings with anyone.

"I don't want to get rid of you. If I did, you wouldn't be the first woman I have taken out to lunch because guys like me don't do that shit. Guys like me are the ones whose fathers wait behind the door with a shotgun when I pick up their daughter for a date, knowing it's to go fuck in a parked car and then drop them off without a kiss goodnight. I'm not soft. You already know that I do not write poems. I slide my fingers through my dark hair, trying to tell her how I'm feeling without sounding like a pussy whipped prick. "I want to be the tip of the bottle you bring to your lips," I say, sliding the pad of my thumb over her bottom lip, knowing it's confusing the shit out of her but not giving a fuck. "I'm everything Dravin isn't. You wish he was. And whatever you want me to be that I'm not, he is."

She closes her eyes, and I know I'm fucking up the plan. I'm fucking up everything we agreed to do with her, but I can't let her think I don't want her. I know she saw the video of those girls and us, and everything got out of hand. The lies we spun like they were gold. We thought we could show her we were unaffected when there was no way she could accept us because of what we did, but all we did was fail her. We showed her she didn't matter when it was the opposite. She's everything. Placed on this earth for us. Only us.

She opens her eyes and angles her head, and I see in the depth of her eyes that we robbed her of the love she felt in her heart for my brother. My brother ripped her apart with his words; what I said to her was like kicking a wounded animal.

"Let's go eat," I tell her, changing the subject and wishing I could say to her I'm sorry. I already went through the loss of my mother. I hoped I could keep her, but keeping her would mean forcing her into a world where she would be unhappy. Losing Gianna would be like watching a burning building full of newborns; you can't come back from something like that. She isn't a wild animal you want to tame by keeping her hidden in your room, hoping to domesticate it when it will do exactly what nature intended, and that is to be free in its natural habitat.

We take a booth facing each other in the back corner of the diner. I can't sit next to her like my brother would. He brought her here, but I am not him. I'll slide my hand down her pants and finger her cunt while she scans the menu, knowing the only thing she would want would be my cock, and that option is not on the menu but right next to her.

Dorothy comes to our table to take our order. She gives me the once-over and then glances at Gia, smiling. "I was wondering when you two would be back. What can I get you to drink?"

Dorothy places the two-sided plastic menus on the table in front of us while I lean back in the shiny red booth, making a noise when my jeans rub against the cheap vinyl, raising an eyebrow. I lean forward, placing my forearms on the white table, the diamonds of my Cartier watch catching the light, and lower my voice above a whisper. "It's our first time."

Dorothy lifts her eyes to me as it slowly dawns on her I'm the dark, evil twin. The one that doesn't bring girls to eat at the diner. Ever.

She looks at Gia like she is afraid of her being alone with me, even in a public space. My reputation proceeds with me. The fucked-up twin that does dirty shit, and everyone looks the other way, but what they don't know is that my brother is just as fucked up as I am, if not more. I'm just the fallout guy. The one that takes the blame to ensure the older twin carries out the duty of the Bedford name.

Gia lifts her head from scanning the menu and orders water and a burger. Atta girl. I'm glad she isn't the rabbit-eating girl who sticks to salad so she won't get fat. Some people think salad is for the rich. Ordered by the rich. If they only knew poor people invented the salad. It was created from leftovers. I saw a documentary about a lady saving a million dollars by making her own candle wax for light, flushing the toilet once a week, walking everywhere she went, and can you guess what she ate every day: salad. She grew it in her own backyard and ate like she was a rabbit. Living poor so she could save to be a millionaire. Like I said, poor people.

"I'll have the same and a chocolate shake." Dorothy writes it down on her pad but lifts her eyes to me with a curious expression. She knew my mother very well and knew my brother was the one she saw the most. She must feel empowered because she knows which twin is seated at her table, and in her mind, she must be wondering why I'm having lunch with my brother's girl. News-flash, Dorothy: She was mine when she was his.

"How's your dad?" Dorothy asks.

"He's good."

"And your brother?"

She wants to get to the point. She wants to be nosey, and what do you give a person who wants to be nosey? The truth they are afraid to hear.

"He's fine, Dorothy. Don't worry, sweetheart." Adding a wink. "Gia is test-driving us both. She is trying to see which one drives better, or maybe she wants to keep us... both," I say to her flustered face, going from ashen to red like a mood ring.

I glance at Gia, and her mouth drops open. My eyes tell her to close it before I find a good use for it, and it's not to eat the burger she ordered. She does.

My eyes zero in on her pouty, plump lips, which I'm dying to taste when they close, and I'm interrupted by my fantasy of pouring the chocolate shake all over her body so I can drink it, knowing it would taste better by my phone vibrating.

I lean back, pull out the phone, and glance at the screen to see my older twin's name flashing from a text next to a face that looks exactly like mine. It's like looking in a mirror and watching your-self calling yourself.

> Dravin: What the fuck are you doing?

Draven: Making sure your baby momma is feeding your kid.

> Dravin: That is my job, asshole. Not yours.

Draven: I'm taking care of our interests while you were too engrossed in the blonde in the hallway. Gia's words, not mine. I'm sure she is also tired of hearing all the girls giggling and whispering shit about her behind her back. I did what you didn't do. Make sure she is eating. The last time I had her underneath me, I noticed she was on the thin side, and I haven't seen her in the cafeteria, probably, so she doesn't have to hear the little voices traveling about how you dumped her and moved on. Get over it. I'm with her, and I'm feeding her.

> Dravin: You're playing with fire, Draven.

Draven: No. I'm lighting the fire and doing what I do best, watching it catch. It's the best part. Oh, and when her lips part, imagining them on my cock when she looks at me like she is right now.

> Dravin: Where are you with my girl?

Draven: Having our first lunch date at the diner.

"Is everything alright?"

I set my phone down on the table and look at her gorgeous face framed by her dark silky hair that I miss on my bed. I wonder if she will let me kiss her.

"Everything is fine."

She nods and averts her eyes, looking around at the people sitting and conversing.

"How are you feeling?"

She knows I mean the pregnancy. Even if I'm ruthless and self-ish, or maybe I'm the type of guy that doesn't give a fuck, but with

Gianna, I do. A lot. I care. She bites the corner of her lip. I notice she does it when she's nervous.

"I get sick some mornings, and others I get hungry, but Jess is always there with crackers, or when she has an early class, she leaves me a bottle of water and a snack so my stomach can settle in the morning. If I smell something like fish or eggs. Even certain perfumes and colognes make me nauseous."

Fucking hell, Dravin. You're not there for any of it. She is doing this alone. I want to kill my brother right now. I get he had to break it off with her, but it's not his responsibility to her. Her room-mate Jess takes better care of her than he does. Watching in the hallways like a creep isn't cutting it. We don't have experience with pregnant chicks, but he could do the same thing I'm doing. Asking her. All he had to do was ask.

"Does Dravin know?" I wave my hand toward her. "About the nausea and needing help in the mornings."

I already know the answer, but I want her to tell me. I want her to give me the fuel so I can punch my brother in the fucking face.

I wait as her pretty eyes look up, hurt and glassy. Her face turns white and then to a shade of green like a cartoon. She slaps her hand over her face to cover her nose and mouth.

A server passes by, and the smell is definitely fried, and I think it's fucking fish. My nostrils flare in anger, not at her but at the plate of food with a dead brown fried fishlike carcass. Its eyes are sunken in its head, staring at the man that would consume him because a grilled cheese was too sophisticated for this asshole.

I look over while the smug bastard sitting in the booth across from us places a napkin on his chest, ready to tuck it in his collar like a fucking toddler getting prepared for his two o'clock feeding. His glasses fog from the steam of the offending plate with the offending odor, causing my girl to struggle with keeping whatever she had left in her stomach, keeping the little being trying to grow inside her from getting fed. Anger courses through my veins like a volcano while my lip curls into a snarl. What is mine comes first, and this asshole squeezes lemon over the offending animal like it's a delicacy.

I slide from the booth just as Dorothy places our plates on the table. She must see the look on my face because her eyebrows raise to her hairline when she sees what has me pissed the fuck off. The twerp looks up as he sees me standing over him.

"C-can I help you?"

My hand grabs him by the collar, and I lower my face when he looks at me with wide eyes. "Throw it out, or I'll throw you out with the Goddamn fish. It stinks, and my girl can't stand the smell. If she can't eat, I'll make sure you can never eat and need to be fed by straw and will have to pee and shit in a bag for the rest of your life."

My head turns like a serial killer in a movie toward Dorothy. "Throw it out. No fish or eggs to be served anywhere near Gianna."

She nods like a bobblehead and quickly grabs the plate. "I'm sorry. I didn't know, Draven. You know I would never—" She trails off.

"It's ok, Draven. Please let him go. He didn't know. Dorothy didn't know." It's just like Gianna to be their savior when she tries to steady her stomach by taking gulps of air.

I let the piece of shit go, not caring if he did. That he would have a meal and enjoy it while she was miserable set me off. I grab the plate and walk over to the front door. The bell on top of the door rings as I push it open and fling the plate with the fucking fish in the road, watching the plate shatter and the fish slide on the blacktop with satisfaction.

I walk back inside, and everyone in the diner has their mouth open. "Go get your fucking fish," I growl to the dork with the napkin as a bib.

Dorothy looks at me with her arms crossed over her chest, shaking her head, trying to contain her laughter. "The trash was over there, you know."

"The smell would still bother her, you know," I mock. I open my wallet, slide two twenties, and hand it over to Dorothy. "For the fish."

Dorothy shakes her head. "Keep it. I'll get him something else." I nod, and she walks away, and I decide to place the money on the table to add it to the bill for her tip.

"Did you really have to do that?" Gia asks.

"I'll do anything to make you comfortable. I would never let another person eat while you're hungry or sick, especially knowing what they are eating makes you feel sick." I nudge my head toward the plate in front of her. "Now eat, Raven. And tell me what you crave."

And she does. Between bites, she tells me everything she craves and everything she can and can't eat. I file this information away in my memory to ensure food is delivered to her wherever she is and whatever she wants. I ask her questions about her first appointment, knowing it's after the winter break.

My brother did the same, but I wanted to keep the conversation going. I want to know her more deeply, not just sexually but mentally. I have found that Gianna is smart and sheltered. My brother was right. She is innocent. She doesn't know about murder and corruption. The crazy part is that she hasn't seen evil. My brother and I are evil. She is eating at the table with evil, fucked evil, and will breed the next generation of evil. God created the most beautiful angel (the devil), but he also made Gia.

My savior and my brother's angel because without her, we are lost. If she only knew how important she is to us. How wanted she is. I never thought I could fall for a woman. How deep I'm falling under her spell.

She takes a bite and a sip of water and cleans her pouty lips with a white napkin. "Thank you. I thought I could never eat without feeling queasy."

My chest swells with her gratitude. I loved that I did something good for her, even though I would have killed him for eating the fish—hung him by the throat. She wouldn't have liked the outcome, but I took the best route possible. Gia makes me a better person—a better man.

Gianna will be the only woman who will have my children. If my brother married someone else and had children with another woman, it wouldn't matter because the only babies Gianna will give birth to are our Bedford.

"What are you thinking about?" she asks, snapping out of my thoughts and placing the burger I just ate on the plate.

I swallow and meet her gaze. "How I'm going to keep you?"

CHAPTER TWELVE

DRAVIN

IT'S dark in her dorm room as I sit and watch her sleep. I miss her dark hair on my pillow. I miss her soft skin, and I miss how her leg wrapped around mine like a vine when she fell asleep in my arms.

I have had no one in my bed since her, and I don't think I could or ever would after her. The scent she left on my sheets and pillow has since faded. I waited until it was unsanitary to have the house-keeper from my childhood home come and wash the sheets. She would shake her head and mumble for me to just tell her how I felt. But I can't.

The worst part is hurting the person you love while trying to protect them. Gia is not from a prominent family and is considered Prey. The members will try to get to her. They will try to talk to her or fuck her, but she will deny them for obvious reasons. I don't trust members of the Order. This is why my brother Draven and I created the consortium.

Discreet selected members that are part of the Order that we can trust. Thirty selected members to ensure our legacies are not threatened by others who wish to eliminate us for control. It is always about power. Religion is used to instill morals in humanity. Without morals or a sense of preservation of humanity, there will be mass chaos, murder, and pandemonium in society.

The catholic church built on this land has allowed the Order to survive using the church as a sacred meeting spot for world lead-ers. Who would question anyone going to church? No one.

They instilled it in the Constitution as our right and freedom to practice a person's beliefs—the perfect cover-up.

My eyes flick to Jess sleeping in the other bed opposite Gia as she turns her body to face the wall, relieved that she hasn't woken up. I came to drop off a wool coat and knee-high leather boots for Gia so she could keep warm while walking across campus. I protect what is mine, and she will always be mine. I inhale, smelling the jacket she left on the chair, which is much too thin for my taste. Her scent is intoxicating, making my cock harden in my black sweats. I have been watching her sleep almost every night since I had to break it off with her. I need to be close to her, even if she hates me.

When Draven took her to the diner, my brother's words got under my skin. She thinks I don't care about her when she is the most important thing in my life. She and our baby.

I need to make sure she is safe. She didn't want me after I lied to her about my twin. I couldn't tell her when I knew she would leave me without giving us a chance if she found out. That blew up in my face because she didn't want to marry me, and I couldn't force her. I also cannot risk her denying me in front of the others and letting them know she is pregnant. She would be a target, and some members would find it going against the rules of the Order.

If a Prey is involved with a member and she falls pregnant, the pregnancy is terminated, or she can marry by choice under strict circumstances. She has to choose, and if anyone speculates it's forced, it violates the Order, and they will vote for her to be eliminated. That can't happen. We won't let it.

I place the note on the winter coat neatly placed on her desk. I slide my hands into the pockets of my matching black hoodie, feeling the metal skeleton key with my fingers. The key works on all the doors in the dorm and the school. It is how I get in and out of the buildings with no one noticing. I have never been a person to stalk someone and thought guys that stalk girls are creeps. I'm one of those people because of my feelings for her. I have to make sure she is okay.

My brother told me she gets sick and hasn't been eating when she smells something that doesn't agree with her. I'm not fond of fried fish, either. He cares about her and feels just as guilty for lying and keeping the truth about us being twins, about him disguising himself as me when she saw him. It is his fault for not coming clean, but mine for going along with it. I guess you do crazy things when you want something bad enough. We both got caught up. One lie bled into the other and another until we had a string of lies that hid the truth.

Her finding out the truth was mixed with the fear of losing her. Losing her is something I can't live with, and the fact that my brother didn't stick to the plan and reached out to her proves that he can't accept it either.

I stand over her, admiring her plump bottom lip, slightly larger than the top. Her lips part every time she is in a deep sleep. Her thin white tank is molded to her perky breast. The outline of her nipples is visible through the thin fabric.

I want to cover her with the thick blanket by her waist and watch her a little longer. I love to memorize her face so I don't forget what she looks like or if I find something I didn't see the last time.

I gently grip the blanket with my fingers and slide it up to cover her body without waking her. I'm tempted to brush my lips against hers, but if I do, she will wake up, and I don't want her to know that I come in here to watch her sleep. There are things she doesn't understand, and I refuse to force her into a life so she can end up, like my mother, depressed. It is her choice; we must respect it, and I will ensure she is safe. I'll do what my father chose not to do with my mother: put her first.

I have already made sure they deliver her meals to her dorm and decided it was time for me to leave. I let myself out quietly, making sure the door was locked.

Someone is walking toward me as I make my way down the hallway. I pause and notice the hooded figure dressed all in black and cross my hands over my chest. What the fuck is he doing here?

"What are you doing here, Garret?"

He pushes the black hood off his head. His dirty blonde hair spiked up from the effort. "I came to see how she is doing?"

I quirk a brow. "Who?"

Garret is your typical member of the Order but also a person the Kenyan sons have found to trust. Garret isn't a bad guy. He fucked up with Jess letting Victoria have her fun with Melissa, and it all turned to shit for the poor girl. The way he talks about Jess is messed up, and I guess he doesn't care about her, but I find it intriguing that he talks about his time with her. He is putting a lot of effort into talking about a girl he supposedly gives two shits about. Reid and Valen have no complaints. If anything, they like her in all the right ways.

"Jess." His green eyes lower to his black books and then land on mine. "I came to see if she was okay. I have checked up on her twice a month since freshman year."

I cross my arms over my chest and lean my shoulder against the wall. "Now, why would you do that, and does she know?"

He slides his gloved hand inside his black sweats. "Nah, she doesn't know. I want to make sure she is alright."

"Why do you care? Why go through all the trouble? You keep the rumor mill flowing about her. The reason I'm questioning you is because of Gia."

He pinches his forehead in confusion. "Didn't you two break up? I mean, it was kind of fucked up. She didn't know she was fucking Draven, thinking it was you."

"Not your problem, but ours. It doesn't change the fact that I love her and will ensure she is okay even if she doesn't want to accept it. Whatever games you play with Jess, make sure it doesn't affect Gia. They are close."

Garret is close to us and knows what is required of us when our senior year is up. He is lucky he doesn't have that problem. There is time for him to choose who he wants. He just has to abide by his parent's businesses. He can fuck and play all he wants.

He lets out an audible breath. "I wouldn't let anything happen to Jess or Gia. You have my word on that, brother. Everything is not what it seems, and like you, we have to do things to ensure the people we care about are safe from others who have too much power for their own good."

I nod, and we fist bump. "You fell for her, didn't you?"

He lifts the corner of his mouth. "Something like that." He snaps his fingers and points at me. "Don't believe everything you hear?"

"You got that, right?" I walk away and then, stop, and turn back. "Garret?"

He pauses and turns around. "Yeah?"

"Don't wake my girl up," I warn.

CHAPTER THIRTEEN

JESS

MY EYES ARE heavy from sleep, but I sense someone hovering over me. Am I dreaming? Is it Gia? Is she okay?

I open my eyes and blink repeatedly. *Garret.* I'm about to scream, but the palm of his hand clamps over my mouth, preventing me from screaming.

"Shh... It's me. I'm not going to hurt you. I swear," he whispers.

My eyes widen, and they dart over to the other side of the room. I sag in relief that Gia is sound asleep and okay.

I shake my head, trying to figure out why he is here and trying to scare the shit out of me. Is this a cruel, sick joke? Hasn't he done enough?

My nostrils flare, and I'm relieved I can still breathe with how hard his hand is over my mouth. His head tilts, scanning my thin t-shirt, and his gaze pauses over my chest when he notices I'm not wearing a bra. I try to squirm, but he holds my body and head in place. Not so hard that it hurts, but enough so that it doesn't allow me to move my head or speak.

He leans in close to my right ear and whispers softly, "I came to see you."

The scent of his spicy cologne that I once loved my freshman year when he kissed me for the first time invading me. I wanted a real kiss and tried to forget what happened back home my senior year. I thought an elite catholic college was a step in the right direction. I soon discovered the path was a gateway into a hell I was never prepared for.

He was my first lesson in how evil the people walking Kenyan halls really are too vulnerable people like me. How much control and influence do they have on people who are not part of their circle?

I shake my head and shrug my shoulders. The light from the top window casts a glow from the moonlight over his features, his smooth face and hard jaw.

His hands slide down my stomach, and he finds the band of my shorts. What is he doing?

"I'm going to touch you. I want to show you not to listen to everything you hear."

I close my eyes. My heart is hammering inside my chest. Why? I have so many questions. Why did he trick me into wanting him so much and letting Veronica and Melissa do what they did when all I wanted was him? I liked Garret and was falling for him at the time. He was perfect. He walked me to class and said all the right things.

Garret is attractive with a lean build and the boy next door's complexion mixed with a bad-boy vibe. He hurt me and continues to hurt me with what he says about me. Going against them is pointless, and I have learned to ignore it.

But it was all a lie, and he used me. I was vulnerable, but he didn't know that. He didn't know what I had just gone through. No one did.

I close my thighs to keep his fingers from reaching the heat between my legs. His lips find that place behind my ear, and he places a warm kiss on that spot that raises the tiny hairs on my skin like an awakening of something dormant inside me.

"I bet you are wet. Sooo... Wet. Do you remember how wet you were that night?" I shake my head because I still can't answer. "I regretted what I did when I felt you gripping my cock. Having them there with us." He slides two fingers on the top of my slit, rubbing me. "Ruining what you were giving me."

My eyes find his green ones. His straight nose rubs the side of my cheek. My thighs widen slightly, and I can hear his breathing pick up. I don't know what to do. I'm confused, but I want to feel.

"You are so pretty, Jess. Do you know how beautiful you really are?" I avert my gaze and stare at a black dot on the wall I made with my shoe when I first moved into the dorm room. I stare at it like it can guide me on what to do with him.

"Look at me," he demands.

My eyes find him, and I can see the inner turmoil mixed with lust. He wants to fuck me. It's plain as day.

"I'm sorry about Veronica and Melissa. But I'm not sorry for wanting you. I know you hate me for what I did and what I have said." He rubs his finger over the top part of my clit, causing blood to rush from my head to the apex of my thighs. "I want you to take me to the showers in this place and hate fuck me. I know about Reid and Valen, and I'm not happy."

Too bad, asshole. I slept with them because they made me forget about my past. I felt free, and they made me feel good, physically.

I roll my eyes, and his lips lift in a smirk. "You like to get me upset, huh?" He rubs faster, and my neck arches. My legs open slightly, giving him more access. I'm wet. Really wet. "That's my girl." He smiles. "Be my little bad girl. Show me how much you hate me, Jess."

The spray of the hot shower falls over our bodies. Garret has me pinned on the shower wall, the cold tiles warming up from the heat of my back. I wrap my legs around his waist, and his eyes lock on mine. He places the palm of his hand near my head and pushes me against the tiles as he puts the tip of his condom-clad cock near my entrance.

"I'm gonna fuck you hard, princess. I want you to ride my cock like you hate me. Or maybe you really do hate me. But that's the best part, the part you'll love the most when I make you come so good, making you forget whatever you're trying to forget."

My eyes widen. It's like he knows my darkest secret—the one I have yet to share intimately with anyone.

"You don't have to tell me," he says, while sliding into my pussy deep with a groan. I gasp at the burning sensation that is welcomed with pleasure.

He stills so I can adjust to his size, and I grip his firm, muscular arms with my hands. "Ready, princess."

"Yes," I say in a hiss.

He moves hard and fast like he is in a race. Fuck. I moan loudly, and he slaps his hand over my mouth. "Shh... I don't want this to end with someone coming inside to see how much I like you wrapped around me. I don't want our little secret to come out."

I turn my head roughly so I can speak. "Fuck you."

He grips my mouth with his fingers and places a hard kiss on my mouth. "I'm planning on it. Whenever you want, I can come over and slide into this tight cunt." He bites my lip softly. "I want to see how much this pussy comes from your hate towards me."

He slams his lips over mine and pumps savagely inside me. My tits bounce from his forceful thrust and I grind on his cock and arch my back.

"Fuck yeah. Damn, this pussy is so good."

The slaps of wet skin echo in the female dorm showers. The sound of the water falling like rain on the tiles. His hand wraps around my neck, squeezing tight but letting me still breathe. His other hand is gripping my ass as he slams into me repeatedly.

He fucks me hard, and I grind harder. A delicious burn can be felt from the tips of my aching nipples to the swollen bud of my clit as he rubs against me with every thrust.

I moan softly, my climax climbing to its peak. My lips find his, and his tongue slides inside my mouth in sloppy, wet kisses. If this is a hate fuck, I want to keep hating him if it feels this good. I don't know why I let him, but I need the release. I need to stop letting him get to me.

"I'm bad a fuck, remember?"

He chuckles. "Yeah, you're so bad. I'm fucking you in the female showers in the dorm at two in the morning. If you only knew, Jess."

He pumps faster, and I can't take it. My eyes roll back in my skull as my orgasm slams into me in a thousand pieces. I grind on his cock, and I can feel it swell.

"Come, princess. Come all over my cock," he says, dipping his head and sucking my nipple. It makes me come more, and I swear I see stars.

He pulls out, lowering my legs from around his waist, and steadies me. "Turn around."

"What?"

"I said, turn around. I'm not done. We're not done."

I turn around, and he slaps my ass. "What the fuck, Garret."

"Hold on to the tiles with your palms and bend over."

"Why?" I ask.

"Because you want to forget."

I hate that he knows that part about me. It's like he knows I was secretly using him.

I was secretly using them.

They don't know from what or who.

CHAPTER FOURTEEN

GIA

WHILE SITTING IN THE BOOTH, I tilt my body forward. "Remind me again, why are we even here?"

Jess is sitting across from me at the Babylon bar off campus. I placed my hand over the beautiful wool coat Dravin left me last night with a pair of black designer boots that probably cost more than someone's monthly salary.

It's the most beautiful coat I have ever worn. I placed it on the booth's far side so it wouldn't get ruined, remembering the note that read:

Gia,
I will always keep you and the baby warm.
Love,
Dravin

Jess leans close, nursing her beer. Her fingers tinker with the neck of the bottle as the suds bubble with the movement. "Because you need to get out and stop hiding. We both do."

I bring the plastic cup of water and take a sip of the straw. "I'm not hiding." She lifts her lips, knowing I'm full of shit.

I am hiding. I'm still determining how I will react if I see Dravin after the note he left. I didn't want to accept it, but I knew I would. I needed a better coat, and the boots kept me warm when walking around campus in the cold.

Jess looks up at me when the echoing sound of the pool stick striking the ball draws her attention.

Her expression turns serious. I turn my head to see what, or better yet, who, has her attention.

Garret is playing pool with three other guys from the swim team. My eyes dart around the pool table, and my heart squeezes.

The twins are standing to the left, watching the game. I still can't tell them apart, but I can tell if I'm around them long enough. *If they allow it.*

I turn to face Jess, and her gaze lands on mine. "What's wrong?"

She shakes her head. "Nothing."

"It's not nothing. Is it Garret?"

She picks up her beer and takes a pull. The sleeves of her black sweater slide up her arms. There is something she isn't telling me. I'm unsure of what she wants to say to me, but I'm here for her. Her lips form a thin line, and she sighs.

"I slept with Garret last night."

My eyes widen, and I pick up the red plastic cup and take big gulps from the straw. "Okay."

I am trying to figure out why or how. She must hate him for what he put her through, the rumors, and how he treated her.

She gives me a guilty expression. "I know you must think—" She trails off.

"I think nothing." I snort. "I'm the last person to judge you right now."

She snickers. "It was a hate fuck."

I chuckle. "A what?"

"A "hate fuck" is what he labeled it. His words."

I raise my brows. "A hate fuck?"

"I don't know why I did it, but I did."

"It felt good," I tell her, waving my hand. "To let it out."

She smiles and laughs through her nose. "Yeah." Then her face falls, and that guilty expression sets in. "I don't want you to think of me as the type of girl that does things like that."

I lean forward, lowering my voice, "It's not like you haven't slept with him before, Jess. It doesn't mean you are any less than anyone who attends here. They have sex with random people and move on to the next."

I know first-hand how easily they can move on. How much it

hurts to be treated like nothing because you didn't agree with what they wanted. To accept.

"I guess." She smiles warmly. "Thank you, Gia."

I tilt my head. "Anytime."

"You liked the coat."

My head angles up, and one of the twins is standing at the end of the booth. His eyes are fixed on the coat by the seat next to me. It must be Dravin since he was the one who left it in my room.

I have yet to notice him sneaking into my room. I used to love it when he would come in the middle of the night. I secretly wished he would keep coming. It means he cares, but the fact that I'm pregnant must be the only reason—the reason I need to stay warm. It's who I'm carrying inside me that matters—his child.

"I nod. Thank you," I say curtly.

He taps his finger on the table, and I watch the ink on his hand move. The tension is thick, like a needle about to prick our bubble.

Jess licks her lips and clears her throat. The rest of the swim team and Draven show up, crowding the booth.

My hands sweat, and my throat suddenly becomes dry. My stomach clenches when Garret leans forward.

"Are you ready for round two?"

My eyes find Jess, and she looks at Garret with a smirk. "I thought I was horrible. The worst you have ever had." He winces. "That was a one-off. I'm sure you can find someone better to meet your expectations."

The guys on the swim team raise their brows, and Dravin looks away.

"Yeah, I get it," Garret says, walking away.

I move to slide out, and Draven quirks a brow. "Leaving so soon."

"Yeah, I wouldn't want to be in the way of your brother's hunt for a better replacement." His head whips over at me, hearing my last words. "Thanks for the coat and boots," I say, as I stand, grabbing the wool coat and sliding my arms through it while Jess slips out of the booth.

"You don't have to thank me, and I'm not looking."

He means he is not looking for his future wife around campus, but it doesn't mean it will not happen. He will, and I know my fate. How easily can I be replaced?

I raise my chin. "You weren't looking while getting your cock sucked off at the party?"

Draven's left eye twitches. It probably bothers him I pointed that out. How could I not? I can't forget what I saw. Since they clarified who I was speaking to by how they answered me, I feel empowered to tell which twin I'm talking to now, what I think, or how I feel.

"I'm sure they kept you both warm." I slide my tongue over my teeth and look down at my designer boots, trying to push the hurt I feel down to my stomach. His words from the cemetery and the video going viral around campus. The tears I silently cried every night. "I'm glad I got a sneak peek of how life would have been if I agreed to be with you both. You just made it easier for me."

I move toward the back exit, following Jess. Dravin's hand shoots out, gripping me by the arm. My head whips up, ignoring what his touch does to me or the leather jacket, which gives off the scent of his clean ocean smell. "Easier for what?"

My eyes are glassy, and the light is bright in the dimly lit bar. The tears are welling up in the back of my eyes at how much he hurt me. How they both hurt me and my love for him.

"How easily you could lie to me. How easy it was for you to hurt me." I lean close and look up at his stormy eyes. "How easy it was to replace me. I hope she was worth it."

"It isn't what you think. We didn't–"

I interrupt Draven. "I know what I saw and what everyone saw. It's exactly what everyone thinks. Now please, leave me alone." I say through clenched teeth, walking out into the cool late afternoon. Jess is holding my arm while she guides me across the street toward campus. The tears I was holding slide down my cheeks.

"I'm sorry, Gia," Jess says. "I'm sorry for taking you there. We need time. We just need time."

I thought I was ready to face him. Face them. She is right. Winter break is just around the corner, and I need time to check my feelings and emotions. My hormones are out of whack. One day, I feel sorry for myself, and then the next, I feel angry. In all honesty, my heart is breaking because I know the truth deep down. I want them. Both of them. I just can't get over his words and what they did in the video.

CHAPTER FIFTEEN

GIA

AFTER THE END OF CLASSES, I stand outside in the cold as the remaining students give me knowing glances about my recent split with Dravin. Thankful that I don't feel nauseous, I ignore the smirks and murmurs that pass behind me and focus on the life developing inside of me.

It's something I receive when I first wake up in the morning, along with the extra crackers that Jess usually puts on my night-stand. She held my hair each time the dry heaving sent me to the bathroom, and she was there when the tears started falling. Because I don't have much of an appetite in the evenings, I managed to shed a few more pounds.

Walking over to get something in my stomach before it sets in again, I decide to enter the café that I tagged along with Warren at the beginning of the year. I hope they have banana nut bread and maybe a hot chocolate.

I don't want to drink coffee in my condition, and I want to do everything right even if I have done everything wrong getting pregnant by a man who doesn't want to acknowledge my baby by name, but I'll survive. I'll give my baby the love he or she deserves. I have enough inside of me for both of us.

The bell of the door rings behind me right before I'm next to place my order.

"Hey."

I glance around to find Warren standing behind me, and I have to question why he is even on campus. Only students from the dorms remain, waiting for rides, and to my knowledge, Warren does not reside in the dorms since he is a member of the Order.

When I turn around, I notice that he must have entered the café by himself, just as everyone else was getting ready to go.

"Hey."

"You're leaving to see your family tomorrow?" he asks.

I nod. "Yep."

"That will be $12.75," the clerk says.

Jesus, for nut bread and hot chocolate? I slide my hand in my jacket to give him my bank card, which has only two hundred dollars to my name. I'm going to have to find a job to save for my little one. I refuse to ask or involve Dravin in any way, even if he offered, but the meal service he has coming by for me and Jess is a Godsend.

"I got it," Warren swiftly interrupts, handing him his card. "Charge for both, please."

"Oh, that's okay. That's nice of you, Warren, but I got it."

"No," he says sternly. The clerk looks at him and then at me, but the change in Warren's expression gives me a chill down my spine. The clerk swipes the card, and the receipt slides out.

I turn to him and give him a fake smile. "You didn't have to do that."

"I want to."

"I could have paid for it."

"It's no big deal, Gia. I wanted to pay for it. By the way, how come you didn't drink coffee? I remember you telling me you liked the macchiato. What changed?"

My eyes dart around the coffee shop, and I realize only three people are inside, and two of them work behind the counter. Shit.

My eyes land on his face, and his staring at me gives me the creeps. It's like he is waiting for me to admit something he already knows, but there is no way he could know that I'm pregnant. I'm alone in a coffee shop and there are no other customers. I must be paranoid.

I raise my shoulders. "Getting in the Christmas spirit with a hot chocolate."

He smiles at me like a clown. There is something off about Warren. He seems nice, but there is just something that doesn't add up.

Walking near the window, I find a seat to drink my hot chocolate and eat my banana nut bread. I expect Warren to leave after he picks up his order, but I see him talking to the barista in a hushed tone. He pauses his conversation and then looks over.

For some reason, a wave of fear begins crawling up my spine. They nod to each other, and he turns to leave, but instead of heading to the exit, he plops himself in front of me.

"I hope you don't mind."

I do mind. I don't trust you, and you give me creepy vibes. Except I can't tell him that. I have to play it cool and maintain my distance. I didn't want him buying me anything, though I also didn't want to argue.

I blow on the surface of the cup, cooling it down enough to take a sip, trying to get a sip so I can get warm.

"So. Where are you headed?"

"Wisconsin," I answer.

He already knew that, but that is all he is getting from me. The first time we were here, he asked where I was from. I should have known better and lied, but it's too late now. He smiles in that creepy, knowing way. Then he slouches in his chair and looks over his shoulder like he is paranoid someone will catch him or something.

He watches me while licking his lower lip. His gaze stays on me while I drink my hot cocoa, his eyes dilating and then closing. It reminds me of the scene in Snow White and the Seven Dwarfs when Snow White bit into the apple.

I blink rapidly, shaking my head out of the crazy thought. Being pregnant makes you self-aware of everything around you. I guess it's because you're trying to protect something precious inside of you. You don't want anyone to hurt that special someone that you love the most in the world.

I inwardly smile, thinking how crazy it is that you love someone so much and haven't even met them. You haven't smelled or felt their skin or looked into their eyes, but you already know deep down inside they are your everything.

"I'm glad I ran into you, Gia. I know it might be premature, but I wanted to see if you wanted to go out sometime."

My stomach clenches into knots. I slide the piece of nut bread out of the paper bag, trying to find something to do with my hands. I suddenly want to swallow the piece of bread and down the hot chocolate so I can get out of here and back to the safety of my dorm room.

I take a bite and swallow, hoping he will take the hint to drop it, but luck isn't on my side. My eyes lift to his, and I lick my lips because I have pieces of food. I hate the way his eyes follow the movement. It makes my stomach churn, except I do have to make it clear to him I'm not interested in him.

He leans forward. "Not all of us that go here are assholes, Gia. Dravin and his brother are just that, assholes. At least we only have to deal with one asshole because the other one makes random visits when he is bored. I'm sure you have realized they are twins by now."

Hoping he changes the subject and doesn't press, I follow along. "Yeah. It doesn't matter anymore though, we're just friends."

He chuckles, placing his forearms on the edge of the wooden table and giving me a smirk. "There is no such thing unless you're still fucking them. Are you?"

"Am I what?" I quip, getting annoyed. He has balls, but I'm not falling for his shit.

"Fucking him or… them."

I lean forward, my appetite quickly vanishing. "I don't have to answer, and I think this conversation is over. Don't come at me again, Warren."

"Or what?" he challenges. "You're getting all defensive

because I'm simply stating a fact. The Bedford twins don't have friends that are female unless they are fucking them, and from what I have seen and heard, you don't strike me to be the type to share your man with other women. He has obviously moved on, and I don't mean that in a bad way, Gia. However, I do think you deserve better than someone who plays with women like the strings on a guitar." He lowers his voice. "Do you honestly think Dravin hasn't written a little poem for anyone else? Do you think you're the only one?"

Warren is probably pointing it out so he can sway me. I already know the things he is telling me and how much it hurts me, but I can't bash Dravin with his child growing inside of me. Like it or not, I have to be civil.

The safest thing to say when someone mentions him is that we are friends. I can't say he is my enemy because he woke up and realized he doesn't want me anymore and that I was a mistake. I can't change how he feels, and he told me how he felt. I can't make him love me or be a father if that isn't what he wants. He wants to find a wife, except that person isn't me. I'm not what he wants anymore.

"I'm not stupid, Warren. He broke it off with me, and I'm handling it just fine. I'm not the first. I don't have to explain myself to you or anyone."

"Then go out with me. If you're fine, let me take you out."

I shake my head and let him down gently. "I'm sorry, Warren, but I'm not interested in you. I think you're nice." *Lie.* "But I don't like you like that. Going out with you won't change that."

His eyes narrow and his upper lip curls. Then he smiles, even though it doesn't reach his eyes and I know he must be upset, but I really don't like him. There is no connection. Every time I'm around him, I feel unsafe. The guy gives me the fucking creeps.

"I'll give you time."

What? Didn't I just tell him that I'm not interested?

I rise from my seat, move my chair back, and collect my bag.

When he approaches me like that, alarm bells start going off in my head. When he leans in for a whisper, he licks his lips, and my stomach knots up in disgust. "You're the one I want, Gia. I will have you, and I'll make you enjoy it, so you may as well get accustomed to the notion."

When his tongue nips at my ear, I move to smack him, but he ducks out of the way and laughs. "Fuck off and stay away from me, you fucking psycho."

He laughs. "I'm the psycho? Baby, you were fucking the campus psycho and look at how that turned out. If anything, I'm doing you a favor. Saving your reputation and all that. I can make it good for you. All you have to do is spread those pretty legs, and I'll show you how to scream."

I move to get away from him and pull out my phone from my jacket to call Jess. My first thought was to call Dravin, but he has made it clear that I should only contact him if I need something related to my condition, not my problems. He made sure I was looked at as Prey. I have to learn to deal with psychos like Warren. I'm on my own now. This just proved it.

Me: Jess, I need you. Where are you?

I sense Warren behind me, and my body stiffens on high alert. Fear crawls over my skin. My whole being goes into fight-or-flight mode, and my skin tingles with dread.

When I shut my eyes, I try to will him away.

"See you around, beautiful," he whispers near my ear, making me want to swat him away like a Nat buzzing near me.

My phone buzzes, and I look at the message, a wave of relief going through me

Jess: I'm in the dorm. Where are you?

Me: Café. Can you come and meet me here? I'll explain later.

The doorbell chimes and he pushes the door with his back. "Who are you calling?" He laughs. "He doesn't give a shit about you. You were just a fuck like all the rest, Gia." His eyes slide down my body, making me want to throw up. "You can run, but you can't hide. I like the chase, and I always get what I want. I'll make sure you like it."

"Fuck you," I sneer.

"I'm planning on it, whether you like it or not. I'll slide in and take it."

My chest begins to rise and fall as I grip my cell phone, and then he turns and leaves out the door. When he disappears into the night, I'm afraid to walk closer in case he tries to grab me.

My head turns to the last two people working behind the counter cleaning up for the night, acting like they didn't see or hear half the things he said.

The guy that he was talking to looks up at me. "We'll be closing in five minutes."

Asshole. He heard, and he is basically telling me to leave. I peer down at my phone, silently begging Jess to show up. It's cold out there and dark. I'm afraid of the things he said he would do to me, but who can I tell if not Jess?. He's right about Dravin, he doesn't want me and is done with me. Tears sting my eyes and I look out the window, hoping she shows up before they kick me out. I could call the police, but then I remember what Dravin said. They're all in their pocket, and I'll just make it worse.

I begin to feel dizzy, coughing it up to the fear Warren brought forth. My stomach rumbles and I close my eyes. Relax, Gia. He let you know his intentions. He laid it all out like the fucking creep he is. I wonder why Veronica is obsessed with him. She's probably just as fucked up as he is.

I look at the guy behind the counter. He glances at his watch and then looks at me, quirking a brow. Fucking prick. I grip my jacket and make sure I'm all zipped up.

After a minute, I see Jess's hair while she practically sprints to the front door with a frown. She pulls the door and the bell chimes.

"What's wrong?" she asks.

I look to the guy with a knowing smile, and I snap. "I know you heard what he said. You're just as sick as he is."

He stands there with an evil grin like the girl in the movie *Smile,* not saying anything. I back away while Jess holds open the door.

Right when the door almost closes, he says, "Bye, Gia." I never told him my name. He heard. He heard everything, and he was in on it.

I grip her arm and pull her along with me as I speed walk toward the building. "I'll tell you once we are inside. It's not safe with that fucking creep lurking out here."

CHAPTER SIXTEEN

JESS

"HE SAID THAT?" I ask once we are inside our dorm.

"Yes," she says, and my heart squeezes for her. She's scared, pregnant, and feels all alone.

"Call him."

She knows I'm referring to Dravin. She should tell him what that creep said to her. How he basically told her he was going to rape her. Memories from my past begin playing in my head like a picture book, but I close my eyes and rub them with the pads of my thumbs.

"I'm not his problem anymore, and from what I have learned about girls like us, we don't matter. That much is clear, Jess. I think you should head out." She lets out a nervous sigh. "I think we should both head out."

"When? Where?" I ask.

"Tonight," she says. "We should head out tonight. Everyone has practically left. The few here, like us, are on their own with no witnesses. It isn't safe for me. We should go home, and when we come back, always be around people. Don't go out on your own."

She has a point. The way that guy in the café acted and what Warren said to her must have scared her.

"Alright. Let's see if we can change our flights to leave tonight, and we'll split the Uber ride to the airport."

She looks up from grabbing her suitcase with a smile. "Really?"

"Yeah," I tell her. "We will meet up when we get back to the airport so you don't show up here alone."

She runs and gives me a hug. "Thank you. You're the only one that has been nice to me here."

"You are, too. We have each other, and it won't be long. We'll graduate and leave this place, but we will always be friends, and I'll help you. I promise, Gia," I say, as we both pull back and laugh and cry at the same time, wiping the tears leaking out of our eyes.

It was the first time I felt good in a while. The first person I could call a friend.

CHAPTER SEVENTEEN

GIA

I'M SWEATING and shaking when the aircraft touches down. With nothing left in my stomach, I go to the restroom for the third time and dry heave since everything is already out. My eyes well up with tears, and I feel them trickling down my cheeks. I'm nauseous and cold all over. I couldn't get my bag from the overhead compartment, especially because my hands were sweating so much.

My mother texted me when I landed, only my hands were so clammy, and I was shaking in my seat so badly that I couldn't reach for my phone. I barely made it to the restroom at the airport.

I flush the toilet, almost falling on the side between the stalls. I wonder why I feel so weak. I feel sweaty and wet. When I look between my thighs, I see blood soaking the floor, and I scream. "HEEEELP ME PLEASE!" I scream.

Everything fades in and out and then everything goes black.

Dravin

I open the door to the main building of the dorm. I have this cold feeling in the pit of my stomach. I haven't seen or heard from her since the day in the bar. I thought by giving her space it would be better for her. I acquired her bank information from financial aid and wired her money into her account. Since my family founded the school, it wasn't hard. Nothing is really out of my reach being a Bedford.

Considering what I said and how I treated her, I can't say I blame her for not calling. I don't know what to do to make her happy anymore.

My brother wants her. I see it in the way he looks at her. I know the feeling, the want, the desire, and the lust that goes through his mind when he looks at her because I feel the same way. We want to consume her. To own her. And keep her forever.

If this is the only way to keep her, then so be it. I will take care of her and watch her with my child in secret. For my eyes only. Under my protection. My biggest fear is when I look at the empty tub in my bathroom, I see her in there, dead like my mother.

My mother, Anastasia, took her life in the bathtub, filling it with water and then blood because she couldn't deal with my father. She couldn't deal with what was expected of her, how her sons were supposed to grow up. What was expected of us and the role she had to play. She lost faith in us, in herself. And most of all, she died sad, alone, and heartbroken. I don't want Gia to suffer the same fate.

I walk down the silent hallway to the door and open it with the skeleton key. The door swings open and I see that both beds are made. I walk over and check her bed and her drawers, noticing most of her things are missing. I pick up one of her shirts and hold it close to my nose to breathe in her sweet scent.

I pull my phone out of my pocket and call her cell phone, but it goes straight to voice mail. I try again and again.

"Fuck!" I scream.

I call Reid and he answers. "Yeah."

"Where are they?"

"I don't know. I tried to call Jess, but she didn't answer."

"Why? What did you do now?"

"Nothing. I was an asshole to her, and she blew me off the other day."

"What did you do, Reid?"

I know he can be a temperamental bastard when he doesn't get his way. He acts out and acts like a total dick.

"I broke the little bracelet she had on her nightstand. It looked like a guy gave it to her, and it was sentimental or some shit. I tore it to pieces and said some fucked-up shit."

"Fix it," I say through clenched teeth. "This doesn't help in any way. They're not here."

"Stalker."

"Hater."

"Why don't you fix your own shit before you get on my case? That is no way to treat the mother of your child. Even if you don't want her. I'm sure everyone is sniffling around."

"She's pregnant. She isn't going to fall into anyone else's bed anytime soon. Only mine."

"Or Draven."

"Fuck you."

"Nah, not my thing. I wouldn't mind watching you three, though. That would be hot."

"I knew you'd love to watch my cock in action."

"Go home and jerk off to the scent of her panties you must have stuffed somewhere, you dick. And wait until she comes back. She must have gone back home to visit family."

"I'll call you back," I tell him, ending the call.

I open my contacts and dial. The sound of the phone rings in the silence of the room. "Hello."

"Find her," I say dryly.

CHAP†ER EIGH†EEN

GIA

A DISTANT BEEPING sound wakes me from the deepest sleep. Wherever it's coming from, it just keeps on beeping. My thoughts are cloudy and hazy. My head hurts, and I can feel it cracking. It feels like an axe has slashed my forehead, and it's about to open.

"Gianna?" I hear my mother's voice. "Gianna," she says again, calling my name. My eyes flutter, and I squint at the bright white light.

"Gianna?" she calls out again.

"Mom," I croak, grimacing at the feeling in my throat. It feels like sandpaper.

"Oh, thank God. I'll get the doctor."

My eyes adjust and I try to lift my hands, except they feel like concrete bricks. Once my eyes adjust, I look around and then I remember. I blacked out.

I try to sit up, but then there is a blonde nurse by my side. "Relax, Gianna. You have to be careful and take it slow."

I look down as she motions to my hand with an IV and then the sound of the curtain being drawn back.

A man with a lab coat appears with my mother right by his side. He unwraps his stethoscope from around his neck.

"Gianna," he says, looking at the monitor where I'm hooked up, measuring my vitals. "My name is Dr. Grayson," he looks at my mother and then back at me. "Is it okay to speak freely in front of your mother?"

I nod, closing my eyes. "Yes."

It's not the ideal way I imagined her finding out I'm pregnant, but I don't want them to send her away. The memory of how I must have gotten here comes back. The blood, my body shutting down, and then blacking out on the bathroom floor at the airport.

"How are you feeling? When the EMTs brought you in, you were in bad shape."

I stay silent. My pulse rate accelerates, and my eyes widen. The alarm starts to sound from the monitors. The nurse turns off the machine, and the tears spill because I can see it. He doesn't have to say it.

"I'm sorry, but you had a miscarriage," the doctor says.

A sob escapes my throat and I shake my head. "My baby. I lost my baby."

"I'm sorry, Gianna, it was early, and there was just too much blood. We ran some tests. I'm afraid you were poisoned. Listeria or some type of food poisoning you ate. It can cause a miscarriage in early pregnancy. We treated you with antibiotics, and after a careful examination, you are still able to have children in the future. In early pregnancy, you must be careful with where and what you eat. Unsafe handling of food can cause a significant amount of bacteria. You were fortunate, young lady. Like I said, you lost a lot of blood. We had to give you a transfusion and IV fluids."

My gaze flicks to my mother and her hand is covering her mouth. The doctor listens and examines me while I lock eyes with her. The loss I'm feeling—the shame and anger for not taking better care of myself.

When the doctor and nurses leave, my mother walks up to me near the side of the bed. "Was it his?" she asks softly.

I nod. "Yeah."

"Where is he?"

I shrug my shoulders as tears run down my cheeks to my chin. "I don't know," I sniff.

"He knows?"

I look away toward the door. "Yes."

"And?"

"He doesn't want me," I mutter. It's all I can say. I can't tell her the whole truth. She would be disappointed in me if she wasn't already.

She wipes her hands across my cheeks and lifts my chin to meet her eyes.

"Then he doesn't deserve you. I'm not going to judge you about what happened. What you are going through is hard, and I'm not going to sit here and give you shit about it."

My eyes widen at hearing her curse. My mother never curses.

"I raised you in this bubble because I wanted what was best for you and tried to instill this image of the perfect family when, in all reality, it doesn't exist. It could, but for us, it didn't. There is no such thing as a perfect family. We all have skeletons we leave in the dark, hoping no one realizes they are there. I was wrong for forcing you to think you had to abide by this ideology."

"It's okay, Mom. I know why you did it. You didn't want me to end up being a girl with no morals. You wanted me to be the good girl who waits until she is married to have sex. To be the perfect wife. To have a career, a house, and a family."

She leans down and wipes my tears. "Now I'm telling you to do whatever makes you feel good. Whatever calls to you, do it. Do things I never did but always wanted to do. I was scared that it was going against my faith."

"What are you saying?"

"Explore your sexuality, and don't let a man make you feel worthless. Don't settle for less because you think that is all you are worth. Live. Have sex. Enjoy life. If you get pregnant and the father isn't around, so what? You won't be the first or the last. I'm sorry about the baby, Gia. You can still have children, but this time, make sure that person is worth it and at least respects you."

"I wanted the baby, Mom." I sob. "I wanted it with everything that I am, even if he didn't."

She wraps her arms around me. "It was early, and you didn't have the support you needed. I feel ashamed as your mother because you didn't feel comfortable reaching out. I would have helped you. I would have spoken to your father."

I shake my head, my eyes widening in horror. "Please don't tell him." I look up, sniffling. "Please," I plead. "Tell him we broke up and that I'm back in the dorm with Jess, and I'm fine. Don't tell him this, please. I was alone. I was bleeding on a bathroom floor, and I was so scared."

"Shh... I know, baby," she says, her voice cracking. I know my mother is crying with me, for me, and for the first time, I feel stronger than ever. With loss comes pain, but it also strengthens you.

There is a knock on the door and we both look up. Eyes that plague my dreams find me. They look at the monitors and the blood bag that was hooked up to the IV pole. His eyes dart around the room and my mother stiffens beside me.

"I think you need to leave," my mother says in a hard tone. She points to the door behind him. "How dare you. Get out."

He gives my mom the cold shoulder while I attempt to identify which of the brothers is standing in front of me. He's putting the phone up to his ear with his shoulder and his head is cocked to one side.

The Phillip Plein logo shimmers in the fluorescent light as it clings to the form of his fitted jacket. His black pants hang low on his hips as he disregards my mother.

She drops her hand and holds my hand in support. Seeing this side of my mother warms my heart. She has my back. I don't know how he found me, and I don't care.

"This is Bedford. I need a private room, now. I want a team sent to the fourth floor." He pauses. "Well, now you know. Send me everything."

He hangs up and walks closer to the foot of the bed. He glances at my mother. "I need a moment alone with her."

"No, you don't. You don't have any right."

He looks at me and says, "I have every right, and I'm not going to say it again. I need a moment alone with her." He looks around the room. "She will be moved from here."

"Oh, so you think by showing up here, you can snap your fingers, and everyone jumps?"

He gives her a devilish smile. "That's right. Everyone will jump."

My mother walks up to him, and I get nervous about how he watches her, arching a brow. "Where were you when she was bleeding on the floor of a dirty bathroom in the airport? She almost died. Where were you, huh? You don't deserve my Gianna. She doesn't need your filth."

"I'm sorry for what happened," he responds.

"*I'm sorry* doesn't bring her baby back," she snaps and walks outside.

When he stares into my eyes, it seems like he's in pain. I shift out of his reach as he tries to touch me. "Don't touch me, please. I don't know who…" I trail off.

He knows I can't tell them apart and my mother doesn't know that they're identical twin brothers. He slides his hand into his pocket and pulls out a black velvet box. It's flat and has an engraving in gold on the top.

"I'm not here to upset you."

"I don't want you here. I want you to leave me alone."

"I will—we will. I just have to give you something first. It's for your protection, and don't ever take it off." A serious expression crosses his face, his eyes look dark and there is a sadness to them.

He opens the lid and slides a necklace out, which is very different from the Raven I was gifted but gave back.

"What is it?"

"Most people call it a necklace."

"Very funny, Drav," I retort.

He smiles. He holds it up and there is a symbol over a circular coin and a bird attached. The bird is black with diamonds on a gold chain glittering in the light. It's beautiful.

"My mother would call me that. It was her way of letting us know she could tell us apart. She would tell me that only a mother would know how to tell her twin sons apart. Besides her, you're the only person that has ever said it."

He holds the necklace close so I can see it better in the light. "This is the symbol of the Order. When it is recognized, they will know. *They.* Only the founding three families have these specifically made. One for each son. This one is mine and now yours." He leans close and whispers in my ear, "I'm the bad twin. The evil one. The crow."

I place my hand over my flat stomach, knowing it's empty. My baby's father didn't make an appearance. Instead, his brother showed up. He slides the necklace around my neck and secures it, and I let him.

I glance up and see tears running down his cheeks, making my eyes well up with emotion. "I'm sorry, Gianna. I'm so sorry."

He places a strand of hair behind my ear and kisses my cheek. "I want you to know that this is going to crush him, baby. Everything beautiful in his life dies, and you are the only thing he has left."

He turns my chin to look at him, and tears are flowing like a river down my cheeks at my loss. *Our* loss. My emotions are everywhere, feeling lost and confused.

Dravin said he didn't want me. He said that I was a mistake. His words repeat in my head like a broken record. I should be mad at both of them, but Draven is here.

The pads of his thumbs wipe my cheeks. He grabs my fingers and leans in so that I can run them up his neck and feel the tattoo that is so similar to the crow pendant on my necklace. I rub it softly and his eyes darken.

"I'm the only one who has this. He has something else that he will show you." He lowers his voice. "That's one way to tell us apart and the other you already know, when we are deep inside you, claiming you." I suck in a breath, and he continues, "I don't expect you to accept me, and he doesn't expect you to accept him, but it doesn't matter, Gianna. You will always be taken care of because, in my eyes, you were already mine."

A man quickly enters the room with a clipboard flanked by four men in black suits. "Mr. Bedford, I apologize for the confusion. She will be moved to a private suite and her mother will also be accommodated. Is there anything else you may require to make Miss Taylor's stay more comfortable? She will have around-the-clock care until she is discharged."

Draven straightens, and the nurse that enters eyes him appreciatively. I give her a stern glare.

"I need all her medical reports sent to me. Her account, and everything else, are to be billed to me," he instructs and then points to the nurse. "I also don't want her attending to Gianna."

My head angles up to glance at Draven, but I can't see his face. I know he noticed me stiffening, or maybe he knows the nurse and the way she is looking at him in front of me after I just lost a baby doesn't sit well with him.

She's practically undressing him with her eyes, ready to pounce. I know that it would happen on campus, but here, after what I went through, I can't help but be grateful.

"Of course," the man says, and then one of the men in a dark suit escorts her out. "I'll send a replacement."

"Make sure he isn't male," Draven adds.

One thing they both are when they want to be is possessive. I'm weak and vulnerable, and something about what just happened to me and how I ended up here doesn't sit well with me. There could have been many things I ate that could have been contaminated, but I haven't eaten anything except what was given to me by the delivery service and a few items from the vending machine on campus.

The man with the clipboard smiles warmly at me. "You're a very lucky young lady."

He looks over at Draven. "He was in the airport when they

found you. He was the one who called to have you brought in immediately. We had to stabilize you first, and you ended up here, but we had no idea..." He trails off. His eyes move a centimeter lower, spotting the necklace, and then he smiles. "Ah... I see it now."

"She left it at home and didn't realize I had it with me the whole time," Draven says.

After being placed in the most luxurious private room, like Draven instructed, there was an older nurse who was very careful in tending to me. I need a shower, but my mother was sent home and said she'd be back. My thoughts are drifting to the talk we had about me exploring my sexuality and looking out for myself, not allowing anyone to push me around or hurt me again. He can hurt me once, but it taught me to know what the sting feels like. I now recognize it. Losing my baby will make me stronger, and I know what I want. I want love, hope, faith, and family, and I want to be happy. But most of all, I want to feel wanted.

CHAPTER NINETEEN

DRAVIN

IT WAS hard acting like my brother around her, but we did it all the time, and I had to see her. I'm the last person she would want to see if she knew it was me. There was too much I said that hurt her.

Leaving her there was the hardest thing I had to do. I left because I needed to be alone to break down and cry. It was the second time in my life I have given in to the emotion—the death of my mother and now the loss of my child. I had them run more tests before she was discharged to make sure someone hadn't tried to kill her, but I know deep down, it wasn't a coincidence.

Is it wrong to lie to her? Of course. I know I did the same thing. I acted like I was my brother. She was calmer, even though my brother was a dick to her, but coming from him, it was more forgivable than it was coming from me.

She thinks I haven't been around, but I have. I have turned into a stalker because of her. Her stalker. When I heard her scream in the bathroom at the airport, it felt like my heart and gut were being ripped open. I found her bleeding and lying on the floor. She didn't look well, and I thought it was the nausea that is common in early pregnancy.

At home, on my computer, I have been drowning myself with information about being a first-time parent. I would never abandon her. If she only knew, I could never have a child with someone else. I had to lie to her to protect her. She isn't my wife, and I can't force her to accept me and my brother. I can't force her to accept the life that will be thrust upon her by being Mrs. Bedford.

My phone rings and I look at the screen. It's my brother, so I answer, "Yeah."

"How is she? I want to see her, but then she is going to tell me to fuck off when she thinks I'm you."

I'm sitting in the back of the car with the divider up so the driver doesn't hear my conversation with my twin. I'm making lazy circles over my pants as I tell him what is weighing on my mind.

"Come here, and let's surprise her."

"I don't think that is a good idea."

"When did you start becoming a pussy?"

"Since the girl we both want and can't have because you have fucked with her in a way she can't wrap her head around. Since she had sex with two identical-looking people when she thought she was in love with only one. Now, what are you thinking?"

I sniff because I've been crying about the baby. Every time I think about it, I want to kill someone. Mainly myself for being careless with her. My relationship with God is sinking at the moment—the loss of my mother, a child, and her love.

I know it was early in her pregnancy, and it can happen, but why me? Why does fucked-up shit happen like that? I get that I'm not a good person because I have done fucked-up shit, but her? Why her?

What the hell did she do to deserve the loss of her baby? Our baby. The pain she was in, she could've died if I wasn't there. If I hadn't gone to her dorm room, they told me she was on a plane to see her mother.

"I'm checking to see if there have been any reports of food poisoning on campus, and so far, there aren't any. She has been eating the food we have delivered for her and Jess," he says.

"Someone tried to kill her," I blurt, my hand shaking in rage.

"Who?"

"It could be anyone that doesn't like us, and we have a fucking list a mile long. Whoever it is, knows that she was pregnant. So that narrows down to someone on campus, and it's within the Order. We have to think about who could have known and who would want to hurt or try to kill her. Once we find out who it is, I'm not going to stop, and I'm not going to wait for a fucking meeting at the church, so you tell our father that the rules don't apply when it comes to Gia. Not when it comes to her life. My unborn child's life."

"If you don't kill the motherfucker, then I will. Either way, the result will be the same. Gianna comes first. Always. Your room is ready for when she arrives back on campus. I will let our father know."

"Yeah, tell him to keep his fucking escapades around the house to his room, or I'll eat my breakfast at the dining table like a good boy."

Meaning, I'll eat my girl's pussy on the dining table, and I'll make sure to make him feel uncomfortable watching his son's ass as I fuck her freely every chance I get.

"That's if she'll let you."

I smile. "Is that a challenge, little brother?"

I can't see him smile back, but I can hear it in his voice. "Challenge accepted. It's going to be fun being you."

I snort. "Don't get used to it."

"Why?"

"Because I saw her first," I say, disconnecting the call before he can respond.

CHAPTER TWENTY

GIA

I GET up from the luxurious bed in a private room in a hotel that the hospital uses for procedures I have read about in brochures and plastic surgery offices. Rich and famous people use specific hotels with private staff and security to cater to the wealthy.

After a long day, I go to the rain shower next to my room, where the dark tiles gleam in stark contrast to the centrally placed light. In the shower, tiny teak shelves are stocked with high-end shampoos and body washes and a teak seat against one wall for sitting while you wash.

To stop the bleeding, I slip down the hospital underwear I was provided and hit the button to turn on the water. It feels like getting a heavy period, the doctor said, and it will pass in a few days. My chest hurts from throwing up so much, yet I feel somewhat stronger than I did yesterday. Assuming I eat well and drink enough fluids over the next several days to restore my strength, I should feel like myself again in a few days.

I was dehydrated and had anemia. I wasn't that far along, but I still felt the cramping and I was in pain. My body begins to shake from being in bed for the past forty-eight hours. I'm in need of a proper shower.

Drav—I smile to myself at being able to tell them apart. When they switch on me like they do, at least I can figure out who did and said what.

I'm figuring out that I have these weird feelings for both of them now. Even if Dravin lied and hurt me with his words, I have a feeling there is a bigger picture at play. The tears I saw Drav shed showed me that the baby and I meant a lot more than Dravin said we did.

What he said confused me, but it was like something inside both of them died. To them, the little being inside me belonged to one, but it also belonged to the other.

I have heard of twins sharing such a strong bond that they share everything. They get used to sharing. They are so equally identical and more so if they were raised that way. I find it bizarre but hot all at the same time.

There were nights I cried and nights I imagined having them both, but they belonged to me and only me. What I did to one, I made sure to give to the other, and in return, they did the same. One night, it was with Dravin, and the other night, it was with Draven.

The IV made my left hand sore. The warm water falls like rain over my head as I wash my hair with shaky hands. The steam rises like fog under the single spotlight in the shower, and then I hear a noise and jolt.

After wiping my eyes to remove the accumulated water on my lashes, I turn around.

Slowly, my gaze travels down to the shower's threshold, where it lands on two sets of feet. My dreams and the real world are both haunted by them. Their presence engulfs everything I think about. It's all connected. They're connected—the way they make me feel. Hate, love, and darkness collide like I'm the sweetest sacrifice.

My eyes train on their necks, and it's like I'm seeing them in a new light. They even share the colors of their eyes. It's powerful when all their attention is on you.

They stare, running their eyes over my body as the water sluices down my curves. Both of their cocks are hard and imposing as they step forward. The water sprays as it hits their bodies, carved like perfect concrete sculptures.

The water wets their hair as one grabs the body wash, and I can see the tattoo of the crow and the other of a wolf in the light. I don't know how I didn't see them before, or maybe they're recent, but they're surrounded by other symbols and markings inked on their skin.

When they turn, the light moves like shadows casting figures, but then I see them as their fingers trail down my cheek, one on the left and the other to my right. The tattoo of a Raven. One near the crow and the other near the wolf. On the bottom, it reads: *We pray for her love evermore.*

"How are you feeling, gorgeous?" Drav says as the suds of the body wash slide down my breasts.

My eyes flick to Dravin, and his eyes turn dark. His nostrils flare, but then I notice his eyes are red-rimmed. His head tilts to look at my stomach and then slowly slides up to my face. He walks closer, but I move closer to Drav, remembering the hurt of his words. His eyes flick to Drav with a glare aimed at his twin.

He shakes his head slowly, then grips my face in both hands and kisses me. My lips are closed, but he forces them open with his tongue, sliding it over my teeth.

"I'm sorry," he says softly while he trails his fingers over my belly. I look down, our foreheads touching as a little trail of blood slides down my thighs.

"I'm bleeding," is all I manage to say.

They both look down at the same time and see a small trail of blood mixing with water down the drain.

"Shit," Drav says with a sniffle.

They are both crying silent tears, and I give them this moment —a moment to mourn our loss, the three of us. They both wash me carefully, not too rough but with gentle strokes over my skin as the rain shower head pours over our skin. We stand under the spray, with the spotlight illuminating the dimly lit bathroom.

They wash my hair, body, and toes while they both kiss my belly. Heat pools between my legs as they inch closer to the apex of my thighs.

Drav's hand stills near my slit and Dravin watches the expression on my face to see if it's okay to wash me there.

"I think it's best if you do it. We don't want to hurt you," Drav says.

I nod in agreement. Dravin hands me the body wash, and I raise my hand to the spray, wetting the palm of my hand and squinting as I reach down to gently wash myself. I watch them and notice the smoldering gaze aimed at my hand as the tension begins to increase.

"So beautiful," Dravin whispers, but the memory of the text with the video slows my movements, and I turn around, giving them my back.

"I wasn't beautiful when they sent me the text of you and those girls."

I meant Dravin, but I recognize that I wasn't just jealous because of one. I was jealous of both of those girls touching them. I close my eyes and feel the sting of tears burning my eyes.

The loss, pain, and humiliation I felt in that moment. Then, the moment after, when he told me I was a mistake and unworthy. That he wouldn't acknowledge his child and that he would marry someone else. Have children that would be considered his.

The fog in my mind clears and I look down, ashamed of myself for letting them hurt me. Guilt for allowing myself to be used, for allowing them to be here with me. A sob creeps up my throat. Fresh tears slide down my cheeks, and suddenly, the shower becomes stifling.

"We didn't sleep with them."

I whirl around and meet both of their stares, but I lock mine on Dravin because his brother wasn't the one I was in love with. He doesn't owe me any loyalty. What he did was fucked up, but I was pregnant with Dravin's child. He didn't know at first.

"I'm going to let it slide for Drav, but for you, I can't because whoever that girl was, sure as hell had your cock in her mouth. You weren't thinking about me then or how I would feel about it, but it doesn't matter anymore because you're free of me. I'm not pregnant anymore," I say, widening my stance. "You have proof.

I'm not your responsibility. The mistake was taken care of, Dravin."

He flinches like I slapped him. My eyes find Drav. "Thank you for the private room and the nice shower. I'm sure I'm not the only woman you have given the same privilege to, and you're right; the girl in the video was better than me. She sucked you off like a champ. That part you did do, right?"

I look up at the bathroom and my surroundings like it's the first time, and that I haven't been standing here feeling numb since I suffered food poisoning and a miscarriage at the same time.

"I'm sorry I hurt you. If I could take it all back, I would. We took things too far and were reckless," Drav says with a sigh.

My chin lifts and our eyes lock. "Me too. I should have listened when everyone told me to stay away from you." My gaze shifts to Dravin. "Especially you. You two are great at deceiving people and are so alike you even treat women the same. When I think of you two, I feel like I'm nothing." I lick my lips and hug myself, suddenly feeling cold. "I would like to go to my mother's and spend the holidays with her, please," I say quietly.

Dravin steps out and hands me a towel for my hair and a fluffy white robe. "Of course."

I hate having to let them go, but I need to. It's the hardest thing to let go of something you love. I can't keep throwing what happened in their faces. I need to move on. I need to let go.

CHAPTER TWENTY ONE

JESS

WE ARE BACK from winter break, and Gia is quiet as she skims over the menu at a bar we decided to try out on the outskirts of Kenyan. We wanted to stay away from campus and the Babylon bar. It's a new semester with new classes and we have decided to lie low.

"Have you heard from them?" I ask Gia while I'm scanning the menu, still deciding between the club or the meatloaf.

"Nope. They dropped me off at my mother's, and they left but made sure to leave two men in suits to follow me and camp outside my mother's apartment."

I raise my brows. "Why would they think you need security?"

She lets out a breath. "I have no fucking idea. All I know is that I need to concentrate on graduating, have fun, and forget about them and what happened. It is in the past. It hurts, but I have to move on. It's over."

I lower my voice and ask, "Have you seen Warren lurking around?"

She shakes her head. "Not since that day at the café when he creeped me out."

"Did you tell them?" I ask, lowering the menu, my eyes locking with hers. "What he said to you."

She shakes her head. "No. Dravin isn't my boyfriend. Why would he care? I'll just report him if he says or does anything else."

I'm about to say something when two guys wearing Ohio State hoodies stop by our booth.

"Hi. We were wondering if you ladies would like some company?"

I look up, and the guy to the left looks at me. His blond friend has his eyes locked on Gia.

I give the guy on my left a playful smile. "Is that what you guys do? You go to diners and pick up girls by asking if you can join them?"

He laughs nervously, sliding his dark hair out of his eyes. "No. Just you two. We've never seen you two around here before. You ladies in school?" he asks, then looks at Gia. His eyes land back on me, waiting for me to respond.

"Yeah," I answer, pointing to his hoodie. "But we don't attend Ohio State, though."

The blond one turns his gaze on me, but then it's back on Gia. "What school do you attend, beautiful? Please tell me you don't have a boyfriend somewhere?" he asks Gia.

She licks her lip nervously and then glances at him. "Kenyan. We attend Kenyan, and no, I don't have a boyfriend. Not anymore."

The blond guy holds his hand out and sits at the edge of the booth next to her. "I'm Dalton, and this is my teammate and best friend, Tate. Since you two lovely ladies aren't seeing anyone, we would love to take you out. How about us four next Saturday night? We can meet up at a local bar. Food, drinks, dancing."

Gia's eyes find mine with uncertainty. Is it too soon? Should we say yes? I can see all her questions cross her face, silently asking me how we should answer. Accept or don't accept.

My need to forget what happened back home claws my insides, and I smile coyly while making my decision. "What time Saturday?"

"We can meet up at six," Dalton says.

"Perfect."

We exchange phone numbers, and he sends me directions to the bar we are supposed to meet at on Saturday. I guess you could call it a date, even if it's just to meet up somewhere. To be honest, I just want to forget what happened back home.

When people ask me how my winter break was, flashes of unwanted kisses and grunts fill my head. Tears burn my eyes, and the sense of feeling dirty and the need to scrub my skin over-whelms me. I hate myself, but before the disappointment sets in, I remember my mother's smile full of relief that she can pay her rent, gas, electric, and car insurance all in the same month. That she doesn't have to go down to the local church at six a.m. to pick up free groceries from donations.

When she told me the sacrifices parents make for their children are worth it, I was eight; I didn't understand what she meant. But I understand now as a grown woman. The sacrifices you make for the people you love most in your life are the ones that count. It's part of surviving, even if you begin to lose yourself. But losing yourself doesn't mean you gave up; it just means you'll rise a different person.

CHAPTER TWENTY TWO

JESS

"ARE YOU SURE I LOOK OKAY?" I ask Jess, pulling the top that is one inch away from spilling my breasts. My dark hair is ironed straight, and I'm wearing black patent leather pants that I found in a boutique store we went to earlier today. I was surprised when I checked my bank account, which had a deposit from Bedford Holdings for fifty thousand dollars. I subtracted the difference I'd had previously and made my purchase.

I know Dravin is trying to keep his word and must be feeling guilty, but I'm going to try and move on. When I got back from my mother's house, Jess thought it would be good to get out the first weekend back. The bleeding stopped, and I had no more cramping.

My eyes scan the room through the reflection of the mirror, and I see Jess dabbing her neck again with some foundation to cover up the marks on her skin. I know they weren't hickeys. They look like marks someone gives you when they want to hurt you.

She looks at me through the mirror's reflection. "You look hot, babe. Just make sure you're ready because when he sees you in that outfit, I'm not sure he is going to just hold your hand," she says playfully.

A blush creeps up my neck at the thought of someone touching me because they really like me and not because they want to use me for some sick game. My mother's words from when I was in the hospital play in my head.

When she dropped me off at the airport, she reminded me to live and to do what feels right. Explore and find what makes you happy, and that is what I'm going to do. I'm tired of feeling guilty and afraid.

"Are you going to tell me what happened?" Her hands pause

from dabbing the concealer with the beauty blender across her neck.

Her eyes lock on mine, and a sadness crosses her expression. Something bad happened to her when she went home.

I turn around and walk closer to her and lower my voice. "You could tell me, Jess. I saw the bruises, and I didn't want to pressure you into telling me, but I want to know if there is a way I can help. A way to make that face you're making go away. You're my only friend."

She nods and her eyes get glassy. Her hands begin to fidget and her lips purse as she lets out a breath, closing her eyes. My heart starts to beat faster because I know what she is about to tell me is going to make me hurt.

She dabs her fingers over her neck on the faded marks. "Well, you know I didn't get these because a boy loves me back home."

I visibly swallow and work my way over to her side of the bed and I give her a hug, smelling her perfume. "Tell me," I whisper.

"It's ugly, Gia."

"All I have felt lately is ugly," I say softly. "Unwanted. Used. And I'm fucking sick of it."

She knows about the miscarriage and what happened over the break. She was sad, and we both cried for hours when I broke down and told her.

She takes a deep breath and begins. "I used to like this boy back in high school. His name is Michael. He was the typical rich boy who had it all. Cars, looks, money, and a killer smile. It was like the devil created him just to fuck with me. Word got around that the trailer trash was at the top of her class liked him, and he asked me out. I felt like I was on cloud nine. I got accepted to come here, and I was being asked out by the hottest guy in school my senior year right before prom. I hadn't lost my virginity because I was secretly hoping that one day it would be him."

She gives a shaky laugh and a sniff, trying to not let her mascara run, dabbing her finger under her eye, and looks up for a second and continues. "Anyway. I was invited to this party in his neighborhood, and I thought the popular crowd was finally accepting me because he noticed me. I dressed up and I went. He was there with his friends. We talked and he was so nice. He did all the right things the entire night, and I was giddy. He knew he had me and I wasn't going anywhere. He told me I was beautiful and that he liked me but didn't know how to approach me because I was quiet. He said he didn't care where I lived or the rumors about me and my mother because we lived in a trailer."

She closes her eyes as I listen to her story. It's like she is reliving something awful every day, and my heart prepares for the blow that I sense is coming.

"He spiked my drink, and they took me to a room. Michael and his friends... they raped me."

My stomach clenches and I blink back the tears. "Did you tell anyone?"

She shakes her head. "For what? No one would believe me. I got tested, and thank God I was on birth control, but I came out clean. I didn't go to prom for obvious reasons and kept to myself. I didn't have money for a dress anyway. It's what I told myself to cope. That is why I didn't want to go back home. I hated to leave my mom, but I have a plan to get a degree and a good job and take my mom out of there, and we can start a new life. A good life."

"When you went back. Was it him that did this to you?"

She nods slowly and I want to go with her and kill the bastard. How dare he. That piece of shit. Then I think of what she said about Garret and what they did with the video. Her behavior with Reid and Valen. She's trying to pick up the pieces. To feel wanted by someone. To forget.

"Does your mom know?"

"No. I couldn't do that when the asshole's father bought the diner across the road. When I went back, she told me she applied there for work, and they turned her down, and to top it off, the owner where she works cut her hours. She didn't want me to worry, but she was struggling. She asked for a raise, and he denied her. It was so she would call me and for me to show up."

"He was there, wasn't he? Waiting like the sick bastard he is baiting you with your mother."

"Yeah, he got what he wanted. He made sure to throw a hundred bucks on my lap after zipping up his pants," she says with a shaky laugh, but it's so that she doesn't break down and cry. "Then Reid called me from a blocked number, telling me I was fun. After I scrubbed my skin raw in the shower, that's all I was worth."

I stay quiet and give her a minute. Her eyes land on mine, tortured and full of hurt and shame. "I just want to forget, Gia. I want to forget what I had to do to put a smile on my mother's face when she came in telling me they hired her. I hate the person I have become."

"Don't say that," I tell her, caressing her hair, which took forty-five minutes to straighten. It's silky and soft. "It's what they want you to become, and you're not that. You're better than they are. They have to blackmail you to get it, but you know what? They may think they have gotten the best of you, but they haven't. They will never have your love, your mind, or your loyalty. Don't let them break what is left of you."

Her voice cracks on a whisper, "I just want to forget. I don't want the memory of his hands on my skin. His tongue on my lips. I want that feeling to go away."

"Then do what you need to do to forget."

She moves to her nightstand and takes a string of condoms out, and hands me two, slipping the rest into her bag. Her eyes lift. "This is the only way I know how."

I get why she wanted to go out with the hockey players who approached us at the booth. They were both good-looking and seemed like regular college guys. Not the kind that would live in a Gothic mansion with secrets and evil twin brothers who are part of a secret society with rules.

We arrive in Jess's car, parking on the side of the bar. Dravin texted me twice on the way here, but I left it as delivered. I don't have time for him right now.

The last three weeks after the hospital, I have kept it curt via text message. He asks me how I'm feeling and if I need anything, but I just tell him that I'm okay and fine. I don't engage in conversation with him. Draven has texted me the same, asking the same questions as his brother. I wonder if they do anything different besides the tattoo markings or the way they have sex.

I clench my thighs, thinking about them and the way they introduced sex to me. I had no experience before them and everything I do know, it's because of both of them. After everything, I love to hate them and hate to love them.

When I think of them, I think of hot sex, pain, hurt, shame, and guilt. Tonight, I hope to move on from all that with someone who can show me a good time.

We both slam the car doors shut and I smile. "Ready?" she asks.

"Yeah. Let's go for it. Remember to keep your drink in hand, and let's stick to beer."

"Good idea."

We make our way to the entrance, and music filters through the door as we open it. The bouncer nods as we come in, taking our coats off.

We notice Dalton and Tate waving at us from a booth in the back. The place has dark gray interior brick walls, a bar in the center, and booths and tables flanked on the sides. Flat-screen TVs hang from the walls at different angles. Some people are dancing from the lit jukebox to the right.

I smile and give them a small wave when Tate stands from the booth, waiting for us to reach them. His eyes take me in from top to bottom and then back up again with a smile.

"Hi," I say, greeting them both.

"Glad you two could make it," Dalton says.

"Thank you for the invite," Jess responds, scanning the bar and the people around us. Ohio State banners and the years of their wins in football, hockey, and even swimming decorate the walls, but there have been very few in the last four years, and I know it's because of the sons of Kenyan. Reid, Dravin, and now Valen. I wouldn't even put it past Draven making an appearance just to fuck with them.

"Of course. You look beautiful," Dalton says, his blond hair sticking up in that messy way that looks sexy. "I love the pants. You have that dark vibe that I like."

I bet he does. He has that hockey frat boy vibe that seems normal, but to be honest, I'm missing my goth boy. Maybe even his twin. I shake my head and forget that I'm supposed to forget about them.

"Thank you."

Tate's eyes keep dipping low to where Jess's heart-shaped mesh top holds her breasts over a black tube top underneath. He slides his dark, straight hair to the side so that it doesn't cover his eyes and he can get a better view.

"So, what would you ladies like to drink?" Tate asks.

"A blonde and a Guinness," I answer.

Jess smiles at my inside joke, and I try to hold in my laughter. I said it to lighten her mood.

After five minutes, the beers arrive. I take the Guinness, and she takes the blonde ale.

"You guys like to switch?" Tate asks, playfully taking a pull from his beer.

Guess who picked up on the joke? Nothing escapes guys nowadays. I tip the bottle and take a pull, and I feel froggy. Some things happen, and they change people. It certainly changed me, and I'm all for it.

"What's the point in switching?" I say, sliding the beer to Jess, taking hers, tipping it back, the taste of her beer mixing with mine while both of their eyebrows lift in surprise. When I set the bottle down on the table and she takes a sip and does the same, I finish saying, "When you can just share."

"Sharing is sexy," Jess pipes up, teasing them.

"So is watching," a deep voice snaking up my spine, belonging to Draven, says as he comes into view by sliding himself next to me on the booth. I notice the tattoo.

I'm sitting between Draven and Dalton, and the hairs on the back of my neck stand. My eyes flick to Jess as she stiffens.

Reid and Valen lean over the back of the booth, and I don't know how we didn't see them come in or why they are here.

Reid curves his lips in a knowing smile as he looks at Dalton and then at Tate, my heart beating wildly in my chest. "You boys like to watch?" Reid asks with an evil grin.

"Depends on what we are watching. Aren't you three on the wrong side of town?" Dalton fires back.

Valen chuckles and leans forward so his lips are close to Jess's ear. He says softly, over the sound of "Mudshovel" by Staind playing in the background, "Did you hear, Jess? They like to watch."

Draven leans forward, the scent of his exotic cologne hits my nose, and his voice turns hard as he looks at Dalton. "We own the town. You're just visiting."

Tate looks at Draven in challenge. "I know who you guys are. You're the sons of Kenyan."

Reid blows smoke in the air from his vape, the tinge of marijuana from the oil permeating the air around us in a cloud. He turns his face, and his lips are near Jess's left cheek. "You're having fun without me, baby?"

Tate's eyes flash in annoyance, and he answers for her, "She was until you showed up."

"Is that so?" Reid says, his nose near her cheek and his lips near her ear. "There is only one way to find out."

His hand disappears under the table, and I see Jess's eyes fill with desire as she bites her bottom lip. After a second, his hand appears above the table and he holds two fingers up to his tongue, flicking the piercing on his lip and showing them to Tate. "Dry as the desert."

Valen leans in again near Jess's ear and says, "That's no fun. Is it?"

Jess's eyes flick to Tate. His nostrils flare and Draven leans forward. "Didn't you just say you liked to watch?"

Fuck this. I slide the beer bottles out of the way and lean across the table toward Jess. Her eyes widen, but she doesn't pull away when I plant my lips on hers and she holds my face in her hands.

Our tongues taste and twirl, the taste of our beer mixing together. We hear intakes of breath around us from the guys. I don't like girls, and I'm sure she feels the same, but I can't stand what they are doing. If they want a show, then we'll give them one, but on our terms, not theirs.

"That's so hot," I hear Dalton's voice behind me.

Strong hands grip my waist, pulling me back down on the bench seat of the booth, and I turn my head and see Draven's stern expression mixed with desire. "No," he says.

I lick my lips from her taste and whip my head toward Reid, his eyes on my tongue as it snakes my bottom lip, and I say, "She's having fun now. I bet she's wet like Florida."

Tate bellows in laughter, taking a pull of his beer and angles the top of the beer bottle toward me. "I like her."

"She's not yours to like," Draven fires back.

He leans forward, cocky as hell, and he doesn't seem to realize the danger they are both in sitting here with us. "Funny, she told us she doesn't have a boyfriend. So that means she's not yours to like."

Draven chuckles and places an elbow on the wooden table with his hand near my cheek. He then places a strand of hair behind my ear, causing a trail of nerves to ignite on my skin. He says, "I'm not a boy, and I'm definitely not her friend."

"She isn't married. That much is obvious. There isn't much left. Then what are you?"

Reid takes another drag, passing it to Valen as they both smile, waiting for Draven to reply. He isn't even my ex-boyfriend, but his twin brother that I ended up fucking, but he doesn't need to know all that.

I watch Valen take a drag of the marijuana pen. The smoke from the vape twirling around the light hanging in the middle of the booth, the tension getting thick. The silence stretches and the music playing fades into the background.

Draven's eyes flick to Tate, hard and threatening, "I'm her fucking god."

Draven slides his hand over my thigh possessively and heat pools between my thighs. I try to clench them together, but his grip tightens.

Tate leans back in the booth with a sly grin. "Funny, but yet she's here with him." He nudges his chin toward Dalton, goading him.

Draven chuckles like it doesn't matter what he says. He will always have the upper hand. "Yeah, but she's so fucking bored. She's kissing her best friend when she would rather be sitting on my cock as I make her pray for me to make her come. You two little hockey boys run along and go play with your sticks. We've come to collect what belongs to us," Draven says, getting up, and so does Reid, taking Jess by the arm.

Valen slides over the booth, plants his feet, and walks out like he is balancing himself on a balance beam. He hops off. He turns around and gives me a mischievous smile. "Let's go, Gia. Let's go have some real fun."

CHAPTER TWENTY THREE

DRAVIN

THE MEN WORKING for me have been following Gia and Jess everywhere they go, whether they're taking shifts at practice or having our meetings. It's a new semester, and we made sure to keep our distance from them. All I know is that she is in danger, and so is Jess. I saw the bruising on her neck if Reid or Valen didn't, but I'll let them handle it.

I have my hands full with Gianna. I've written so many letters to her but haven't had the courage to leave them on her bed where she can wake up to find them.

We pile in the matte-black SUV, and I let Valen drive while I sit in the back and act like my twin brother so she doesn't run away from me.

Acting like Draven around Gia takes some patience because she knows me intimately. I've seen her watching me. She is studying my quirks and if he is around, she will study his. She isn't stupid, but I never thought of her being anything but intelligent. She's smart and sexy. I have to up my game, or I'll lose her forever. Her seeking out another man that isn't me is driving me insane.

Seeing her next to that asshole in the bar had me wanting to yank her out of there and pummel his face until I split it in two. The way his eyes were glued to her breasts and thighs. Those pants had my cock straining to be released; I wanted to bend her over and sink into her.

I lean into her while she sits next to me, our thighs touching. "You must be feeling better. Are you trying to escape me so I can chase you?"

Her head angles toward me. "I thought guys like you don't

chase. It wasn't the fact that I was here. It was who I was with that bothered you. I never thought you were the jealous type."

I give her a side grin. "I'm not jealous."

"I can tell. *I'm her fucking god*," she mocks. "Real smooth, Goth boy. I wouldn't be surprised if you turned green next to me."

The smile on my face falls. My stomach clenches. Does she know I'm me and not Draven? Shit. She called me Goth Boy. Has she called him that?

I turn her chin toward me, and I watch as her pink tongue licks her glossy lips. She must have applied lip gloss at some point and the image of that glossy mess all over my cock has a tingle snaking up my spine.

I arch my eyebrow. "Goth Boy?"

She snickers, and so does Reid. "Where are you taking us?" Jess asks.

"To a party," Reid chimes in.

"What kind of party?" Jess asks.

"Members-only type of party," Valen says, looking through the rearview mirror.

"What kind of party is it? We aren't members," Gia points out.

"If you come with us, then you're allowed in. The rules are…" I trail off.

My eyes follow the wetness of her lips. My thumb touches her bottom lip, pulling it down slightly, feeling the stickiness and I chuckle. "There are no rules. We… are the rules."

Her breathing is slow and shallow, but I can see the desire pooling in her eyes. The clenching of her thighs. My Raven wants to get fucked. She's ready. My eyes trail down to her top, partially hidden by her jacket. I bet her nipples are straining, and I know she isn't wearing a bra.

When she leaned over and kissed Jess, I was green with envy. Jess was tasting what was mine and her pussy was wet for her. My Raven wants to break the rules, but I want to be the one she breaks the rules with.

I lean close, and my lips brush her neck and rasp against her skin, "Tell me, Gia. Do you think about me when you play with your pussy? Or do you think about him?" I place a small peck against her neck, and she squirms.

I know she wants me, but I want to make sure she wants not just one. I'm okay if she wants us both, but if it's one of us, it has to be me. "Or... maybe you think of us both."

Her head turns, and our eyes lock while the car moves over bumps in the road toward Garrett's house. The younger members of the Order are throwing the party there. I'm not sure how Jess will feel about it when she finds out, but I have faith in Reid and Valen. I don't want to ruin their night.

"How did you know we were there?" Gia asks.

"We've had you followed for your safety," I say, peppering a kiss on her cheek.

I notice she is still wearing the necklace I gave her. It is usually reserved for the sons of the founding families or their wives. She's mine in my eyes, and there will never be another. It's her or nothing.

The car slows down two miles from campus and proceeds through a gate that opens. A guy in a suit exits the security booth Garret's family has on their estate. He sees Valen and nods to proceed through.

The mansion comes into view, dark and gray. Expensive cars line the driveway, with drivers sitting inside waiting until the members leave for the night.

"Wow," Jess says from the seat next to Gia.

The lights glow against the dark pillars with a tinge of red. It's cold, but the party is indoors with an indoor pool.

Music filters through the house as we step inside. The staff takes her jacket off her shoulders. Her skin flushes at the warmth of the changing temperature. Valen leads with Reid, and Jess follows in front of Gia.

I'm walking behind her when she slows down and asks softly,

"Where's Dravin?"

I want to say I'm right behind you, and I'll never leave you, but I can't—not yet. Instead, I say, "He's inside by the pool with the others. He's expecting you."

Draven is dying to see her, but I keep that bit to myself. He's been grumpy all week because she refuses to stay in the main house. I have offered, but she repeatedly turns me down. I don't think she's comfortable in the main house. I prefer to be at my house in my bed, but that is my own fault.

The indoor pool comes into view, and she stops as she takes in the scene. Candles dimly lit. The steam from the heated pool comes from the surface of the water. Women are swimming topless, laughing, and drinking. Servers with trays walking around serving champagne and hors d'oeuvres.

There are private cabanas with lounge chairs that have sheer curtains, but you can see people fucking. Moans filter through the music, "More Human Than Human" by White Zombie plays.

She looks at me. "Is this—?" She swallows, looking as one of the girls considered Prey rides one of the guys on the swim team that is part of the Order. Her tits bouncing as he pumps into her from below.

"Yes. It's all consensual. Prey choose who they want. Parents know we need to let off steam, or we will do it out there, and they can't have that."

She knows what I mean. She chooses. Girls are dancing in the pool. Some I have had sex with smile coyly at me, hoping they'll get lucky with a Bedford. Fat chance.

She turns and faces me, her head lifting so our eyes lock. "Cold" by Breaking Benjamin plays as my hands slide over her arms, and she watches me touch her. My brother Draven comes up behind her, shirtless and in his Versace board shorts. Flashy bastard.

Her head tips up, and her lips curl into a sexy smile. My chest flips inside out. He grips her by the neck gently as his mouth crashes down on her lips, and I slide her top down an inch, making her breasts spill out as I feast on one nipple and then the other. Her pink nipples are begging for my tongue.

A gasp escapes from her lips, and I remove my shirt, her neck straining and exposed while she kisses Draven. I remove the rest, not giving a fuck who is watching. The three of us crash into the warm pool water. Hands gripping and touching, removing clothes.

Her groans mix with mine as we desperately seek to be inside her, like an empty cup waiting to be filled. We go at it like two predators devouring our Prey, but it's the other way around. She's the predator, and we are her Prey.

She's ours, and she knows it, and so does everyone here. Untouchable. Her pants come off next and the black lace thong is left, but my brother shakes his head no. We leave it on. We will work around it.

I bend my legs and slide into her wet heat first and she arches her back. My brother's tongue is on her breasts as I pump into her from behind. She gasps as I slide my tongue, licking her neck.

"Mine," I growl.

"Don't forget. I'm right here," my brother says.

She smirks and holds onto his shoulders.

I slow down inside of her and Veronica saunters up. "Damn. She's beautiful."

"Fuck off," I warn.

"I didn't come for her. I came for the one who fucks me."

Gia stiffens and my eyes flick to my brother. Fuck. This bitch.

My brother turns his head, and Gia turns her face away.

I grip her waist. "She is looking for Draven," I whisper in her ear. Knowing she thinks it's me. Veronica can only tell us apart because I moved out of the main house. She's pissed that Gia has us both right now.

"Then go to her," Gia responds.

"I can't."

"Why?" she asks through clenched teeth.

"Because I'm not the one who's fucked her."

As my confession dawns, my dick swells inside her as I pump into her, the water making waves and the steam so thick it's making us sweat. From where we are, you can't see people across the long pool.

"Drav," she says, a moan escaping her lips.

"I've been here next to you." *Thrust.* "Watching you." *Thrust.* "Always."

I pump into her. I know she is on birth control, and I haven't stuck my cock in anyone since. The blow job was only for show. Pulled out and sent the girl packing. No one is like her.

Her pussy clenches around my cock and Draven's gaze looks at Veronica watching us. "I'm busy with my girl. Fuck off," he tells Veronica.

Her lip curls and she snarls, "She's his girl."

"I shared a womb with him for nine months. She's mine just as much as his." His eyes trail over her perfect tits, licking her torso while she gets fucked.

Gia's moans mix with my grunts. "Can I come inside you, baby?" I ask.

"I'm on the pill," she gasps, and I know she's about to come. I pull out and flip her around so that my brother has his turn. This will only happen occasionally, us at the same time. I want my time with her alone uninterrupted. I'm sure Draven does too, but he can't have another if he chooses her.

The way he slides into her to the hilt, balls deep, making her lift off the pool floor, I don't think he plans to have another woman. He pumps into her savagely and her eyes roll back in her skull. Fuck.

I take her lips with mine, and she grips my cock in her hand and starts to jerk me off. Her eyes land on mine, and the look on her face as she comes has me about to bust. I grit my teeth, holding on. My brother comes in her, and she dips her head underwater and we both look down as she wets her hair coming back up. Her fingers run up my torso.

"Put it in the other side," she whispers.

Jesus. I close my eyes, wiping my face. I turn her around and the tip of my cock nudges her puckered hole. She gasps and my brother begins to play with her as I slide in inch by inch. The pressure from the water easing me inside of her.

"Deeper, Drav," she says.

I close my eyes and look down at her ass backed up against me. My hands slide on her hips, and I push in all the way.

She moans. "Yes. More. Yes."

"Fuck, she's there," Draven says with his hand on her clit.

Her hands are on his shoulders, gripping him in a vise as I pound her ass, biting my lip as my orgasm crests and I finally spill into her tight ass. "This ass and pussy are ours, baby. No one fucks them but us."

She nods and mewls. "Yes. I'm… coming."

Draven dips his fingers, sliding inside, and I feel her pussy contract even from my cock deep inside her ass.

"I feel so full."

"You're always going to feel full, baby," I tell her.

I slide out of her and kiss the side of her neck, smelling her sweet scent, hoping this is what she truly wants because it's what I want. Her.

CHAPTER TWENTY FOUR

JESS

Winter Break

AFTER CHANGING our flights and saying our goodbyes, we planned our return flights to arrive forty minutes apart on the same day the next week. The Uber driver pulls onto the road leading to the trailer park where my mother lives. As much as she tries to work, she cannot save enough to move out on her own.

I'm hoping when I graduate, I can change all that. I want to take my mother out of here. She deserves better and has sacrificed so much for me. She's never cared what people think of her living in the trailer park. Like always, they assume shit that isn't true.

As the vehicle leaves the trailer park, dust and smoke billow from its rear bumper. The heat and age have turned the bottom of the trailer's once-white door a dingy yellow. I drape the strap of my duffel bag over my shoulder and step toward the small concrete steps.

Inhaling deeply, I glance across at the nearby parking spot with one car and know she's home. When I would get home from school, I always knocked twice. She always worked the schedule that got her home in time to have supper ready for me every night. I would be surprised if she had kept the same shift since I left for Ohio. I'm about to double-knock, but the door swings open, and I see my mother's eyes widen and hear her squeal in excitement.

"Jesse!"

"Surprise, Mom," I say, waving my hands out wide.

"Get in here. Oh my god. You made it!"

I walk up the last steps of the shaky wood that leads between the concrete to the front door. Once inside, it smells like Dollar

Store air freshener and old carpet. My mother could never make enough to change it because she saved every last dime she made to send me to college.

I embrace her tightly, shutting my eyes to keep the tears away. She's clearly working double shifts; I see the tired lines around her eyes. "How are you, Momma?"

"Oh, honey. I'm doing great now that you're here," she whispers as I hug her tight. She smells like the peach cobbler she always bakes at the diner. It's their signature favorite because she makes it.

"I miss you," I whisper back.

God, I missed her. It's been almost four years since I last saw her, and I'm only keeping in touch via phone.

We break apart and I close the front door, walking farther inside the small two-bedroom trailer. It is old but clean and doesn't smell like stale cigarettes, like the neighbor's next door, where my mother would tell me to drop off leftovers.

"I'm going to make you something to eat, and then I have to leave for my shift, but you could drop me off and keep the car if you want."

I smile. I'll drive her just so she can relax, and I'll pick her up until I leave—anything to make her life a little easier. I tell her, "I'd love to take you, Mom. How's work and the diner?"

"It's okay. I guess. Jim cut my hours last week, but I've been saving. I'll be fine."

Shit. That means she's struggling while I'm at school, not worrying about rent or utilities. She didn't tell me, so I wouldn't worry. She knows I would drop out if I knew. She's all I have.

"I'm almost done, Mom. I can get a job on weekends if you need help. Did Jim give you a raise yet, at least?"

She shakes her head, setting two plates on the small, chipped counter. "He was, but business hasn't been going well since the bar opened across the road."

Not comprehending, I furrow my brows. "What bar?"

She slides mayo on each slice of bread. "Michael and his father opened a biker bar, and it has affected Jim's diner. I tried to apply for extra shifts, but…" She trails off.

I stiffen hearing his name, and she looks at me. "I'm sorry, Jesse, I forgot. Jesus, I'm sorry."

"It's okay."

I swallow, knowing why he wouldn't hire her. Michael was the guy I fell for in high school. The one I lost my virginity to, or better yet, he took it by spiking my drink at a party. He thought it would be fun since I was out of it. His friends thought so, too. She doesn't know what really happened and probably thinks it's because we live in a trailer.

CHAPTER TWENTY FIVE

JESS

I DROP OFF MY MOM, and my stomach drops when I see Michael in a late-model Mustang across the street. He gets out and looks over when he sees my mother. The sound of the creaking door of her old Oldsmobile slamming shut.

He walks across the street, looking both ways. My hands shake because I want to run him over. Over the last three years, I have thought of so many ways to make him pay.

My mother, not knowing what would happen or what seeing him in the flesh was doing to me, greeted him, "Hey there, Michael."

He watches me with a brilliant gleam in his eye like he's struck gold. "Hey there, Mom. I didn't know you were bringing my Christmas present early. I've missed her so much. I hope she can forgive me. We went out, and I said something I shouldn't have, but we were younger, and I think we have matured since then," he says with his smug smile.

Bastard.

"She surprised me! I didn't know my Jesse was visiting."

Through the open window on the driver's side, he glances up and smirks before fixing his gaze on my thighs. Even though my mom's air conditioner is broken, we seldom need to use it since the weather is usually cool. My legs, covered in wool leggings I found in a consignment store, were warming up thanks to the vents blowing hot air on my thighs.

"Did she now?"

It's really annoying that he continues talking to her and staring at me. I despise him. He needs to be locked up, him and his friends, for what they did to me, but nobody would believe me. In this town, he has the police in his pocket. Around here, he'd be treated like a prince, while I'd be the lowlife trying to take advantage of Michael Levine's celebrity status. The Levine family owns half of the town, and if they see a business, like Jim's restaurant, doing well, they will set up shop and attempt to steal their customers. They will make it appear as if they are helping the community, but they are just trying to make a quick buck off of Jim's success.

He looks over at my mother from the roof of the car, and I see that he's gotten bigger and stronger. I wonder how I fell for someone like him. His leather jacket over his fitted sweater and black jeans. He isn't unattractive, but he's a predator. A manipulator.

"I heard you applied for a shift at the bar. I'll talk to my father and Jess. We will come up with something," he says with a gleam in his eyes.

Motherfucker. He turned her down to get what he wanted. Me to come around or contact him. To plead with him for his father to give my mother work because he knows that we are broke. He doesn't know where I went exactly, he just knows I was accepted to a college in another state.

"Oh, don't you worry. Jess and I always work something out. Don't trouble yourself." She bends down and looks at me through the open window of the passenger side. "I'll see you in a couple of hours, sweetie," she says as she walks away, her pride not allowing her to ask for any favors.

He waits until she's inside, and he lowers his head. "Take a drive with me. It will be in your best interest, Jess."

"No."

He angles his head, making his handsome face look ugly every second I watch him look at me. "Now, don't make this difficult. You want your mommy to have a job, right? Then do as you're told."

I look at my mother through the diner window, knowing she is

worried deep inside about how she is going to pay rent and utilities, car insurance, and food. I'm sure she's been saving up and
that my being here will prompt her to run out and buy me
a Christmas present—a Christmas present we both can't afford.

My fingers are shaking, but I recognize what he wants. He
wants what every other man I've ever met has wanted from me:
my body. Unlike other situations, I really don't have a say when it
comes to Michael. He will make me pay through my mom, and he
will take whatever he wants anyway. My mom puts on a fake grin
for a couple who just walked in, but I know she's dying of exhaus-
tion on the inside as I watch her.

My head snaps up to see Michael open the door, which swings
open like the devil welcoming me to hell. I swallow the bile that
creeps up my throat. The ball in my throat tightens as he waits for
me to slide out.

"Come on, Jess. I know you miss me the way I miss you."

The engine rumbles as Michael maneuvers the car in an abandoned warehouse on the other side of town. He finds a secluded
area in the dark and parks the car. He glances over at me, leans
back, and unbuckles his pants, and I hold back the tears that
threaten to spill.

"I'll make sure your mom has a job. All you have to do is take
care of me once in a while. It's all I want. I'll show up, you open
your legs and give me that sweet cunt of yours, and all is good."

"And if I don't? What are you going to do? Drug me? Rape me
like you did before?" I quip.

"Don't act like you didn't want to fuck me. Girls like you
always want the rich guy. I made it easy for you. We all had fun. "

"I said *no*."

"Then you fell back, and when I touched you, you opened up
and let me slide into that tight cunt."

"You bastard," I snarl. "Drugging me until I'm almost uncon-
scious. That's called rape."

"Who the fuck cares? No one cares about you except your trailer trash mother. Your daddy doesn't even want you."

My teeth are clenched so hard in my mouth that I can hear them grind together. He lowers his head while he palms his cock, making me want to throw up.

"Do as I say, or your mom suffers. Do what I say, and she'll have a job with a raise. You won't have to worry about her. She will make her chump change and live happily ever after in her trailer. Worry free. I'll even give her a little extra for Christmas and a bonus for your trouble tonight."

"Fuck you, Michael. I hate you."

"I know. That's what makes it so good. I get what I want, you leave, I want more, and then you leave again. You think you're smarter than me because you're away at school in some college you managed to get into? You don't have a pot to piss in. You will never have a pot to piss in unless you sell what you have between your legs because that is all anyone will want from you. Now, be a good girl and give me what I want, and I'll give you what you need. You can't run from me, Jess. I know where you go to college. It's not in another state. It's here in Ohio, right? Some Ivy League Catholic university that admits poor trailer park trash like you just to look good on paper."

He chuckles and leans closer, whispering, "Are you trying to find God?" His hot breath fans my cheek, and I want to fold inside myself. He slides his fingers across my cheek, and I flinch.

"Stop it."

He grips my neck hard, knowing it will leave a mark for resisting, pushing me to where his cock is. I close my eyes and know this is my fate. *I'm doing this for my mother*, I tell myself. My demon has come to collect, and all I can do is be the sacrifice. There is no way something evil didn't create Michael. It makes me wonder if there really is a God because, right now, all I see is hell.

CHAPTER TWENTY SIX

JESS

I SCRUB myself in the tiny shower in my mother's trailer until I'm red like a lobster. I can still smell his cologne on my skin like the first time. It's strange how some guys' scents are more appealing than others. Reid's scent is heavenly, and so is Valen's.

When they touched me, the memory of Michael faded. It was like a bad dream that could be easily forgotten, but now it's vivid. It's real, and he is blackmailing me with my mom, and I know he can make her suffer. Except I don't have a way to get her out of this situation until I graduate. I would have to tell her everything, and I couldn't do that to her.

We live in a small town in Ohio near a small road that leads to the trailer park called Cedar Lake. There isn't even a lake, and I always wondered why they decided to call it that. There are old trailers with old AC units hanging off and some stuck with duct tape. The majority of the guys who hang out here are either on meth or sell meth.

Guys like Michael were a girl's dream guy back in high school until I saw his true colors. He can make any girl feel special and lure her in like a fish on a hook. He had me fooled with the nice guy act. I thought he actually liked me, but all he wanted was a quick lay, and anyway, he got it. Willing or unwilling. To a guy like Michael, the word no doesn't exist in his vocabulary.

He wants me as his paid whore and will use my mother to get it. I lean back, tired, my throat raw from crying, silently wishing he would have just drugged me again. At least I felt numb and could only remember bits and pieces.

I hear the slam of the main door of the trailer, indicating my mother must be home. I left the car and keys with her at the diner when I left with Michael. I closed my eyes, trying to figure out how I could face her. I'm officially a paid whore. I slept with a guy so my mother could get a higher-paying job, or she would lose the one she had.

Jim decided to cut her hours because Michael forced him to do it so my mother would reach out to me. Michael knows how much my mother means to me. Back in high school, he made sure I fell for his charm, and I sang like a canary. I told him about my wishes and dreams and who the most important person in my life was. My mother.

"Jesse, are you almost done? I have some wonderful news. We have to celebrate," she says with happiness pouring out of her voice.

I know, Mom. I know, I say to myself, closing my eyes. *You will have enough money and a solid job as long as I sleep with the boss's son whenever he wants. I can do this. I'll graduate, and then I can take you away from here.* I promise myself.

My phone dings, and I turn off the water and slide the plastic green shower curtain my mother bought at the local dollar store. There are some cool things you can find in those little stores.

I wrap the towel around my stinging body, raw from scrubbing. There is only one way I have been able to cope after that night when Michael and his friends did what they did to me. Have sex with someone I'm at least attracted to.

It replaces a bad memory with a better one. I could imagine someone I actually like instead of remembering the one who haunts me. I hate his name, his smell, and the way his hands feel on me.

It's funny how you can daydream about a guy for so long, and then when he shows up and proves how nasty he can be, you doubt your judgment. I threw up as soon as he dropped me off. I was disgusted and hated myself for what I had to do.

The irony is that you don't want to be labeled as a trailer trash whore, so you try to avoid it but end up becoming one. I can't be a simple girl who just happened to have been raised in a trailer.

It didn't matter if I graduated at the top of my class, helped my mother instead of going out with my so-called friends, or waited for the right boy to come along and sleep with him. It only got me to be the thing I despised the most. The one thing I didn't want to become. A woman who sleeps with a guy for money.

I look at the hundred-dollar bill near the sink like it's a serpent. Michael threw it in my lap right after he was done with me. My bonus, he said. I'm worth a hundred dollars and a bottle of shame.

I look at the text messages and my heart drops. Oh my god, Gia.

I lift my cheap pay-by-the-minute cell phone to my ear as it rings.

"Hello," Gia says, her voice croaking.

"Tell me."

I sit on the old, ugly, worn carpet at the foot of the single bed in my old room and cry over what happened to her after I hung up. Dravin, or Drav, as she now calls them so she can finally tell them apart, is there with her. One of them followed her, thank God, and was able to call for help in time. She could have died. Whatever the deal is with the Bedford twins and Gia, it's a great mystery. One minute, they want her; the next, they don't.

My phone rings from an unknown number. I furrow my brows and answer the call. "Hello?"

"You don't know how to call and say goodbye?"

I close my eyes. Reid.

"What do you want?" I ask.

"What do you?" he counters.

Of course, the typical guy only sees me as a piece of meat. "Look, I already told you. I'm not interested in being your fuck buddy."

"Oh, you're Valen's now?"

"Last time I checked, I don't belong to anyone. I'm not your whore that you pass around. Find some other Prey on campus to meet your twisted needs."

"I have, but they're all boring."

I snort. "And I'm so much fun, right?"

"Of course, you're fun. It's why I'm calling."

I look at the cheap mirror hanging on the wall and notice I have bruises on my neck from Michael when he gripped me in the car. My fingers trace the handprint of his fingers over my skin as I look at myself, not recognizing what I see. I'm not the girl I thought I was. I'm a cheap nothing. I can't escape my fate. I tried to find a higher education and ended up back to where I started. This is what they all want. What people in this town expect.

"I'm sure to you I'm just fun," I volley back in a rough tone.

"Hey, are you okay?"

"I'm fine. Why wouldn't I be? You just made me an offer. A girl like me should feel honored. She should be grateful she is receiving a blocked call from you for sex. You know—that way she won't call you back when you're done with her. I'm sooo lucky. So, what do you think my going rate is?"

"What the fuck are you talking about? You think I would pay you for sex?" He scoffs. "If you need money, just ask. I have plenty. So how much do you need, Jess?"

I hang up. He calls back, but I press the power button on my phone to turn it off. The numbness is taking over. *I know, Reid. You just want to have fun. The last thing I want is your money.*

I've never been asked out on a date. Back in high school, I didn't have money for a prom dress. Even though I wanted to leave here so badly, I couldn't wait until the year was over so I could start college. I wanted to start fresh. I didn't want to return here unless it was to pick up my mom and move somewhere else. I wanted a new beginning. A better life away from the scumbags and naysayers.

CHAPTER TWENTY SEVEN

REID

Pool Party

JESS IS DISTANT, and I'm trying to keep my emotions in check. I don't lose my head for a girl. Ever. Especially Prey. There is just something about her. Something that calls me to her. The fucked-up parts of me. The first time I fucked her, I wanted to take her home and keep her there locked up until I fucked her out of my system.

I love her hair. It can be wavy, curly, or straight. She looks hot any way she styles it. It's like a man has many options with her. A fantasy. But fantasies are not real. I can see her weakness, her darkness, and the monster inside me feeds off it because it releases her body in the most delicious ways.

She's fucking something out of her, and I'm here to take it. So is Valen, but he's young and loves to fuck around with free pussy. Enjoy it, kid. Once you're a senior, your parents throw down the gauntlet, and the rules you heard of are thrown into the mix for you to follow. The Order. The wife. Killing whoever needs to die. The deceit, lies, and betrayal come into play, and if you aren't ready, it will break you.

Jess can see her best friend getting deliciously fucked by the Bedford twins through the mist from the heat of the pool. Lucky girl. But, honestly, I think they're the lucky ones to have such a nice piece of ass, and despite everything they've done to her, she's still wrapped under their spell. Dravin won't let her out of his sight after what happened. He's like a stalker. She could have died, and she doesn't deserve to die. She's just Prey. A girl just like the one next to me, watching how her friend moans in pleasure as her men make her feel like she is the only woman. In their eyes, she is the only thing that matters. She is their future.

I come up behind Jess and press her to tell me how she got the bruises on her neck. "Are you going to tell me what happened?" I ask as I slide her pretty hair to see the faint markings on her neck.

"I fell."

My hand makes a fist. That's what every woman says when a man hits her. My teeth grind together, and my jaw hardens, and I want to shake the name of the fucker who did it out of her.

"You know, that's what all the women say after a man beats them. It's cliché. You might as well say." I lower my voice. "The fucker hit me, but I can't tell you who. I'm afraid or I liked it."

Her eyes snap to mine in anger. Of course, no woman likes that, but I had to say something to get her attention. It was for effect. I would never hurt a woman.

Valen flanks her other side. "Hot, isn't it? It's beautiful to watch when two men love a woman so much. They're in their own world. Nothing matters more than pleasuring her. Making her feel wanted and needed. They will do anything for her love."

"How do you know that?" she asks, ignoring me and what I asked.

"You see it in her eyes. It's there. The love she has inside her, and they want it. They just have to come to terms with it."

"Terms?" she asks.

Valen is a sentimental jerk. He knows emotion when he sees it, even if he doesn't possess it himself. He is like a machine. You switch him on and off. That's it. It's easy and uncomplicated.

One thing I have noticed is that he talks to her more than he ever talks to other women. He's dirty in bed, and she likes it for some reason. It's like he is throwing dirt over something she is hiding. I just have to find out what it is, and I love a good mystery. I like hunting and killing, too. Let's hope it's both. I like to get my hands dirty from time to time. And for her, I think I'm going to enjoy whoever I have to fuck up.

"Why did you meet those pricks at the bar?" I ask, snapping her attention back to me. I don't want to talk about the twins and the woman they have claimed as their own.

"I wanted to go out and needed a change of pace," she says uncomfortably.

"Why not with me? Why not with us?" I ask.

The silence stretches as she shifts from one foot to the other. I stand in front of her, and she has to look at me.

"You don't want to tell us what happened to your neck. So why the hockey pricks from Ohio State? What do they have that we don't, except small dicks and ugly faces."

She snorts. "They weren't ugly."

"They were ugly," Valen chimes in. "That fucking dork with the Justin Bieber haircut sitting next to you, he kept leering at your tits every five seconds. He was lucky I didn't crush his fucking skull against the lamp."

Valen makes a mocking motion every two minutes, flicking his hair out of his eyes. "Fucker looked like he had Tourette's syndrome. At first, I felt bad, and then he opened his mouth and I realized he didn't have it."

She laughs, and I smile, watching her. "Tell me. Why him? I would have let it slide if it was Valen."

Valen pushes me playfully on the arm. "If it were me, she'd be bent over moaning my name by now. While you watched."

I slide my finger under her chin, ignoring his attempts to piss me off. "Why?"

Her expression is torn, and I watch as she pinches her brows in a frown. "I wanted to go out with a guy. I've never done that before."

"What do you mean you've never gone out with a guy before? You're out with us," I tell her.

"She means on a date, dick. She's never been out on a date."

She looks away, but now I'm curious. "That wasn't a date. It was two girls showing up at a bar to meet two guys. That's not what I think you had in mind."

Her head whips toward me, and she crosses her arms over that sexy mesh top she's wearing. "Maybe I just wanted to fuck and not have to look at his face again."

Valen snorts. "I knew it. You were down to fuck."

I'm pissed. She was going to spread those pretty legs for that smug asshole. I am the only one she should be spreading those legs for, so I can feel that wet cunt.

"Let's go," I demand.

"I'm not going anywhere with you. I'm here because of Gia. I know how shaky things are between her and Dravin or the other one with the same name." She lifts her hand toward them fucking her friend. "The twins," she corrects.

Sometimes, I can't tell them apart except for their attitude and demeanor. It's almost as if they don't want you to know which is which. The show they are putting on here is to show the members of the Order that she belongs to them. It has a purpose. Everything we do has a purpose—a darker motive.

Veronica walks up with a pissed-off expression. Her eyes darting to where the Bedford twins are fucking Gianna. Draven must have turned her down. She could never have the fun Gia is having right now. Veronica and her sex addiction can be too much for some people. Her gaze lands on Jess and she licks her lips.

What the fuck?

CHAPTER TWENTY EIGHT

JESS

THE SONS of Kenyan showing up at the bar messed up my plans. I wanted to have casual sex so I could forget. I woke up this morning with the scent of Michael in my nose and the feel of his rough hands on my skin and sprang up, feeling like I needed air. That I was suffocating. It woke up Gia, but she just turned on her side and watched me calm down, so I turned over and gave her my back. She asked if I was okay, and I assured her I was fine.

"Just a bad dream," I told her. I like that about her. She doesn't press. She listens and doesn't judge. The kiss at the bar shocked me, but she did it so that I wouldn't feel cornered. It was hot. I'll give her that.

Reid's interrogation is getting to me. I'm not telling him shit. I don't trust his kind and all he does is play games. That is what all the guys in Kenyan do… play mind games, and I'm tired of losing. I'm tired of feeling guilty.

Veronica leans in close. "You want to play?" she asks, her eyes undressing me, but she knows I like men and only had her touch me once with Garret. Melissa did most of the work on her, but I remember when I looked down, my legs spread open, she was the one sucking my clit, cleaning me up.

I didn't think anything of it because I was trying to please Garret and give him what he wanted, and at the same time, I was trying to forget what had happened back home. But now I think Veronica likes women more than she likes men.

I'm not sure where Warren fits in, but that is her issue, not mine. As long as she stays away from Gia, I don't care what she does.

My eyes follow her as she slides her manicured nail down her arm. "Pretty please," she coos.

"She's definitely one that won't look at your face in the morning," Reid says in a derisive tone.

My eyes snap to him with his smug smile, slick mouth, and sexy body. He's an asshole. But a fine asshole. I'll give him that.

Valen is the lighter version, with a darker appetite. His hair isn't as dark, and his body is leaner than Reid's. I haven't had the pleasure of exploring that tongue piercing yet and have only had the pleasure of the one on his lip. Brief kisses and flicks over my nipples are as far as I have been acquainted with it.

The second time we had sex, it was quick, and I fell asleep in his bed soon after. I was shy and couldn't believe what I had done, but he took it away. He took away the feeling. The feeling on my skin. The one I'm trying to get rid of now. Both of them did. Valen and Reid. They have so far been the only ones.

Valen shakes his head at Reid and takes my hand.

"What are you doing?" I ask Valen as he tugs me toward a dark hallway.

"Shutting him up."

He opens the door to a private room that looks like a room set up for massages. There are tables and couches. There are curved chairs in deep red velvet and teal colors, but to the right, there is one curved red chair that looks more like a chaise.

Valen looks over at it and then back at me. He lifts the hem of my shirt over my head and begins to remove all my clothes, leaving me topless and in my red thong.

He looks down at the color and smirks. "It was like fate brought you to this moment. A moment where I'm going to fuck you. I'm going to fuck you so good, Jess."

Veronica enters, and my head turns. I watch as she stares at us. Valen is fully clothed, and I'm clad in only my thong and standing in front of him. I feel comfortable with Valen and Reid. Veronica is a wild card, but I don't feel threatened with Valen or

Reid nearby because they wouldn't let anyone physically hurt me.

Valen lifts his head and I'm a lot shorter than he is, so he can see over my head at Veronica. "This is all for her. If you're interested in a fuck, you're in the wrong room."

She snorts. "I'm here for her, not you. She likes me," Veronica says, like I'm not here.

"I'm not fucking you," he snaps.

"I don't want you to. I want to pleasure her."

"Fine, if she wants to, but you only get to clean her when I'm finished." He leans down and whispers, "Are you on the pill?"

My pussy throbs at the way his breath fans my ear. Valen is fun and crazy, and he always makes sure I come before he does. I'm not sure what he has in mind right now, but I want to feel good. I want him to take it away. I want Michael's memory to go away. I know it's temporary because he will show up to collect my body as payment soon, but this is better than what I had to endure.

Veronica's gaze lingers on my breasts and then moves down to the apex of my thighs. "I'll clean her up. I love the way she tastes. If she lets me, of course." Her eyes land on mine. "Rules are rules. Prey chooses."

Fuck. If I turn her down. She will make me pay somehow. She loves to mess with people's heads, but I think she has an agenda, and I don't know what it is yet. I can see it. She hides something.

"Fine, but no fingers."

She walks closer to me while Valen is behind me. His warmth was like a warm curtain against my skin. "I wasn't planning on using them. I want my tongue on your pussy." Her eyes trail over my body. "Maybe other places, too. You know I love to suck," she says, making an emphasis on the *K*.

Valen picks me up from behind and places me on the chaise. The smooth velvet on my skin keeps me warm while the cool air teases my nipples.

He moves between my thighs as he pulls down the zipper of his dark jeans and slides them off, followed by his boxers. He removes his shirt, his lean muscles rippling from the effort. His tattoos snake up his torso, then down to his washboard abs. His hair is sticking out in all directions with that messy look that I find attractive. He quirks his lip the way he does, showing a glimpse of his straight white teeth.

I widen my legs and he slides his index finger over my slit. I'm so wet his finger is coated with my arousal as I watch him slide his fingers in his mouth and suck them clean with a beam in his eye.

"Are you ready for me?" he asks.

"Can't you tell," I volley back.

Veronica walks closer, but then the door opens with a slam and in walks Reid. Valen turns his head with his hard cock in his hand as he strokes it up and down. "Someone is upset," he says softly, raising his eyebrows up and down.

"What the fuck is she doing here?" Reid growls.

"She wants me," I hear Veronica tell him.

Reid stomps over, looks at me with my legs wide open for Valen like an offering, and then glares at Veronica. "Playtime is over. Get out."

She opens her mouth, but Reid points to the door. "Get out!" he roars.

She scrambles and leaves without looking back, out the door like her ass is on fire.

Reid points to Valen. "Put your dick away and get dressed," he demands.

"What the fuck, dude. What is your deal?"

I get up and cover myself with my hands.

"It's a little too late for that," he says sarcastically.

Anger courses through me, but his next words are like guilt clawing at my skin, making me feel worse about what I was about to do. What I was about to let happen.

He bends down and collects my clothes from the pile on the floor as Valen glares at him. "You are not a whore."

"No one is treating her like that."

Reid straightens, handing me my clothes. "You were about to. You had her in here with that psycho bitch like she was some prostitute. Just because she had sex with you, Valen, doesn't mean she's a cheap lay you can run a train on."

"Yeah, like you treat her any better."

Reid snorts. "I've treated her better than those assholes out there."

His gaze lands on mine when I slide the mesh part of my top over my head. He walks over and hauls me up by my arm.

"What the fuck is your problem?" I hiss.

"*You* are my problem," he seethes. "You want to fuck for whatever reason, fine. But not here, and not with that bitch in the room."

My chest aches as guilt begins to seep in. I feel mortified. He's right, but he doesn't know what I deal with or have to deal with. He doesn't know what I'm trying to forget, what I have to hide, or how I have to survive.

This is all fun and games to them.

CHAPTER TWENTY NINE

JESS

"WHERE ARE WE GOING?" I ask Reid.

Valen left with Gia and the twins, who gave him a ride back to Dravin's house to pick up his car.

He stays silent as he maneuvers the car that he had in the garage at Dravin's home. It is a sleek black sports car I have never seen before. While I wait for him to respond, I hug myself for warmth.

"Are you cold?" he asks.

"A little."

He pushes the button, and my seat begins to warm. Then he says, "I'm taking you somewhere."

"Okay," I say, looking out the window.

I'm tired of arguing with him. He can be so dry and cold. He's moody, but sometimes I like that because when he is angry, it means he cares. For some reason, he cared about me back there. He cared that I was in that room, and even though I trusted Valen, he didn't like the idea of Veronica.

My finger reaches out and rubs the red stitching on the black leather interior of his car. He gazes briefly at my hand, and I yank it back into my lap like I was caught doing something I shouldn't.

"Sorry," I mumble, embarrassed that I was caught admiring his car like I just came to Earth from another planet and had never sat in one before.

The truth is, I have never sat in a car like this before. It is truly a work of art. Inside, it looks like a spaceship. The car is matte black, like the SUV we rode to the party, with a black interior, a fancy screen, and red stitching.

"It's okay. I'm not mad. You can touch it."

I look up at the roof of the car. The smell of expensive leather touching every part of my body. Even the carpet feels nice. I feel bad that I'm touching it with my black boots. "What kind of car is this?" I ask.

He turns his head briefly. "An Aston Martin DBS."

"It's beautiful. It's way better than what I drive or ever had growing up. My mother's car doesn't even have AC, and my car hardly turns on sometimes. I really should go back and get it."

I pause when he doesn't say anything. He remains quiet and looks straight ahead, gripping the steering wheel. Shit. Why do I always ramble when I'm nervous? I shouldn't have said that. He wouldn't be interested in the car I drive or the life I had growing up.

"Don't worry about your car." He leans forward, sliding his cell phone out, and opens his music app. "It's taken care of. I had someone get it."

He did ask me for my keys right before we left in the SUV, when we were at the bar nearby. I guess that means I should shut the hell up if he is going to play music.

He presses play on his phone, and because it's connected to his car, the sounds of Breaking Benjamin's "The Diary of Jane" play through the car's sound system. I look down and grip the strands of my hair that are turning wavy, sometimes wishing that I had straight hair.

After fifteen minutes, we pull into the valet of a five-star hotel surrounded by trees and, from its appearance, very private. There are gas sconces that are lit with a firepit in the center instead of a fountain. He rolls the car forward and places it in park.

The valet rushes over and opens the door. "Welcome, Mr. Riordrick. They are expecting you and your guest."

"Thank you," I hear him tell the valet driver. I see his jean-clad legs pause. As my door opens, he turns around, and I can hear him say over the roof of the car, "I've got it."

The door is pushed closed, and I'm sitting in the seat. He doesn't even want the other valet to open the door. Weird.

I see Reid look at me from the front of the car as he makes his way to the other side. His eyes find mine, and they are black as night. His bottom lashes are so thick that they almost seem lined with black eyeliner.

The door pops open, and he sticks out his hand so I can take it. I slip my hand against his warm, gloved palm and slide out. The door closes behind me, and I look up at the grand entrance of the hotel that is in the middle of nowhere. The fire in the center lights up the entrance, with wood doors handled by two doormen flanking both sides and allowing people to enter and exit.

"Where are we?" I ask, my breath coming out like fog.

"My hotel."

My eyebrows rise as he gently tugs me forward to enter the lobby with its dark red carpet and gold accents accented with dark wood. I feel like I'm in the Neri Hotel in Barcelona, which I saw on the travel website while researching a school project.

Every luxury hotel has a concierge and a check-in counter. Not that I have ever stayed in one, but I have seen them in movies. The closest thing to a building I have stayed in is Kenyan and a motel when my mother couldn't pay the light bill. It was one of those hourly motels, but at least we slept for four hours and had a hot shower. Whatever she paid, it was worth it.

He walks up, and the older woman with her gold-plated name tag that reads Shelley warmly greets Reid. "Hello, Mr. Riordrick. Your room is ready," she says, sliding a room key across the desk. "Will you be requiring anything further?"

"No," he answers softly, picking up the key card and holding it up. "Thank you, Shelley. Was your holiday bonus this year enough for the grandkids?"

Her expression warms, and my heart skips a beat. I've never thought of Reid as being thoughtful, but you can tell by the interactions with the employees when we arrive that they hold him in high regard. He also nods and greets everyone by their first name.

He is quiet most of the time but has a mean dark streak that I find appealing because he directs it when needed. This is the side of Reid that I find most attractive, and I secretly wish he was always like this. What he did back there with Valen made me angry and relieved all at once. He was protective and pulled me out of there when I was at my lowest.

Valen is young and doesn't take things seriously but loves to have fun. The few times I have been around Valen, he has had this carefree lifestyle and loves to push the limit and live on the edge. No consequences. No judgment.

Reid guides me by my hand, and to my surprise, no one looks at me like I don't belong. No one is looking at me like I'm worthless or poor, but my joy is short-lived when I see a woman enter the elevator wearing a long coat over a short red dress and suede cream-colored boots to midthigh. She looks like she just stepped out of a Vogue photo shoot. Her hair is mid-length and chestnut in color, and she has green eyes. The woman is drop-dead gorgeous and pauses midstride when she notices Reid.

"Miss me?" she says coyly.

He grins. "Not tonight, Tara. I have company."

She doesn't even look in my direction. It's like I don't exist, and he makes no move to introduce me as his friend, but then again, why would he? He brought me here to have sex and nothing else. I'm no one. I'm just considered Prey. Used and discarded. So I tell myself I'll use him right back so I can forget about my demons for a while until I have to face them again, or him, the one who keeps coming back for me. Michael. This is just a temporary reprieve.

"Well, later then." She steps closer, sliding her palms over his chest and a pang of jealousy hits me in my solar plexus. I try to move my hand out of his grip, but he squeezes, wrapping his fingers tighter, keeping me from removing my hand.

I don't know why he won't release me. Tara looks over at me with amused annoyance. Like I'm gum on the bottom of her boots, and she can't wait to get rid of it, and I feel like telling her he's mine. That she can go fuck off and freeze her ass outside while I warm him up upstairs.

I don't know what has come over me. He isn't nice to me most of the time, except when he's fucking me. He isn't rough but demanding, like a guy possessed with need and knows what he wants. He doesn't snuggle me or spoon me after. He doesn't caress me or give me tender kisses the way girls fantasize about sex with the right guy.

To Reid, sex is like a transaction. Once it's over, he leaves, and it's never mentioned. Sometimes, you even wonder if it ever happened. He is so quiet, and he doesn't talk about himself. Which works for me because I don't have much to say about myself. It's not like he would care what I have to say about myself anyway. He isn't interested in me in that way, and at times, I wonder if he even likes me.

Right now, this is a reminder. A reminder that I don't mean shit. I might as well be invisible next to him. Then my mind wanders to what Gia said about people in the Order. Members conduct business, and everything is filtered through the higher members, which is like a hierarchy of needs.

Business connections, meetings, parties, alliances, and, of course, private parties that involve sex. And hotels owned by founding members in the middle of nowhere, with no one knowing what happens inside.

Reid looks down at his chest, where her palms are firmly planted, while her eyes, full of promise, gaze up at him. I manage to yank my hand from his grip and rub my wrist.

I roll my eyes. "I'll just go sit in the lobby while you two catch up. You guys are clearly having a moment."

I walk away, while Tara snickers, and find a spot near the fireplace in the lobby. A man is sitting reading a document from a folder and looks up.

"He let you go already?" he asks with a grin.

I stroll over to the man dressed in slacks and a crisp dress shirt opened at the throat. "Excuse me?"

He grins, looking at me, and his eyes flick to Reid talking to Tara. Only he has stepped back so that her hands fall off his chest. I can't hear what is being said, and at this point, I don't care. My sole goal is to forget and avoid falling asleep, where my memories will take over and send me spiraling into self-destruction and misery.

The man doesn't look old but like a wealthy stockbroker who belongs in New York. His gray eyes look at me, full of promises he probably doesn't keep. I watch as he places his hand on his phone, his biceps flexing under the crisp fabric from the movement while he watches me. Did he just flex so I would notice him?

Ignoring him, I slide my phone out of the pocket of my jacket to see how far I am from campus, kicking myself for leaving with them instead of Gia and me following them in my car.

He leans forward, rests his forearms on his knees as he looks behind me, tilting his head to study me, and says, "She has nothing on you. Just because you don't have money or wear pretty things doesn't mean you're less beautiful. It just makes you flawless. The natural ability to look that stunning no matter what you wear, now that is true elegance."

Did he just say I'm beautiful? Prettier than Tara? That's not possible, this guy is just preying on the fact that I'm vulnerable.

"Who are you, and what are you talking about?"

He chuckles, wiping his mouth with his hand. "I'm the hated cousin. I run things sometimes until Reid graduates. I was surprised to see him walk in with you, but now that I can get a better look, I see why."

His cousin. I don't see a resemblance, but why would he lie?

Compared to everyone that walks through here, I stick out. In a poor way, people stick out.

"I guess you have me all figured out."

He smiles. "It isn't common to see Prey from Kenyan come through here. I'm surprised he brought you to his hotel. He's never done that."

"If this is an attempt to get me to stay because you saw me scroll through my Uber app, it's not helping. Look, I know I don't belong, and to people like you, I don't mean anything, and I'm okay with that. Where I come from, I don't mean much to people, and I know where I stand. I'm not part of the happy ending in my fairy tale, I'm the tragedy."

He leans back, his right elbow on the arm of the chair, two fingers over his lips as if lost in thought as he watches me. "Let's play a game," he says.

"Why would I want to play a game with you?"

He gives me a dark, knowing smile that curves his top lip. "Because it will get you what you want, and I want to teach my cousin a lesson."

I'm intrigued. How would he know what I want? After scrolling through my poor excuse of an old-model smartphone while flipping through my thoughts, my gaze lands on him.

"How do you know what I want?"

"You stated that you knew exactly where you stood. If that's the case, then there is only one reason you walked in here with him, and it's not to sleep. It's to fuck."

My pulse is going haywire from my heart beating so fast, a mixture of anger and annoyance. I guess someone like him, being part of the Order and if he is indeed related to Reid, would know that. In their eyes, it would be obvious why I was brought here or chose to come here, but it's a different matter altogether when someone points it out. It becomes real. If he noticed, then so did everyone else.

I don't look behind me to see if Reid is done talking to Tara. I don't want to witness her touching him or him smiling back. If I see it, I'm not sure I'll be able to stop myself from walking over there and dragging him to the elevator to get away from her. I shouldn't care. He isn't mine, but I can't help the way I feel. Maybe it's because I want him to take away the memory of Michael touching me. Maybe I want to use him the way he wants to use me. Maybe it's because I find him the most attractive. I like that he is discreet. I like that he is quiet. I like when he touches me and doesn't expect anything after. He goes back to ignoring me like I don't exist, and it works for me in my current situation. I have two options right now. Play their game and get what I want, or leave and let the memory of Michael haunt me when I fall asleep.

My gaze returns from the screen of my phone to his gray eyes staring at me. "What do you have in mind?"

"This is going to be fun."

"I'm sure it is."

"My name is Alaric Riodrick."

I quirk my eyebrow. "Alaric?"

He smiles. "Say it again, gorgeous."

He wants to play games, but I'm not easily played. I don't know him, and all I know is it's obvious he doesn't get along with his cousin. I'm just annoyed with the way Reid treated me just now.

"No."

"Fine."

He flicks his eyes to his right, where there is a bar. The bartender is cleaning a glass, holding it up to the light to ensure that all the spots are gone before placing it on the black mat and preparing a cocktail.

"Have a drink with me, but first, hand me your phone," he says, standing up.

I look up as he stands above me. "What do you need my phone for?"

He looks at the phone in my hand and bends down so that his eyes lock on mine. "So I can call you. Have dinner. Fuck. Whatever you want." He glances up and lowers his voice. "There isn't much time before he starts looking for you. He shouldn't let something so intriguing and beautiful go."

I move to stand, causing him to straighten and step back. He is almost a foot taller than me and very handsome. Not the type of guy I usually find attractive, but handsome all the same. I like Reid's dark hair and body full of ink, but most of all, I like his darkness.

Alaric peers down and takes my phone from my hands. "Come with me to the bar."

I nod, and we walk side by side until we reach two barstools and take a seat. "What would you like? You can have anything you want. It's on me."

The bartender glances up at me, waiting for me to ask for what I want. I take a deep breath and scan the bottles behind him, lit up by the neon lights behind the shelves. There is a mirror, and I can see Reid in a heated discussion with Tara. At least she isn't touching him, and he isn't smiling.

I'm trying to find something to order that doesn't sound like I'm immature or an idiot and settle on the first thing that comes to mind. "A black vodka ghost martini."

The bartender raises his left eyebrow and his lips curve in a grin. "Excellent choice."

"I'll have a merlot," Alaric tells him.

"Right away, sir."

I shift slightly to my right while the bartender mixes my drink and pours Alaric his wine.

"Wine?" I ask.

He is entering his number into my phone, and for some reason, I let him. I'm not going to call him, and I don't care if he calls me or not. I'm not going to have sex with him. This is all a game to him, and I don't trust him.

"I don't look like a wine guy?"

"You seem more like a gin and tonic type of guy."

The bartender places my drink in front of me and does the same to Alaric with his glass of wine.

I grasp the stem of the martini glass and take a sip. The flavor and alcohol explode on my tongue, followed by the slight burn of the alcohol, warming me up on the inside.

"So, where are you staying? Dorm?"

"Yes," I answer. "But you already knew that. It's where we all usually stay."

He places his wineglass down on the bar counter and licks his bottom lip. "Actually, I would have thought you were staying with Reid."

I snort, shaking my head. "You mean in Dravin's Gothic mansion? Highly unlikely. Reid doesn't strike me as the type to have a woman stay with him."

"Have you?"

I angle my head, confused. "Have I what?"

"Slept in his bed."

A blush begins to creep up my neck. I did more than just sleep in his bed. I did stay the night, but he asked me to leave the next morning. It stung, though I understood. It was just sex, and he served my purpose.

The dreams. The nightmares since the day it first happened. It was the first time I could sleep without having a nightmare or that feeling you get when you wake up after being drugged and see blood and sperm coating your thighs.

Sometimes I wake up and I remember the same sting. The pain I felt between my thighs that day was still there the next morning. The way Michael laughed the following Monday at school when he told me I wanted it and he gave it to me. They all did.

I swallow down the memories and meet Alaric's knowing grin, no different than any other guy I have encountered. They all want one thing, and that is to use my body. To them, the rest of me doesn't matter. I'll never matter to these types of people. Men with privilege, money, and connections who feel they are above all others. Manipulative and selfish. To me, they are all the same. Except Valen. I can't say he hasn't been truthful with me.

I rub my lips together, grab the martini glass, and drink it all at once, hoping the burn will melt the feeling and what's left of my emotions. The sound of me placing the now empty martini glass on the bar with a clink of glass meeting wood. The fire in my belly gives me the liquid courage I need to answer what he wants to hear. I feel brave, not caring. He can ask and find out anyway. Why hide it?

"Yeah. I slept in his bed. Reid and his friend took turns with me all night. Isn't that what you want to hear? With people like you, that's all I'm good for. It shouldn't matter, so why are you asking?"

He looks at me with a surprised expression and raises his eyebrows. I know I'm being a bitch, but he's being a nosy prick, and I'm annoyed.

"I apologize for upsetting you. I didn't mean it to sound that way."

"Whatever," I mumble.

"Would you like another one, miss?" the bartender asks with a soft expression. He probably heard every word, but I'm sure he hears a lot of things working as a bartender. My mother would sometimes come home and tell me town gossip she overheard waiting tables at Jimmy's diner.

"I'm good. Thank you."

He nods, looking over at Alaric with a hard expression while he watches Reid. One drink is all I'm having. I don't mind a buzz, but I'm not close to campus, and I'm in a room full of potential predators. There is only one I feel comfortable with, and he isn't paying attention to me. The hairs on the back of my neck stand up like a magnet. I can feel his presence consuming me by the minute, and I know he is behind me because I see Alaric stiffen.

Awareness creeps down my spine and the rumble of his voice

slides between my thighs. "Never fails, Alaric. I'm not surprised. You were always interested in what was mine, and you always wanted to play with and borrow my things without asking."

My eyes land on Reid. His expression is murderous, cold, and very angry. The glare aimed at Alaric is laced with pure hatred. These two clearly hate each other, and it is the type of hate that is built up over the years. What has me squirming in my seat is him pointing out that I'm his. I should feel giddy, but how he says it also makes me think he sees me like an object. A toy you play with and put back in the toy box with the others.

Alaric looks at me and then at him with a smug grin, taking his wineglass and tilting it slightly so that his lips meet the rim. He takes a sip of the wine and places it next to my empty glass as if pointing out that he is interrupting our conversation.

"I was just entertaining your guest. You obviously were engrossed in your chat with your ex-flame. I was trying to help you out since you were rude and left her there waiting for you. I saw she was about to order a ride and convinced her to have a drink with me. You should be thanking me, little cousin."

Reid's fists clench at his sides and then he turns his head and glares at me. His eyes flick to my empty glass next to Alaric's.

Reid signals for the bartender, and he says in an even tone, "Her drink is charged to my tab. Understood?"

"Yes, Mr. Riordrick," the bartender responds.

Reid gets up in Alaric's face in a stare-off. His jaw is clenched. His teeth are grinding, sounding like they're ready to snap. He is so angry at Alaric, and I wish I knew why.

His nostrils flare, and people walking by stare briefly but swiftly look away. "Go near her, and I'll kill you," he growls.

He grabs my hand and almost yanks me off the barstool.

"What the hell, Reid?"

"Shut up," he snarls.

I try to give him resistance without causing a scene as he practically drags me through the lobby, but he's stronger, and the anger coming off him in waves is making me tread cautiously on how to deal with him right now.

He slides the key card near what seems like a private elevator and the doors open. He practically drags me in the car first and cages me inside so I don't walk out.

"What is your fucking problem?" I snap.

The doors close behind him, and I'm trapped inside the elevator with Reid, and the look of fury in his eyes has me shrinking back, turning my head with a grimace.

He backs me up against the back side of the elevator and reaches with his index finger to hold the elevator. Fuck. His face is inches from my cheek, and he is breathing like he has just finished running a marathon, but it's from anger and not exertion. He isn't even breaking a sweat; he is just pissed.

He opens my jacket and feels my breast over my mesh top. My nipples harden under the thin tube top and my thighs clench.

"You need cock that bad?" he asks against my cheek. His lips snake roughly over my skin down to my neck, and he licks the spot over the yellow bruise on my neck. "Huh? Is this what you want? For me to fuck you? You can't wait, can you?"

His hands slide down my torso to the band of my skirt, and he glides his fingers under the hem of my panties to feel how wet I am and cups my soaked pussy. "You're so fucking wet it's pathetic."

My cheeks heat in embarrassment at how turned on I am. I'm so wet for him; I'm drenched. The way he touches me with rough hands but with gentle fingers is confusing. He knows how much to push me before it's too much, and I feel like he's going to break me. The things he says to me while he's inside me are dirty and cold, but it makes me feel alive.

I want it.

I want him.

It's a secret.

My secret. But I'm good at keeping secrets hidden. No one has to know how much I want him.

He undoes his pants and slides his hard cock out, stroking it with his hands between his legs while he watches me. "Take off your jacket."

I look up and notice a camera in the corner of the elevator. "There're cameras," I say.

"I know," he says, his lip curling and his voice barely above a whisper. "That's the point. I want them to see how desperate you are for my cock because you can't wait. You'll go with anyone to get fucked, won't you?"

"Fuck you," I snarl.

"Baby, I'm going to fuck you so hard you won't be able to stand when I'm done. I'll make sure to ruin you."

I turn my face, my lips inches from his, and I meet his dark gaze in a challenge. "Then what the fuck are you waiting for? Do your worst. Finish breaking me."

His eyes flick up like a serial killer before he commits a murder. Something flashes in his eyes, although I can't decipher what it is. I want him to take it away. I pray in my head for him to please kill the memory that haunts me. He's my reprieve before reaching insanity. I want him to fuck it out of me.

He growls and pushes my winter jacket down my shoulders. The camera is long forgotten. He rips my top and slides my skirt roughly down my body. I'm hoping he doesn't see the bruises between my thighs. The lighting was brighter than the dimly lit room I was in with Valen.

The tearing of clothing mixed with the tearing of the wrapper of the condom assaults my ears. The palm above my head lies flat on the wood paneling on the elevator as he holds himself while he slides the condom over the head of his cock. The angry veins running down his shaft, almost too big for me and looking like it's about to burst, have me closing my eyes and getting ready for its onslaught.

Reid fucks like an animal devouring its prey, ripping it limb from limb as it feasts. "Open your legs so I can fuck that tight cunt, or I'm going to ram it in there."

I raise my head and open my legs, my neck arched. My breasts are exposed and I'm completely naked except for my thigh-high pantyhose and black boots.

The tip of his cock is at my entrance and in one hard thrust, he rams his cock inside me, causing me to gasp at the delicious burn. He lifts my legs and wraps them around his waist. "If I catch you around another man that I don't approve of, I'm going to make you pay, Jess. I'm going to fuck you so hard I'll ruin you for anyone else. The only cock you will be begging for is mine."

"How about Valen?" I tease. "What if all I want is his cock, his tongue, inside me?"

In truth, I like his cock, but I would never admit it to him. I would never give a man power over me like that again. I'll never tell them how I feel. I fell for a man once, and he broke me. All they do is take from me.

My body.

My innocence.

My heart.

They break everything. Reid's promise of him trying to ruin me should have me running for the nearest exit. But what he doesn't know is I'm broken. I'm already ruined. It's too late. There is no turning back for a girl like me. His sex is a Band-Aid for the wound left by another. There will be more. I just have to hold on until it's over. The pain will go away and leave scars, but I'll still have the smile from a mother's heart. The only light I'll have in the darkness left inside me is when they leave me picking up the pieces.

CHAPTER THIRTY

REID

I'M THRUSTING into her while her legs are wrapped around my waist. I know I'm giving security a show, but I can't take it anymore. I want her. Since the first time I laid eyes on her. I almost told Draven to fuck off when he said to watch over her at the party. Valen saw the same opportunity, and I didn't want to show him I was interested because I was never interested in a girl. To me, they are all the same—a wet hole to stick my dick in and get my fix.

Prey is all the same to me. Poor girls coming to a prestigious school for an opportunity. When they see a rich guy on campus, it's a dollar sign in their eyes, and Jess is no different. She was practically drooling over my car. Gold diggers waiting for a payday. I almost felt bad when she told me her mom's car back home didn't have AC and that her piece-of-shit car doesn't start sometimes. Almost.

I have never lived a day without luxury. I was born into it. It's not my fault she was dealt a fucked-up hand, but that is not my problem, it's hers.

"Yes," she moans.

I continue to savagely pump into her, making her pay for being spread out in front of Valen and another hard thrust for her having a drink with my asshole cousin, who will only fuck her like a savage. He's brutal with the women he fucks. Some come out screaming after he is done with them. I was doing the right thing. She doesn't know the danger she was in by letting him get too close.

The Order doesn't care how many women he does it to. He chooses the most vulnerable ones with no money and no connections, and if they open their mouths or report him, he will kill them and bury them somewhere. He's done it before when he went to Kenyan.

I'm thrusting deep inside her, playing different scenarios in my head of other ways to punish her for her stupidity. I keep pumping into her, and I can't help myself. I place my hand over her mouth to keep her from moaning too loud. Security knows not to interfere and to call maintenance about the elevator.

"Shut up and take it like the whore you are."

I know it sounds fucked up to call her a whore, but that is what she was acting like. Like a bitch in heat needing a hard cock. She wants dick, I'll gladly give it to her.

Her eyes flash in anger, and I know that calling her that bothered her. Good. Maybe next time, she won't act so desperate. I check her mouth, making sure she can breathe. I'm an asshole, but I don't want to kill her. I just want to hurt her a little.

Her pussy begins to clench on my dick, and I know she is close. She's grinding her hips, seeking more, and I meet her thrusts. I slide my hand down her mouth to her throat. Her lips are slightly parted, flushed, and red, waiting to be sucked. I look down at her perfect breasts, bouncing up and down with every thrust I pump into her. Fuck, she's beautiful. She's perfect. Too bad. She's considered Prey. Good for only one thing, to be fucked and used. I was surprised she didn't have a boyfriend somewhere. But I'm sure there aren't any good wealthy prospects where she comes from.

I saw her get jealous when Tara walked over, wanting to jump on my cock. Her father and my father are business associates, and I don't have a good relationship with my own father. That is why I moved in with Dravin. He understands my frustration. We have to take over when the time comes and find a wife.

My father wants me to marry as required by the Order, to take a wife and be one of the founding members. One of the prodigal sons of Kenyan. They want me to marry within the Order. Preferably, Tara. And as tempting as she seems in bed, I can't stand her. I hate her laugh, her smell, and her cunt. It doesn't wrap around my cock like the girl I'm currently fucking in the elevator who's about to come.

My cock swells, and I'm holding on for dear life, not wanting to come before her, but I can't, and anyway, fuck her. She wanted dick; she got dick. She took too long.

"Please, more. Don't stop," she pleads.

"Too bad. I'm not your boyfriend. You're just a wet hole."

Her body goes slack, and she averts her eyes. My words hurt. She tries to slide down my hips, but I pump one last time, emptying myself into the condom.

She won't give me her eyes as I come so good and hard. She tries to hold herself without touching me, and I know I fucked up. I pushed her too far. I said something I can't take back.

"Are you done?" she asks without looking at me.

Fuck. What did I just do? Why do I feel so fucking guilty?

I look down as I slide out of her and tie the condom. She looks down, picks up her clothes from the floor, and slips her skirt over her legs. Her panties are in shreds. She looks at her unsalvageable shirt and balls it all together, slipping on her jacket and zipping it up all the way to her neck, almost choking herself.

I get dressed and press the button so the elevator can climb up to the floor of my suite. She stands silently, watching the numbers change with each floor the elevator passes on the way up.

I shouldn't care about the way I treated her. I should tell her that I'm sorry. I should, but I don't. I can't. I'm not that guy.

When the elevator reaches my floor, the door opens, and I step out, expecting her to follow me to my room. I stop and look behind me with a frown, noticing she hasn't exited the elevator.

"Thank you, you were great," I hear her say as the doors close, leaving me alone in the hallway.

Fuck. I march over to the elevator and press the button, then swipe my card on the card reader repeatedly, but I'm too late. I look up and see the elevator descending to the lobby.

I messed up.

I pushed her too far.

And I know she will never look at me again. I don't know what she meant about thanking me or telling me I was great. I wasn't great. I was horrible. I acted like a total asshole. I shouldn't care about what I did or how I made her feel, but somehow, now I do.

CHAPTER THIRTY ONE

JESS

FUCKING REID. He took her away from me. It was wrong to bring her to the back room and have my way with her, but I get why he was upset. We were at Garret's house with Veronica. I'm not sure if it was because of that or because I was about to have sex with her. I allowed Veronica inside and didn't tell her to fuck off because I didn't want Veronica to target Jess.

She didn't deserve what they did, but the children of Kenyan love to play games and break people. She's Prey, and we give them opportunities after graduation, so they should pay the price, and if not, they die. To everyone, she's no one, but to me, she's different. I see it in her eyes—the tortured pain of someone wronged by people.

It's the same look I've seen when I've had to kill. The look right before you die. Acceptance of your fate. She thinks this is it. She believes that being Prey is her fate, but she's wrong.

I drive back to Garret's house after picking up my BMW at Dravin's. Draven and Gia went up to the house to continue their night of fucking.

I didn't want to interrupt or hear them. Reid disappeared with Jess, and if he treated her like shit, I'll kill him. Not really kill him, but I'll break his face. He has this love-hate thing for Jess, and I think he has it all wrong for her.

I walk back into his house toward the pool where I last saw him. Garret is seated on a lounge chair with Jasmin sucking him off, bobbing her head like a chicken.

"Yo, Garret," I call out.

His head looks up over Jasmin, attempting to deep throat his cock but failing miserably.

"What the fuck, man? I'm busy."

The party died out, and now there are only a few guys from the swim team fucking random girls.

"She sucks anyway, ask Reid."

"Fuck off."

I walk up with the perfect opportunity. I pull my fist back and punch him in the mouth. He falls back from the impact of the blow to his mouth. The sting on my knuckles causes me to shake my hand.

Jasmin shrieks, covering her small breasts with her hands and my eyes land on Garret, who is covering his mouth with both hands while howling in pain, blood is dripping down his chin from his busted lip as he sprawls on the floor with his pathetic excuse of a dick out.

I pick him up off the floor by his hair. "W-what the fuck did you do that for?" he grunts in pain and asks.

I grip his hair hard, almost tearing it out of his scalp. "Ahh! The fuck, Valen!" Garret bawls as he howls in agony.

I bend down close so he can hear every word. "I'll come back and finish you off if you ever go near Jess or spread rumors about how your pathetic excuse for a cock fucked her. Got it!"

"Come on, man," he cries, spitting blood on the floor. The pool water mixed with the blood flowing like a crimson river down the floor from his mouth. "She's Prey. It was all orchestrated by Veronica."

"I get that you're a little shit, but you're such a pussy that you have to keep telling everyone about her and how she fucks in bed. Leave her the fuck alone. Stop spreading shit about her. This is your only warning, or I'll tell Veronica the truth about how you love Jess," I warn, shoving him roughly when I release his hair. "Don't play yourself, Garret."

I watch him, satisfied that I split his mouth open, walking backward toward the exit.

"Why? You fucking her?" he spits.

I laugh. "Maybe."

I'd never out Jess like that, but I love fucking with his head. What I do in bed with her is my business. No one needs to know. Especially a jerk like him. If he cared so much about Jess, he could have said no or warned Jess about Veronica.

I slow my steps as I watch him get up, almost slipping on the wet floor in the process of trying to pull his shorts back on. "I'll fucking kill you."

I snort. "Try it, bitch. I'm right here," I say, holding my hands out.

When I see him bluffing and not making a move, I point my finger at him. "Stay away from her, and don't let me catch you talking about her. You've done enough," I warn, turning away before I take the piece of shit and drown him in his own pool.

We were at Babylon two weeks ago and he was drunk. He started talking about Jess, and I wanted to kill him right then and there over the pool table. But what he said caught me off guard. He started slurring and saying the opposite about her.

Sometimes, when people are drunk, they tell the truth. My teammate on the swim team nodded, confirming that what Garrett was saying wasn't a lie. He wants Jess. Veronica manipulated him and Melissa to get to her.

Garrett had been interested in Jess since the beginning of her freshman year. He would follow her and sweet-talk her before I started Kenyan. I overheard about it when I started my sophomore year. He told her he wanted her to be his girlfriend, but it was supposedly all a lie.

He caught feelings and played it off that it was Veronica he wanted. In his drunken stupor, he stated that he did not want Veronica to go after Jess and hurt her in order for her to save face. He confessed that Veronica liked Jess in bed. I understand that Veronica is a sex-crazed bitch, but it still bothers me. They took it too far with her. I get that she's hot as fuck, but now I'm involved, and I don't like the fact that he won't drop it.

He was jealous that they touched her and angry with Jess for the wrong reasons. He was falling for her, but it was too late. The damage was done, and she wants nothing to do with Garret.

He's a salty asshole and wants to hurt her because she rejected him for the right reasons. I can't say I blame Jess. The reason I'm here is that I have a problem with it all, or maybe I'm falling down the Jess rabbit hole. I like her. I like the way she tastes. The smell of her pussy. I shouldn't want her that much, but I do. I want her a little too much.

CHAPTER THIRTY TWO

JESS

I'M IN THE SHOWER, scrubbing myself in self-loathing with my loofah, but at the same time, I like that Reid was the last one to touch me. I just hate his words and how he called me a whore. I wasn't going to sleep with his cousin. He pulled me out of my jealous thoughts about the scenario playing out with Tara and him. It was self-preservation. I didn't want him to know it bothered me, because then he would know I liked him more than just for sex.

He didn't let me come. The way he did it reminded me of Michael. At first, I thought it was no big deal, but then disappointment and disgust crept in. When I saw him put on his clothes and not care what he said or how he treated me, I didn't want to be in his presence a second longer.

I wanted to get away from him. I hated that I liked him more than I should have. It brought memories of the past. The feelings and emotions that got me to that room in the party. The way you crush on a guy you like way too much, and they use it to lure you in with a false pretense. Exploitation of your emotions in order to break you. To use you. To take advantage of your feelings as an excuse to rape you.

I was craving for Reid to touch me, but the way he did tonight only reminded me of the man I was trying to forget. He said the same things Michael said to me. I was weak for him, and I hated myself for it.

Tonight, Reid reminded me of Michael.

I close my eyes as the hot spray from the shower head in the communal shower bathes my skin, rinsing the soap off my body.

Since I got into the dorm, I knew I would be alone, but the

room was dark and empty. Gia is with her twins tonight, and I can't blame her. Those men are crazy, but they worship her even if they fight to hide it. I expected a blocked call from Reid after I abruptly left, but when I checked my phone, there were no missed calls, just a text from Gia saying she was at Dravin's house. I wasn't surprised Reid hadn't called to see if I was okay or if I arrived safely, like I secretly wished he would. He got what he wanted, and whatever that was didn't include the real me or my feelings.

I'm afraid to go to sleep. I have to admit that to myself and decide to take my time in the shower while everyone on the floor is asleep. I slide the pads of my thumb and index finger over my eyelids to wipe away the water and turn around to give my hair a thorough rinse when I sense a shadow looming and a scream crawls up my throat.

A hand is placed over my mouth. My heart is beating in pure fear, but when my eyes widen, I calm myself. Valen.

"Shh, it's me. I'm sorry, but I didn't mean to startle you," he says, sliding his hand off my mouth.

"Are you out of your mind?" I whisper-yell.

His upper lip curls in a small grin. "Maybe."

My eyes travel down, and I notice he is completely naked. Yes, definitely insane to be naked in the women's shower.

"How did you get past security?"

He chuckles softly and whispers in my ear as I slide under the warm shower spray. "Do you not know who I am, Jess?"

Right. One of the sons of Kenyan. He can do whatever the fuck he wants, and they will just look the other way.

"Yes, I think I do. A crazy guy breaking into the girls' shower wholly naked in the middle of the night."

"You weren't in your room. I figured you would be here since I was the one who took care of your car," he says, looking down at my naked breasts pushed up on the pecs of his lean muscles with pure lust in his eyes. "I wanted to see if you wanted to finish what we started since we were rudely interrupted."

He brushes his nose with mine and the drops of water slide down onto my chest, creating small goose bumps on my skin. "Where did he take you, huh?"

He means Reid. I guess since they are very close and didn't mind sharing me that one time, I guess it's safe to answer him.

"To his hotel."

He caresses his firm lips over mine; his lighter eyes and blonder hair are a strong contrast to Reid's. "Why are you here and not there?"

I pull away slightly, but not too much, so I don't bump my head against the tile behind me. His forehead pinches, and his expression is laced with confusion. No, not confusion, but worry.

"Did he hurt you, Jess?"

I shake my head, not wanting to talk about it. It's not like I matter to him in that way. I don't belong to Valen, and he isn't mine. He's young and fun to be around, with a hint of an edge of darkness. He probably would laugh in my face.

"He didn't hurt me physically. It just didn't feel right with him. Alright." I swallow the lump that is crawling slowly up my throat. "He called me things I didn't like while we were…" I trail off on the last part.

The sound of the water from the shower falling over our bodies like a rain cloud sliding into the drain. The silence stretches longer and tighter, causing his expression to tighten.

"What did he say to you while you were with him? What did he call you?" he asks in a severe tone.

He means while Reid and I were having sex. My eyes fill with tears, and I hope he can't see them, and if he does, I'll blame them on the water from the shower.

I bite my lip and look down between us. His cock is semi-hard against smooth skin filled with scripture tattoos all over his body. I take a deep, shaky breath and tell him what bothered me the most.

"He said I was so wet that I was pathetic, and he also called me a whore. There are other things, like the camera in the elevator where we were." I shrug, a watery smile on my lips. "It doesn't matter. I just couldn't stay there," I tell him, meeting his eyes. "I don't want to see him again. He reminded me of things I want to forget."

"And the bruises on your neck. How did those get there?"

I shake my head and avert my gaze. "I can't tell you that. Please, don't ask that of me," I say softly, a single tear sliding down my cheek like a knife slicing my skin.

He slides his finger from my belly button up my torso to my breast, making my nipples strain for his attention. He doesn't press me for answers and appears relieved for some reason, as if a heavy weight has been lifted from his chest. His eyes follow the movement of his fingers until he stops on the hollow part of my throat.

"I almost didn't let him take you out of there, but I see it wasn't the time or place. I'm sorry Veronica was there, and I should have known better. Sometimes, I don't think; I just want to feel."

"What do you want to feel?" I ask on a gasp when his other hand grips my waist, bringing me flush to his groin.

"Me, inside of you. I want to taste you. I want to fuck you."

My hands rest on his chest, over taut muscle and ink. I look up into his eyes, the water making lines like streams down my face and chin. My chest is rising and falling. The feel of his dick teasing my slit.

"I was with Reid a couple of hours ago."

I want to tell him so he can stop if he wants to. I don't want him to think any less of me. It's better to actually say it, even if he already knows it.

"Did he make you come, Jess? Did he make you feel good?"

I shake my head. "No. I didn't come."

He closes his eyes. "Bastard," he mumbles with a grin. "I guess I have to be the one to make you come."

He slides his hands over my ass, spreading his big hands over my skin. Valen is about an inch taller and leaner than Reid but is strong for his build. He lifts me, and I wrap my legs around his waist as my back hits the tile behind me. He bends his knees slightly, his gaze not leaving mine, when he slides the tip of his cock inside my pussy inch by inch and we both groan.

"Fuck, you feel so good."

My pussy gushes, my arousal coating his cock as it makes noises while he thrusts inside of me.

"Yes," I say on a moan. "Don't stop."

I wrap my arms around his neck, giving him a better angle so he can plunge into me deeply. He places my lower back against the tiles, holding me at a certain height while angling his body.

"What are you doing?" I ask with a gasp.

He feels so good. He's hard but soft at the same time. He knows what he's doing and how to hit me in the right spot that has me falling off the edge. He may be younger than Reid, but he sure as hell knows how to make a woman come.

"Making sure I come inside this pussy. I want my cum dripping out of you in the morning while I eat my breakfast."

I grind my hips, hoping he reaches the right spot. Fuck. His words are hot. He grasps my thighs with his strong hands as if I were nothing.

"Do you like that, baby? Is that what you need? Me inside you."

"Valen," I mewl. "Right there."

He pumps into me while I gyrate on his shaft. I'm swollen and dripping. The water feels hotter, but I know it's my body and what Valen is doing to me. He has my body on the verge, and god, he's perfect. It's a shame he isn't the relationship type. This is just a good time, and I need a man to make me feel good, so he's perfect, and I don't want him to stop. I want him inside me, taking me away from my reality just for a little while. I'm on the pill, and I've only had sex with Valen without a condom. Except when Michael raped me. Valen has evolved into a guy I can trust with sex. A guy who doesn't judge and is comfortable in his own skin, and when I'm with him, I'm free. I feel like that girl in college exploring what she likes. He gets tested monthly like I do, which we only share with each other.

He places his lips on my neck, placing soft kisses. "I want you, Jess. I want you so much. Come on my cock, baby, it's all yours. I want to feel you milking me."

I meet him with every thrust over and over until my orgasm crests, and I feel him going at me deeper. His grunts and my moans echo in the shower against the sound of water hitting the tile. It's hot, and it feels forbidden. He takes what he wants, and I want to give it to him.

I glance down and watch his cock disappear inside my pussy, hitting my clit and causing me to clench my pussy.

"You're coming, baby. I can feel it. Let go, Jess. Give me what I want."

"What do you want?" I ask breathlessly.

He grins and slides his tongue up my neck and over the seam of my lips.

"To fuck you whenever I want," he responds, sliding his thumb over my clit in circles, and it throbs, pushing me over the edge. "Tell me I get to fuck you whenever I want. Tell me," he repeats.

My pussy floods in response, and I scream, "I'm coming! Fuck. Yes!"

He pumps into me and grunts with a smile, spilling inside me, jerking his body as his cock spasms, lighting me on fire from the inside.

"You're dirty and swollen now," he says, holding me steady while my heart rate slows down.

The door to the main shower opens, and I stiffen. "Fuck, someone's in here," I whisper.

He places his index finger over my lips, telling me to be quiet as he helps me slide down until my feet touch the tiles.

My forehead is touching his chest, and I wait, closing my eyes.

My skin prickles in awareness at being caught naked in the shower with Valen.

I hear footsteps, but he remains still. Once they stop hearing the only shower running in the middle of the night, it is evident that we are the only ones in there.

I hear a snicker. "I knew he wouldn't keep her."

Veronica's voice booms inside the quiet bathroom. Shit. She saw us. How the fuck did she know we were here?

"I'll handle this," he whispers. "Don't be afraid."

"I'm not," I say, looking up at his beautiful face full of mischief.

"Play her at her own game. She wants you. Are you up to play, baby?"

It depends on what kind of game he wants to play, and I can't ask him with her right here. I wonder what she wants with me besides being a sex-crazed idiot.

She walks close to the curtain to the changing area right before you reach the shower curtain. The curtain is like a barrier. But you can still see who is inside the shower stall if you walk into the small changing area with a bench.

Valen turns around, not caring if she can see him completely naked, shielding me behind him. Valen is the type who doesn't mind who sees him. It's what I like most about him. He doesn't care what anyone thinks or says. He does what he wants and with whom he wants.

I can't see her, but I can hear her next words. "You're fucking her raw," she says, with a smile in her voice. "I like it. Did you come in her?" she purrs.

"What do you want, Veronica, and more importantly, why are you here?" Valen says with a firm tone.

"I was curious to see where you went. I had a hunch after you stormed in and punched the shit out of Garrett in her honor, and I guess I was right. You couldn't resist her. Could you?"

He punched Garrett? For me? My stomach clenches, and

butterflies swarm, mixed with tears burning behind my eyes. No one has ever cared for me besides my mom. I feel bad for Garret in a way. He is fucked up, and his motives don't add up, but no one has ever defended me that way. Why would he risk himself for me?

"Your point?" he snaps.

"I was surprised, that's all. I would have thought it would be Reid, but then again, he doesn't care about a Prey. He had me confused earlier when he saw us and called me a bitch."

I snort. He called me a whore. I guess I got the short end of the stick. Being referred to as a bitch is preferable to being referred to as a whore.

"What was that, Jess? Did he say something to you, too?" she asks in a singsong voice.

Like she would give three fucks what Reid would call me. She's a manipulator. She sure as hell got me by screwing me over. But that was then, and this is now. I'm tired of people using me.

"I'm going to my room," I say, quietly moving from behind Valen and coming into view. She steps aside, but her eyes dip as she watches me walk with pure want in her eyes. Valen wasn't wrong. She does like to bat for the other team.

CHAPTER THIRTY THREE

JESS

ONCE I'M in my room, I don't expect Valen to show up. I'm combing my hair in a fresh pair of pajama shorts and a cropped tank top. I hear a knock on my door, and looking at my phone, it's already three a.m.

I open the door and see Valen fully dressed, minus his jacket and gloves or the beanie he likes to wear. His light hair is a sexy mess, and his eyes roam over my body. Veronica is behind him, and they walk in and close the door, flicking the lock.

Veronica sits on the chair by my desk and watches Valen as he walks closer and tips my chin up with his finger. His eyes find mine, and the look he is giving me is different.

"Remember what I said," he says.

Veronica raises her brows, but she is so fixated on me that she doesn't grasp the hidden meaning in his words. He pushes me down on the bed, and I break my fall by placing my hands behind me.

"What are you doing?" I ask softly, my eyes locked on his.

He smiles and looks over at Veronica and then back at me. "Showing her how much you like me. She wants to watch your cunt swallow my cock."

What is he doing? My elbows shake at the intentions behind his words. He wants to finish what he started, or rather, what almost happened at the party. The part with her in the room.

"I'm tired."

"It will be quick, I promise," he says, removing his shirt and pants.

Veronica bites her lip, but she isn't looking at the beautiful man standing in front of me, sliding his boxers down his muscular, solid thighs full of tattoos or his hard cock. She's watching my reaction to him.

"Yeah, Jess. It will be quick," Veronica parrots, her eyes transfixed on me like I'm a shiny dot in a dark room.

"Sit on my lap, baby," Valen says, sitting beside me and stroking his cock.

I should ask him to leave and get the fuck out or, better yet, kick them both the fuck out. But then I'll be left alone with my demon coming to remind me at night that I'm his.

How bad can it be? He's here to make me feel good. He won't hurt me, and he says all the right things—things that make me forget. I know he's saving me from her for whatever reason. The problem is, I don't know what that is exactly.

I sit up straight, and he reaches for me, pulling me so that the backs of my thighs rest on his muscular ones, the contrast of his tattooed hands against the bare skin of my thighs. My back to his front, I can feel the heat of his hard cock ready for me.

He slides my hair away from my neck and places a soft kiss near my ear, the little spot where my pulse beats wildly when his firm lips touch my skin.

"I want you to ride me this way. Reverse cowgirl," he says, nibbling my neck. "She wants to watch you take my cock. She wants to see how much you want me."

He kisses me again, and my body melts. My skin is on fire with goosebumps from the heat. My nipples are hardening under my shirt like I'm cold.

His other hand slides the neckline of my top down, exposing my breasts and pulling it down so that it stays in place beneath my tits like an offering—a sample for someone to taste.

Veronica gets up from the chair and kneels between our legs. "You're so beautiful, Jess. Has anyone told you how beautiful you are? How hot and sexy your body is?"

I shake my head silently, telling her no, and watch as her forehead creases in a frown. She tilts her head to the side, licking her lips.

"Really. I guess we have to change that, don't we? Right, Valen? We have to show her how pretty she is and how good she tastes. What she does to us."

She glides her small white hands on my thighs. Her straight hair sliding forward like a curtain. I hold my breath, stiffening as she reaches for the hem of my shorts and slides them down my legs in one motion, exposing me.

Valen reaches around my waist to flick my clit and I explode from the sensation on a moan.

She looks up and bites her lip like she's in agony. "Does it feel good?"

I nod. "Yes."

She looks up at Valen like he's a disease but is only here for my benefit. "Make sure she's wet, Valen. Make sure it's good for her."

"It's always good for her. She's my favorite," he says, smearing my arousal all over my lower lips while playing with my clit.

"I know she is. I've never seen your cock work so hard or go... bare for a girl."

She looks at my pussy and then looks up at me, biting her lip so hard I think she is breaking the skin. "Did you know Valen has this special appetite? Not like mine, of course, but an appetite so bad it's crazy and borderline insane."

She angles her head, mesmerized by how wet Valen is making me, breathing fast and steady. "He loves to fuck, and I like..." She sticks her tongue out, wetting her upper lip. "To suck pussy."

"You don't like cock?" I ask.

I don't care, but I need to keep my cool. She's a lesbian, which is fine. No judgment. I don't like women, but this is just experimenting, I tell myself. I'll be clear: this is a one-time thing. I'm not going to touch her or let her stick anything inside me. It will just be a kiss, I tell myself.

Valen slides the tip of his finger inside my pussy, and I arch my back against his chest, and he widens my thighs.

"That pussy is so wet," she purrs. "Ready to be fucked. I like to call it a pootie." She smiles. "Do you know why?"

I don't give a fuck, but I can't tell her that. This sex-crazed bitch is insane. It's no wonder Warren dropped her like a bad habit. He's a creepy asshole, but this bitch is crazy. They're like a match made in heaven.

"No, why?"

"Because it's what my daddy called it. It's what I like to call it since I found out for the first time that I like them," she says.

"Fuck," I gasp as Valen slides a second finger inside me.

"Ready, baby?" he says in a rough voice.

His cock is hard like steel, and it's throbbing under the crack of my ass. He lifts me, and I impale myself on his cock, holding my breasts. "Yes," I moan.

"You feel so good, baby. You're always so tight and such a good girl," Valen says, pumping inside of me.

With my hips riding him, I meet his thrusts. He grunts and groans.

My nipples are hard and aching. Veronica kneels and leans forward, flicking her tongue on my nipple, causing me to jolt. Valen stiffens slightly but keeps going.

"I'm just going in for a taste."

Her eyes flick to my hooded ones. "Let me make you feel good, Jess. I need you to tell me I can suck your pussy and those pretty nipples aching for a touch."

I moan. Valen's cock is so hard and is swelling inside of me, stretching me. The sound of wet noises bounces off the walls, with only the lamp from my nightstand casting a glow on the wet nipples she just licked, causing my body to react biologically.

I want to feel good, and she licks it again, placing her lips over the tight bud. "Please," I whimper.

"More?" she asks.

"Yes," I moan.

God help me. I can't help myself. It feels so good. I'm hot and wet.

"Fuck, that's hot," Valen says behind me. "That is so hot, baby. You're in control, Jess. I got you."

I close my eyes, and she begins to suck my left breast and then the other. While Valen's cock is fucking me, her fingers play with my clit. I moan and he grunts.

She moans against my skin, releasing my right nipple with a pop. "So good and so beautiful. She's gorgeous, Valen. Look how wet she is for you."

She leans closer to my lips. "Tell him. Tell him how much you like his dick inside your tight pink cunt."

"I like his dick inside me. It's so hard and big. I love it when he forces me to come," I whisper.

He grunts in response, going faster. "Yeah, baby. You're so beautiful, Jess. You're exactly what I want. I'll be inside you, pounding this pussy whenever you need me."

Veronica smiles and snakes her tongue down my torso to my clit and begins to suck my pussy like a woman starving to eat. "Oh my god. Yes!"

I grab her head, holding her in place. I lose myself, not believing what I'm letting her do to me. She makes circles over my clit, licking it and sucking my pussy at the same time Valen's shaft disappears inside my folds. Fuck.

"Mmm," she moans. "This pussy belongs to the Order. You choose, and we fuck," she says as she twirls her tongue against my clit.

This bitch is fucking nuts, but she can eat pussy. Fuck, I'm about to come. Valen increases his thrusts as I turn my head and he devours my lips.

His tongue fucks my mouth, and I can't take it. Her mouth on my pussy while Valen is fucking me is too much. I break.

"I'm coming!" I scream.

Valen places his hand over my mouth so no one can hear me scream while he grunts. "I'm coming. It's a lot of cum, baby. I'm going to fill you up so much," he says on a grunt, spilling inside me. He stills, letting his release, and I can feel his cock throbbing as it promises what his words just did.

I'm breathing hard after he's done, and he slides out of me, his cum leaking out. He places me on the bed with my legs open. My pussy used, swollen, and leaking.

Veronica kneels on the bed while Valen kneels beside my head. I turn and the tip of his cock is coating my lips. "Open. Clean me," he says.

I open my mouth and he slides his cock slowly inside my wet mouth. I can taste his salty cum on my tongue. It is not nasty but tastes a little sweet.

"Fuck, your mouth is perfect," he rasps.

He looks at Veronica. "Clean her," he instructs.

"Yes, sir," she says without protest.

Her mouth is on my pussy, and I lift my ass off the bed at the intense sensation. I'm sensitive and swollen, but her tongue is soft as she licks his cum from my pussy.

I moan when she places pressure on my clit. She dips her tongue inside, and I clench my thighs around her head. She places her hands on my outer thighs, caressing me. "Open, baby. I need to get all of it. He wants you clean."

I relax my thighs, and she finishes cleaning me off, sucking her lips when she is done feasting on me.

"All done."

He looks at her. "Good, now get the fuck out. You're done."

"Fine," she growls, getting up. "But I did what you wanted. Reid is going to be pissed when he finds out."

What? He called her? Did he lie to me?

I stiffen, but he is already between my thighs, sliding his cock inside me, thrusting. He leans over me with his hands on the side of my head.

"Shh."

His lips move closer to my ear while the door clicks after Veronica exits. "You heard her. Your pussy belongs to the Order." He looks down as his cock slides in and out, making me whimper. "When you want to fuck, you call me, and I'll fuck you so good."

"You'll fuck me whenever I want?"

CHAPTER THIRTY FOUR

JESS

I BOLT upright from the bed after being jolted awake. I look down, and my legs are open with a sense of relief. I was dreaming. Valen is between my thighs. My eyes are closed. I was talking in my sleep.

He nods, letting out a breath, sliding his hand behind my neck. "Whenever you want. Wherever you want. I'll come over, and we'll fuck." He lifts my head, allowing our lips to brush against each other's. "You were talking in your sleep. What you didn't hear me say to Veronica in front of you was that she wasn't allowed to touch you. Don't let me catch her touching what's mine. If anyone touches you without your consent, I'll kill them. Do you understand?"

I nod, my gaze fixed on his. He slides inside me in a hard thrust, causing my orgasm to crest again, and I tighten around him. His nostrils flare while he peppers kisses on my lips.

His words fill me with warmth, with the hope that someone cares. Veronica wasn't here. It was a dream. I must have fallen asleep, and he found his way inside my room. He cares right now, and that's the most anyone has ever done for a girl like me.

He's not my boyfriend, and I'm not stupid enough to believe he can offer more than what he's giving me.

The way he looks at me while he's inside me is the closest I have ever felt to feeling wanted. To feel free and be able to enjoy sex without being haunted by memories because of my bad decisions.

He runs his nose against my cheek, just the way I like when he does it. The smell of his skin mixed with my body wash.

"You're not a whore. You are not a bad person simply because you want someone to make you feel good sexually. You're sexy and beautiful, and if anyone can't see that, then fuck them."

"Valen," I mewl.

His words make me fall. I can't say it's love, but it's something I have never felt for someone.

"I know, baby, you're almost there. I can feel it. I want you to let go. I don't want you to hold back and not enjoy this. Enjoy us."

That's when I come. I come hard from his soft words. Tears pool in the corner of my eyes because it's all I want. I want to forget. I want someone to treat me right, even if it's just for a minute, to caress me like I belong to them, to love me for a second, to know what it would feel like when someone truly cared for me like I would care for them.

Some type of love. Even if it's a lie. My mind tries to make sense of why I dreamed of Veronica and Valen pleasuring me at the same time. Was it because Gia kissed me, which triggered what happened with Garrett, and I was at his house with Veronica before Reid saved me from doing something I would later regret?

I close my eyes, trying to make sense of it all. I'm losing myself, but I secretly crave two men and hate another. One is inside me, and the other treats me like the thing I hated the most, triggering a memory I'm trying to forget. Then, the other allows me to use him.

The sacrifice I had to make for the only person who truly loves me and sees me as a saint, despite the fact that all I have become is a sinner. I'm using their want for sex on a primal level to forget the monster that comes for me, but now I'm feeling things that I want. With them.

CHAPTER THIRTY FIVE

GIA

WALKING into Babylon after a late class on Monday, I scan the bar and spot Jess talking to the bartender. I smile as she animatedly waves her hands with a smile on her face.

Making my way through the crowd, it is surprisingly busy tonight, being a weekday, but it's Monday night football, and there isn't much to do so…

When I finally make it up to the bar, Jess smiles at me. She turns and sees me in my fuzzy jacket over wool leggings and UGGs on my feet. "You look so cozy, I miss you," she says, giving me a hug.

She turns her head, and the bartender she was deep in conversation with gives me a nod and asks, "What can I get you?"

Before I can answer, Jess blurts, "Cranberry and vodka, but not too strong."

I giggle. "I'm not a lightweight, Jess."

She waves her hand, taking a sip of a fruity cocktail she is drinking. "Yeah, but I'm not taking any chances with your man, or should I say…" She trails off.

She means the twins. I have been holed up in Dravin's house, being waited on hand and foot by two hot-ass men. My body is deliciously used, but I'm not taking anything seriously and just enjoying feeling safe. Wanted.

I didn't tell them my fear of being alone with Warren lurking around or his threats. I should have told them, but I was as caught up with both of them as they were with me. There were no discussions of the future, just being in the moment, and I was okay with that for now. No pressure. They held me at night when I cried about the miscarriage. They took turns holding me. When I was in the shower, the other was there supporting me and telling me everything would be all right.

Dravin repeatedly apologized for his actions, but what was done was done. Do I trust them? Not entirely. Do they want me? Maybe. Time will tell, but I'm not in a hurry to find out right now. I need to find myself, explore what I want, and discover what I truly need.

Jess twirls her glass between her fingers, the drops of water sliding down the glass. She looks happier—not entirely happy, but happy for now, if that makes sense. I heard she left with Reid, but then I heard Valen slept over, and I'm not sure what the deal is between them.

"You look happy," I say over the music playing from the jukebox.

She gives me a smirk. "Not as happy as you. So, how was your weekend?"

"You first," I counter.

She takes another sip of her drink, and I see her eyes are glassy from the alcohol. She's buzzed. I can tell with the way her mouth curls in a grin and her upbeat attitude. Usually, she's more reserved and borderline paranoid half the time.

She swallows and watches the bartender place the drink I ordered in front of me. When he walks away, she spills everything that happened with Reid, Valen, and Veronica, causing me to down my drink in one go.

"Hey, chill with that, or I'll have to call back up," she teases.

"I think it's too late for that," I say, nudging my head to where Drav, Draven, Valen, and Reid are making their way through the crowd. They are all dressed in black like they are part of a cult, except they look like cover models. All the females turn their heads to get a good look as they approach us. Some make it obvious, and some try to hide it by giving them a glance behind them as they pass.

Once they see us, I notice Reid standing a few feet away

from Jess, unsure how she will take the fact that he's here. She doesn't look at him, though. Her eyes are locked on Valen, and they share a silent language that only the two of them can understand.

"Hey, gorgeous." Drav is the first to greet me, but Draven places a kiss on my neck. My lips rub together, nervous at their display of affection. People are staring at them because they look like two clones that were made in a lab somewhere. The good news is that I can tell them apart. The tattoos. A particular touch that is different. I have also been smart enough to share certain things with one and not with the other.

"Hey," I say softly.

Valen gives me a knowing smile, looking between the Bedford twins and me. My cheeks must be red because Draven leans close and says close enough to my ear but out of earshot. "Relax, or I could take you right now to the bathroom with Dravin and fuck you. No one would know the difference."

I bite my lip and Valen quirks an eyebrow. I swear nothing that has to do with sex escapes him.

"What are you guys doing here?" Reid asks.

Jess stays silent, but her eyes swing my way, telling me to answer him. She doesn't want to talk to him directly after how he treated her, and to be honest, I wouldn't either.

My eyes find his a few feet away. "We decided to meet up after classes were over. We wanted to catch up. We were both busy this weekend and didn't get to hang out," I answer.

He nods, though I can see he is trying not to look over at Jess. He tries to break the awkward silence by talking to Valen since he knows where the twins and I were all weekend.

"What did you get up to this past weekend after the party?" he asks Valen.

Jess stills and rests her forearms at the bar, facing the bartenders and giving them her back. She reaches for the glass and drains the rest of her cocktail.

She was screwing in our dorm room with Valen all weekend. It is obvious Valen didn't mention that part to Reid.

After a few seconds, Valen rubs the back of his neck and faces the opposite direction, leaning on the edge of the bar next to Jess. "I was with someone the rest of the weekend." He licks his lips and looks down and then back at Reid.

"No shit. Who was she? You're not the type to hang out with one chick all weekend," he says on a laugh.

My hand slides into Dravin's hand and squeezes it for support. His eyes land on mine, and it dawns on him to be quiet. Not to say shit. Draven, behind me, chuckles, but he gives Draven a look that tells him to keep his mouth shut.

Valen sucks his teeth, trying to keep his cool. "No one you care about," he responds.

Shit. He's keeping it from Reid. It must have bothered him the way Reid treated Jess. I look over at Valen and smile, seeing him in a friendly light. He's looking out for her. The things she told me she went through, and keeps enduring, and he's actually not being a dick about it and putting her out there.

Reid is quiet, not entirely convinced by his answer. It's like you can feel the uncertainty of Valen's response or the way he isn't talking like he smashed some random chick he usually does. He is typically vocal about the girls he sleeps with the few times he's been around. He's a total player.

Jess turns around and nudges Valen playfully. "So, who was the lucky chick? Was she good?" she asks.

Draven snorts and I widen my eyes. He takes the cue and looks over at the bartender, twirling his finger, silently motioning for another round of drinks.

Reid finally glances over at Jess while she isn't looking, totally checking her out. She's wearing tight skinny jeans and over-the-knee boots with an off-the-shoulder sweater. Her cute bra strap peeking out. Her hair is in loose, messy waves. She looks hot. It's no wonder even Veronica has a thing for her, but Jess clearly said it wasn't ever happening again after that time with Garret. College experimenting, she said on a laugh.

Valen pulls his bottom lip with his teeth, and he is totally going to talk about her in front of Reid without him knowing he is talking about her and what he thought of her in bed.

Fuck, she's playing with fire, making me smile at her. Well played. He deserves it.

Valen snakes his gaze over her briefly and tilts his head. "She was hot and tasted so good I didn't want to leave, so I stayed the whole weekend."

"You slept with her in bed?" I ask him, acting like I don't already know.

He gives me a mischievous expression, licks his lip where his teeth are, and then chuckles. "More like fucked nonstop. More fucking and less sleeping, and I stayed. The sex was so good I didn't want to leave. We even ordered food in between."

Drav scratches his head when he looks at Reid, but he notices he doesn't catch on.

"How about you?" Valen asks Reid. "What did you do after?"

Reid looks at Jess, but she's already turned away, disinterested in what he has to say. I can see the frustration in his brows as she continues to ignore him.

After the way he treated her, why should she feel the need to acknowledge him? He's lucky I don't punch him in the eye, but I'll let her handle it.

Reid swallows, trying to find the right words. "I had some family business to take care of after Jess left," he points out.

She snorts yet doesn't turn to look at him. When the bartender arrives with our round of drinks, he smiles at Jess and says, "I made this one just the way you like it."

Draven's eyebrows rise, and Reid slides his hand on the bar, his forearms taut with corded muscle and ink, tilting his head toward the bartender.

Oh, shit. Someone's a little pissed.

"How would you know what she likes?" Reid asks with a growl.

The bartender glances at Jess and answers without looking at him. "Because she told me. She told me what she likes."

Reid and Valen both chuckle, and my pulse begins to pound when Jess glances at me. The twins are flanking me on each side but make no move to intervene. They want to see how this all plays out. It's like watching two lions fighting for a lioness, waiting for someone to attack so they can pounce. This isn't about the bartender; this is about the way Jess smiles and is comfortable with Valen, and how Reid doesn't like the way she doesn't acknowledge him. She looks down her nose at him like he's no longer a factor. The way she is flirting and sharing what she likes with the bartender.

Reid's eyes travel down her body, making a point that he's undressing her with them. That he's seen her without her clothes on. It's obvious to anyone who is watching him next to her that they have been intimate.

The bartender watches him with annoyance and then flicks his eyes to Valen, who tilts his head, watching Reid make his next move with a devious smirk. It's like the rest of the place fades away, and we're the only ones trapped in our own makeshift bubble.

Jess raises her head and stares at the bartender with a worried expression. She must be nervous because Reid is unpredictable when pushed. He's mostly quiet and keeps to himself. Although the few times I have seen him, you wonder what is going through his head. Like right now, he may be looking at Jess with interest or maybe it's just part of their game. Games they like to play just to fuck with you.

He makes it seem like he's interested in her, but then, you never know with Reid. He could walk away and go to the back and get his dick sucked by some random chick in the bar. Jess is a memory all forgotten until… next time.

Two distinctive pings sound on either side of me. I look up to see Draven pull out his phone and then I look to my left to see his twin do the same. They both received texts at the same time.

I hear Draven mutter, "Fuck."

"I would love to see how this all plays out, but we have to leave."

Valen darts his eyes to Draven. "What's up, brother?"

"Family business," Draven answers for him.

"Let's go," Dravin whispers in my ear.

Jess turns around and our eyes meet. "Are you okay to stay, or do you…" I trail off.

"I'm good. I can have Valen take me back."

I nod, and Dravin places his hand on my lower back, signaling that we must go. I don't know how that involves me, but the twins have been very adamant about never leaving me alone. I wonder why?

CHAPTER THIRTY SIX

REID

Present

MY ARM IS CAGING Jess from her right side, and the sideways glance she gives Gia tells me all I need to know. She's nervous when I'm near, and I'm going to show her she should be. Especially when she's flirting with the bartender.

She thinks I haven't been watching her since I entered with Valen and the Bedford twins. Her sultry smile and the way her snug leggings are hugging her perfect ass. Her bra strap is visible from her shoulder. The asshole in front of her keeps looking at it, probably imagining sliding it off to see her creamy breasts and what color her nipples are.

My gaze moves over her shoulder, down her arm, and back up to her neck, where I'm sure I can feel her pulse beating if I place my lips there. Not the same way it beats when I'm inside her, but close.

I stare at the bartender and can see the look of annoyance aimed right at me. I smile when I rub my lip piercing and inhale her flowery-scented perfume. Intoxicating right to the head of my dick, straining in my jeans. Fuck, she is addicting. I hated the way she left my hotel that night. The way I let her go when I fucked up. It wasn't the way I wanted to end the night, not with her. I shouldn't give a fuck, but there is something that draws me to her, like a moth to a flame, something that needs to be awakened. There is something inside her that I see that is dormant, but once it is unleashed, I want to feed off it. I want her to want me. I'm just so fucked up when it comes to her. I was raised in a world where I was taught to not care.

To take.

To control.

"You don't want to look at me?" I whisper in her ear.

Nothing. No answer. She just stares at the bartender. The music fades in the background. My heart begins to pump inside my chest. My cock is rock hard, but I'm going to rectify my mistake. I didn't let her come. In my jealousy, I punished her. It's hard to admit that to myself, but that's what it felt like. The same way I'm feeling now with her attention on Valen. His attention on her doesn't bother me—or perhaps it does. I'm not sure yet. But the bartender? Now that I have a problem with. Him—or any other man she smiles that way for.

My hand finds the waistband of her pants, and she tenses. "You don't want to look at me, fine, keep looking at him."

Her face turns to gape at me. Her stormy expression is in those brown eyes.

"What are you doing?" she hisses.

My lips are just inches away from hers. "I'm finishing what you started. You didn't let me finish, but I will now."

My hand quickly slides inside her stretchy pants, and I find the elastic band of her panties and slide my finger over her clit.

She turns back to the bartender and parts her lips. At her entrance, I make languid circles with my thumb, teasing with my index finger, and softly say, "Tell him everything you like."

She doesn't say anything. Valen tilts his head forward to glance at me over the bar, with Jess between us. People are drinking, and the place is filling up quickly, which is perfect. No one will notice.

My name escapes from her lips, which are so soft, in almost a whimper. "Reid."

"Tell him."

The bartender pinches the skin between his brows in a slight frown. He doesn't realize I'm finger fucking her in front of him while he watches. She doesn't tell me to stop or scream. She wants this. She needs to come. She craves it. And I want her taste on my fingers.

"Hey, man. It's all good," the bartender says. "She's good. She doesn't have to repeat the types of drinks she likes."

"Oh, you thought that this was about drinks?" I ask, plunging my finger inside her tight cunt. She takes a deep swallow.

Fuck, she's wet and tight. I want to slide into her right here so bad, not giving a fuck who watches, or maybe I do. I don't want this asshole to see her perfect cunt or the way her perky tits bounce when I'm inside her or when her neck arches when she comes on a scream.

I slide my finger in her faster and swirl my thumb on her clit. She grips the bar with her hands, and I'm right behind her. My lips are inches from her neck, under her ear, while I look at the bartender with a grin. She's about to come, and I plunge into her one last time, and I feel her walls clench my fingers as she breaks.

"Yeah, baby. Come. Show him what you like. Tell him you love my fingers fucking you in a roomful of people."

Her mouth is parted, but I can't see her eyes. The bartender looks at me and shakes his head with his lips curled.

I raise my head, my eyes challenging him to say something so I have a reason to slit his throat. He sets her empty glass to the side so the busboy can retrieve it. A couple of girls across the bar are waving their money to get his attention. He hears them calling, but he's pissed. I'm not sure if he knows what I am doing to her or if she allowed it.

I remove my fingers full of her cum from between her leg and raise them to my mouth, tasting her. "One thing you will never have is her." I suck my fingers clean.

"I get it," the bartender says. Then he looks at her, but she turns her head away.

"Make sure that you do, or I'm going to have to pay you a visit," I tell him with a sigh, placing a small kiss on her hair. "And you wouldn't want that."

Valen laughs through his nose at the nervous look that crosses the bartender's face and he leaves to take the other orders.

Jess whirls with a glare. "Why? Why did you do that?"

"Because I can. Last time I checked." I wave the scent of her pussy under her nose with my fingers. "You didn't protest, and you sure as hell loved it. I owed you one, remember?"

"Fuck you."

"I plan on it."

"No."

"We'll see."

She sidesteps to the right to go around me. I'm about to stop her, but I let her go. I'm surprised Valen doesn't follow her. Instead, he stares at me with a glare.

"What?" I snap at him, annoyed.

He shakes his head. "You didn't have to do that."

I take my vape pen out, place the tip between my lips, press the button so it heats up, and inhale without giving a fuck. "I did," I say, releasing a cloud of smoke tinged with marijuana into the air. Some people can make out that it's marijuana in oil from a vape pen, and others don't notice. I couldn't care less. It's just convenient, and it relaxes me.

Valen walks away, pissed at me, but I don't care. I was making a point, which I'll keep making when it comes to Jess. She is mine, and I'm claiming her. She just doesn't know it yet.

CHAPTER THIRTY SEVEN

GIA

I'M in the back seat of the black Rolls Royce with Dravin and Draven sitting next to me while their driver is taking us to the Bedford estate. Apparently, their father wants to see the three of us. Dravin to my left and Draven to my right. I know this because I have picked up on some of their quirks. Dravin likes to place his hand on my knee, and the other twin likes to watch him do it.

I wonder if it bothers him to see Dravin touch me and for me to allow it. Draven isn't affectionate in public. He isn't soft or emotional like Dravin. He's more to the point, but he does have a soft side, which I saw when I was crying.

He's seconds younger, and by default, he doesn't get to marry. He has to share the woman who bears his children with his brother, but it doesn't appear to bother him. Maybe it's because of his freedom to choose who he wants to be with.

Feeling Draven tense beside me, I look down at his hand resting on the red leather seat. I glance at the rearview mirror and see that the driver is looking straight ahead and I look to my right and see that we are passing the cemetery. It's dark, and the glow from the pillar near the gate illuminates the front door of the old church. I see suited men leaving discreetly to the awaiting vehicles parked in a line by the path near the opposite entrance.

Trying to get a better look without being obvious is straining my eyes. I'm beginning to sweat under my jacket, and my feet feel suffocated inside my UGGs.

The Order. They had a meeting. It must have been between the main leaders and that didn't include the sons of Kenyan because they were with us. All of them, so that could mean that something is wrong.

I feel Draven next to me, and he seems restless, which causes me to feel nervous. Dravin must feel that I'm nervous and begins swirling his thumb over my thick winter pants. My right hand moves slowly down by my thigh and I reach for Draven's hand. I can hear the small intake of his breath when my fingers brush against the top of his left palm. His head angles slightly, and I can feel the burning gaze, watching our hands touch.

Slowly, I place my left hand on Dravin's, and my right hand grips his brother's. My skin prickles with awareness, and my body reacts to the warmth of their hands on mine. Identical hands from two different men. It's crazy but so erotic. Memories of their touch on me the whole weekend flashed back into my mind. When they were on me. Inside me.

When the car turns on the same street Draven took me on his motorcycle, I snap out of my thoughts. This time, it feels like I'm on my way to meet the devil. Mr. Bedford is a very powerful man. He serves a purpose: the Order and himself. Everything else is inconsequential.

The black iron gate opens slowly like it's taking its time, or maybe it's giving me time to flee. But I know deep down I won't. I'm not going to run. There are threats in the name of Warren. He threatened me. I haven't told the twins and fear what they might do. I'm sure they will kill him. It means they will risk their lives for me if they find out. Do I want the death of Warren on my conscience because of his threats? Do I want the twins to risk their lives for me? I know the answer in my heart is no. As much as they have hurt me, they have also made me feel like I'm a woman. They have made me love myself. Warren hasn't touched me or physically hurt me. Not yet, but I wouldn't put it past him. I'm stuck in a hard place. Tell them or don't tell them. Either way, there is a risk.

The driver pulls in around the fountain with the gargoyle. The reflection of the red light on the pillars gives him red eyes. The front door opens, and the staff, I assume, is present. Maybe they only appear when their father is home, or maybe that day Draven had them dismissed.

The driver places the car in park and opens the door on Dravin's side to let us out. Dravin slides out of the car first, but when I move to place my foot, Draven pulls me back. His hand grips my jaw, turning my face to his. His lips come crashing over mine. I gasp when his tongue plunges inside my mouth, and he groans. His soft tongue sucks my top lip and then my bottom.

"Are you done?" I hear Dravin's annoyed tone snapping me out of the kiss. For a moment, we weren't in the car. Dravin wasn't outside waiting for me to slide out. I was transported into another world—another moment—with Draven.

Draven releases me and tilts his head to look at his brother. "It was the kiss, or I was going to take her in the back seat."

"He's waiting, Draven. If he gets into one of his moods, you know how the night will end."

I frown and look at Draven to see if there is a hint. How will the night end? He sighs and gives me a peck on the nose. "Let's go. He's right."

I slide out, holding Dravin's hand, and he tugs me to his chest. "I'm not mad at you. I'm not mad that he kissed you. I just don't like being here."

I look up at him. The smell of the cold air and the way it's seeping into my clothes causes me to shiver from the change of temperature when exiting the warm car. His childhood home must bring him memories and thoughts of his mother.

"Okay," I say softly.

He smiles and slides his fingers down my cheek, and places a kiss on my forehead.

"Let's go," Draven says as he passes by us, walking ahead.

The front door is held open by a butler or doorman or whoever rich people hire to man the door—unnecessary if you ask me. The place looks like no one lives there, and it feels dark and haunted.

When Draven walks in, I follow him to the west side of the

house. Just Draven's room on the east side of the home is the only part of the house I've seen. We make our way down the stairwell toward the middle. The gargoyles are just looking ahead, uninterested, as though they've seen it all before. The only sounds in the house are the sound of our feet on the red carpet runner and the thud of the front door closing. I wouldn't be so fearless if it weren't for the fact that I have the twins with me. It's almost as if they're stepping in front of me and behind me to protect me from... something.

Dravin's decision to go off on his own is understandable. His home looks sleek and sophisticated, yet it's rather dark. This house is dark, ancient, creepy, and holds secrets—secrets that could destroy you. These walls have seen things—terrible things—things that would have you question your existence. You can feel it in the bones of the house. It's solid, evil, faithless, and deceiving, like the people who own it.

CHAPTER THIRTY EIGHT

GIA

WE MAKE it down to the end of the west wing, reminding me of Stephen King's *The Shining*, where the twin girls appear at the end of the hall. Dravin takes a right and turns the knobs of the double doors that appear to be an office.

His father is seated at a very old wood desk that looks antique and completely restored. It seems like it belonged to the house when it was being built. Not a piece you would find in an auction or a gallery.

"All three of you are here. Good," his father says, seated in his chair, which looks like a king's throne. In front of the desk, there is a young woman, probably a few years older than me. She looks at the twins with a smirk. A protective instinct flares inside my chest at her expression.

Three wood chairs mirror the one Mr. Bedford is seated at, but they're smaller versions. There is a floor lamp to the right and a painting of what appears to be old family members from their past. Men like their father. Their eyes witness everything that goes on inside the room. To the left is a bookcase filled with books. The carpet under the desk has the symbol of a family crest. When I take a seat in the chair, both men are at my sides. The young woman doesn't move except to lean close to Draven and whisper something in his ear. From the corner of my eye, I see him nod. A pang of jealousy snakes up my spine. *What the hell?* I look to Dravin, who is eyeing his father.

His father is watching me with his self-aggrandizing grin. He knows it bothers me that the woman is close to his son. The intimate way she touches his shoulder and the way she leans close so he can see the low cut of her black dress. The dress is formal in a way. A cross between office attire and a housekeeper's uniform. But not the way she bends at the waist. What throws it off is it's completely black and tight. It's deceiving. Fucking with a man's imagination.

Thinking about what Jess told me about showing no emotion, I'm trying to go with indifference, but my thoughts move into anger and rage. I want to claw her eyes out and hope an animal eats her face off when I'm finished with her.

Mr. Bedford clears his throat when he sees that I'm not amused by the woman or that she's touching him inappropriately for being an employee. If that is what she is. I'll soon find out. If Draven wants to mess around, then all he has to do is tell me. I'll accept it, but he isn't touching me ever again. It's his choice what he decides to do, and right now, it looks like he's making it.

"It has come to my attention that you were pregnant with my grandchild."

I raise my chin and cross my legs, one over the other. Mr. Bedford watches me, and his eyes slide over my thighs. I notice Dravin gripping the arms of the chair. Is his father checking me out? Gross. I get that he is a very handsome man. He doesn't have a protruding belly, it's flat. His dress shirt is open at the throat, and he looks like an older version of his sons, except he has a sprinkle of gray in his hair by the temples. He is muscular and toned, with a couple of tattoos peeking out from his chest and left arm by his wrist. He keeps them well covered by wearing tailored suits that must cost a fortune. The twin's father is a very attractive man for his age. He looks like he is in his late forties, maybe early fifties.

"Yes." I finally say. "I was, but I..." I trail off. It's still too painful to think about it. The sting of tears causes needles to prick my throat and I avert my gaze.

"You were poisoned. My son gave me the medical reports, and I had an investigation done on campus, as well as your where-abouts. I had a meeting with the leaders and it has been concluded that someone made an attempt on your life. Has anyone threatened you? I also need the last places you were before you ended up in the hospital. What you ate and where? Who was with you? And don't lie to me."

"Be careful how you talk to her, Father. I get you are upset about her losing the baby, but don't you dare threaten her," Draven warns him, to my surprise.

Dravin, to my left, is quiet, but he straightens in the chair. His glare, aimed at his father, is laced with fury and full of hate. It's obvious that Dravin hates his father. Resentment bleeds off of him in droves.

"Or what?"

"You will not like the outcome, I assure you," Draven replies.

Mr. Bedford trains his eyes on Dravin. "What? You're going to crawl over the desk and hit me."

"Maybe," Dravin challenges. "It all depends."

"On what?"

"If you look at her that way again. You know exactly what I'm talking about. Make no mistake. You touch a hair on her head or look at her like you are undressing her with your pathetic eyes, I will kill you."

Mr. Bedford laughs, and a wave of fear chills my spine. "You touch me, and you're dead, and your brother will have nothing. It is a stipulation within the Order. You might as well secure everyone in this room's death sentence if you go through with your threat against my life. I have treated you better than your mother ever could." He nods toward Draven. "Gianna knows too much to let them keep her alive."

He looks at the woman and nods. She kneels in front of Draven and my eyes fly to her as she slides her hands up his thighs. What the hell is she doing?

"What is she doing?" I ask.

The woman looks at me. "Taking what you didn't want," she says coyly.

"You said you didn't want to marry my son, so I'm going to

show you what happens when you deny a Bedford. When you go against what you agreed to."

They already showed me the video they released to go viral on campus. It bothered me and hurt me to see it. How would they feel if I did the same thing?

"They have already shown me how easily they move on."

Draven tries to push her away, but his father's eyes darken, full of malice. This man is evil. He cares about himself and the control he has over everyone. He cares about me losing my unborn child because, in his eyes, someone took his legacy from him, even if it was inside my body. To a man like the twins' father, someone attempted to kill me because they knew I belonged to a Bedford and wanted to kill his legacy and get control.

This isn't about love or having a family. This is about power and manipulation. A pang of sadness consumes me for the twins and their mother. He didn't love her. He used her, like he expects the twins to use me. And if I don't fall in line, he will make me pay or, worse, kill me.

It's too late to turn back. I can read between the lines. He said I knew too much already. He isn't going to let me go. I either toe the line or pay. I look at the woman undoing Draven's pants, and my heart sinks. He wouldn't? He wouldn't let her. Not with me right here.

Dravin glances at me and then to his father. "I have done everything you have asked. I have sacrificed my entire life and future. "

"I'm helping you out," his father says with a smirk. "Trust me. I have never steered you wrong. You're not a momma's boy like your brother. You don't cry. You're just like me. You take what you want, which is why you are free and he isn't. You think you have sacrificed everything, but we all pay. She will look at him differently now, and maybe she'll think about the consequences the next time she decides to deny a Bedford." He looks at Draven. "Let her, or you'll be sorry. She needs to learn."

My chest tightens, and I close my eyes, not wanting to look at her grip Draven as she slides his cock out of his pants and slides her mouth over him like the greedy bitch she is, moaning while sucking him off, looking at me with a satisfied expression. Draven's cock goes rock hard while she is sucking him off and I turn my head away.

"Be a man and enjoy when a woman is sucking you off. What are you, a pussy? You like dick in your ass? Is that it? You're lucky I don't make her fuck you with her cunt."

"Fuck," Draven snaps. He grips her head and shoves his cock down her throat, and she almost dies of pleasure, and I want to claw her eyes out. The bitch.

He begins to fuck her mouth savagely. "This is what you want, you greedy cunt. You want my cock? Take it."

He grunts, and a wave of nausea climbs my throat. Bastard. He's enjoying this. The wet sounds echo in the room, and my eyes are trained on Dravin beside me, but he is silent. He doesn't look. He stays still, and I'm confused. He doesn't look at his brother or the woman. He is frozen, staring at the window behind his father, where there is nothing but the pitch-black night and a glow coming from what must be a garden or backyard. I have never been to the back of the house, so I don't know what the view is like. I'm trying to think about anything. Does the backyard have a pool or just manicured lawns like the front?

"Look at her while she takes his cock," Mr. Bedford says to me, snapping me out of my thoughts. "You want him? Now you will have him, but with the knowledge that you're not the only one that can make him come. Your cunt isn't anything special. Just a wet hole a Bedford sticks it in. You will dress appropriately and stay here for three days."

My eyes snap to his. "Why?"

Why do I have to stay here for three days? I don't want to stay in this creepy fucking house.

"Because I said so, and you will spread those legs and fuck my son until you cool off. You will learn what your duties are in this house. Your soon-to-be husband likes to live in his little playhouse. You will learn to play house in both. If you deny one of my sons again? I will make sure you pay. Trust me, it will be fun. There are other ways to make you pay. You will get pregnant, and you will have security. No contraceptives from here on out. Once you're pregnant, you will wed Dravin. You will accept that this is your life. You belong to the Order."

He thinks he can control me. That I don't have a say?

"What if the wrong son gets me pregnant?" I counter. I can feel the twins stiffen beside me.

One is getting his knob stroked, her moans and his grunts giving me the courage to challenge him. I'm not going to have sex with Draven, but I want to push. I want to annoy their father.

"It doesn't matter who gets you pregnant. Either way, you will give each of my sons a child from your cunt. My oldest son Dravin wanted you; he got you. There is no turning back. You belong to us, and you will learn to act, dress, and obey. You will not only honor your husband, but you will honor the Order."

Reid's evil smirk when I found out I was pregnant is coming full circle. The meaning behind his words comes at me in full force. *I belong to the Order.* Choosing to be with Dravin also means choosing to go along with everything that he is part of, including his brother.

"Tell her to stop," I say, turning to look at the woman as she is playing with herself while his hips lift and his hand is in her hair. "Better yet, tell them to leave and continue outside or in his room."

Their father raises his eyes in surprise and her mouth makes a pop when she releases his cock. "You don't care?" his father asks.

I lean forward, placing my long, dark hair to one side. "They don't leave anyone a choice once they accept and come here, do they? The ones you call Prey."

"I'm afraid not. It's the price that is paid when you accept. Tuition has nothing to do with it because when you graduate, you will make enough money to cover the tuition and more. The only problem is when they go against us. If you threaten us or our way of doing things, it messes with our purpose. Our control." He bends forward. "This is how we maintain the Order and control the world. We choose."

"You mean you choose people based on where they are from. People that have nothing else to lose. People you can manipulate and control."

"Let's not forget. Fuck and discard."

I snicker when I glance over at the woman with swollen lips and a smirk on her face. Her face falls when she sees that I'm not angry. I'm pissed off, but I'm not going to show anyone in this room that I'm devastated about my situation or, more importantly, that she is pleasuring Draven. I'm doomed to a life in a hell of my own choosing. Choosing Dravin or any son of Kenyan is accepting their life and rules that have you questioning what is right and what is wrong. If I have no choice but to accept Dravin and his twin, I'm not going to share them.

The memory of the painting in Dravin's room comes back to me: the woman depicting Lilith, the snake, and the man devouring what appears to be a woman's body, even if the history of the painting says otherwise. I know what I saw in the painting, and it was not about history. It is what they represent to them–the Order, lust, control, manipulation, but most of all... power.

I sneer at the woman with a look of hatred. "So, how did I taste?"

Her eyes widen but then she looks at Draven, but I can't see his expression.

"Answer her," Mr. Bedford demands.

She licks her lips and the rage burning inside me boils, causing my hands to grip the handles on the wooden chair.

"G-good. You tasted good."

I roll my eyes because I wanted her to say something slick so I would have a good enough reason to slap her across her face. I know she is a puppet for the puppet master, but it was the look she gave me when she had him in her mouth. It was supposed to be my mouth and now I can't look at him. It's one thing seeing it on video and another to be in the same room. He isn't mine, and he is allowed to do whatever he wants, but he was enjoying it. His grunts and her moans replay in my head.

My indifference is my armor. I shouldn't care, but I'm left with no choice but to care. I'm trapped in this, and it's obvious there is no way out. But I cannot lie to myself and say I don't want them. I crave them. My head lifts, and I see their father's smug face, watching the woman adjust her clothes and stand.

"I don't find this funny," I say, watching their father with his air of arrogance and devilish smile. "I'm not going to have his child. I'm not going to pollute my womb with her filth or any other's filth. That is sentencing me to hell."

He chuckles. "I know the only cock that has seen your cunt is from my two sons, but you actually expect my sons not to screw around? All men have mistresses. You need to accept that this is the present and your future."

His words are like sandpaper across my skin, burning with every word spilling from his mouth.

I'm about to tell him what I think, but Draven is quicker. "That's enough," Draven growls.

I'm relieved that he is defending me from his father, but I refuse to look at him. His father's eyes are like a pit of snakes, intimidating and always looking to strike. He chortles, and I have never hated someone the way I do their father right now. If evil had a face, it would be his.

He places his elbows on the wooden desk and leans forward. Dark eyes are fixated on Draven seated beside me. He made sure he gifted each of his sons a piece of the evil that lurked inside of him to ensure his agenda was carried out. They each have a dark eye that matches his as a reminder.

I can hear Draven adjust his pants in the chair next to me, and my head turns to look at Dravin to my left. He is silent, and I wonder why. I wonder why he hasn't said anything else to his father. He just sits silently, glancing at each person in the room as they speak. He doesn't reassure me or hold my hand. He is just… silent, like he isn't in this very room.

"You're playing a dangerous game, my son. Bringing a Prey to our circle has served no purpose. I applaud your efforts in trying to save her, forcing her to accept you both, but she denied you the first time and was against what was required."

"Save me from your incantations. Tricking her into believing a false pretense isn't fair. She didn't know that she had to accept both of us," Draven fires back.

He's trying to defend me, and my reasons for rejecting Dravin, but the truth is that I'm interested in both of them. I'd want to keep them all to myself and not share them with anyone else. I can't believe that their dad expects me to allow them to have mistresses whenever they want. There's no way I'll let it happen. I don't see why, but I just can't imagine choosing between the two. My dilemma is how to proceed without being destroyed by them or, worse, losing who I am. Now I know why their mother chose to end it. This is the reason she gave up. If you fall in love with a man, how do you bear to see him with someone else?

Their father chuckles. "The sins we remit on earth. I see it in your eyes. You want her for yourself. You were always the confrontational one, but you know the rules."

"Fuck the rules. They tried to kill her, and they almost succeeded. They killed our unborn heir," Dravin seethes.

"There will be others. It means she was weak. Unprotected. You failed her, but you will never admit that. Especially to her."

Recalling Dravin's hurtful words brings back painful memories. He assured me that he would provide for me and our child, that I would never have to worry about him or her, and that he would eventually marry someone else. Trying to recall what he said as he pushed me away, I stare down at my sweaty hands in my lap.

My eyes glance at their father, and it dawns on me that he is saving me from this—a life where heaven and hell make a pact among the scavengers of the damned. Children being born in the eyes of God corrupted by evil. He was trying to save me from this life. A life where they will try to kill me. They tried, but...

Everyone turns to gaze at me as I let out a startled sound. In my lap, my hands are shaking. Warren. It was definitely Warren. The café and the way he watched me sipping hot chocolate, the barista's knowing grin as I left the shop. How Warren found out I was pregnant is a mystery to me.

"Warren. It was Warren," I blurt.

His father's expression hardens as he stares the lady in the eye and motions for her to depart. She moves away from the desk, but her hand passes across Draven's shoulder, causing me to lash out. Getting out of my seat, I give her a backhand across her smug face.

She screams and covers her mouth, then looks down at the blood trickling down her chin from her split top lip and sees her hand-painted scarlet.

"Touch him again, and I'll split the other one," I sneer. "Now, do as you're told and get out."

She scrambles and exits the room, and Mr. Bedford gives me a diabolical grin. A deafening silence falls in the room when the door shuts with a click. Dravin gets up from his chair and moves over to the bar to pour himself a drink. The clinking of ice falling inside the glass and the decanter being uncorked. My hand begins to sting from the slap.

Dravin turns, his eyes resting on my face. "Tell me everything, and don't leave anything out," he says while he raises the glass to his lips.

His countenance darkens when he stares at me and at this very moment, watching his neck as he downs the full glass of amber-colored liquor in one go, I know there is a monster being unleashed. The man behind the black flowers and pretty words on paper is gone. A murderer is standing in front of me—a cold-blooded killer, to put it bluntly. Draven wasn't the crazier or more dangerous of the two, as I had assumed. Dravin is worse. In a more far worse way. I immediately think of Jack the Ripper.

He walks closer. Draven and his father quietly wait for me to tell them about the night I went to the café, and Warren showed up and how the barista acted. How afraid I was.

CHAPTER THIRTY NINE
GIA

I'M SITTING on Draven's bed while he talks to his brother outside the door. I can hear their loud whispers but can't make anything out. I'm upset about having to stay here in this house. I have to get my clothes from my dorm, and the only reason I don't stomp out of here is because of Warren and his threats. If he attempted to kill me by having me poisoned so I could lose my baby and die, who knows what else he is capable of? I'm about to hop out of bed when Draven enters the room and shuts the door.

"Where's Drav?" I ask when I see that he doesn't come inside with his brother. I have begun to shorten his name and use the nickname his mother gave him to identify them in conversation.

Draven lowers his head and wipes his hand over his face. He looks up and takes a deep breath. "He'll be back in three days to pick you up. He has to take care of business while you're here. He left you a note."

I frown when he hands me the note. "What do you mean, he left? Why didn't he tell me? Why did he just leave me here? I don't want to be here."

I scan the note similar to the ones he always leaves for me in his handwriting.

Gia,

I would search the world if you were lost. I would ask the stars for guidance. The moon to be the light in the dark and the sun to shine bright, knowing it would all lead me to find you.

Love,

Dravin

I look up and meet Draven's gaze, feeling my heart squeeze.

"You don't have a choice. He asked that I take care of you while you're gone. He doesn't need to ask, but he needs to hear it from me."

I shake my head. "I don't want to be here with you. I want to leave."

"I'm afraid that isn't an option. You will have everything you need," he says while he walks toward his en suite bathroom.

I slide off the bed and follow him inside, not caring if he has to take a shit. I'm pissed off at what he allowed that bitch to do to him.

He whirls around and begins to undress. When his clothes are off and he is standing naked in all his delicious glory, he raises a brow. "Are you joining me?"

I snort. "I'm good. I'll be on my way."

When I turn to leave, he grips me firmly on my arm and pulls me toward the shower, pressing the button that causes the warm water to spray like rain against the tiles.

"What are you doing? Let go of me!" I seethe in fury.

"What is your problem?" he asks, pulling me under the spray.

"Are you insane?" My clothes and hair are drenched, and my shoes and socks are soaked. I'm relieved I left my phone on his bed.

"Just a little."

I back up to leave through the shower door, but he pins me against the tiled wall. "No. You're not going anywhere."

"I don't care. I'm wet."

Draven begins to tug at my clothes, and I stiffen and pull away. He rips off my shirt and bra.

"What the hell?"

His lips slide over my jaw near my ear. "You are in hell. You're just my heaven."

"I'm nothing of yours. Now let me go. Go ask that bitch to be your heaven. You were certainly enjoying it. Now, fuck off."

His lips form a smirk. "You're jealous."

I turn my head away. "I'm not."

I am, but I won't admit that to him. I won't tell him that he hurt me. I don't know why he did it, but he did, and I can't look at him the same way. It's stupid, and I should only have these types of feelings for his twin, but I feel them for him, too. Dravin's words in his letters hit that part of me. The part that I felt when I fell in love with him. It's crazy and weird, but the feelings are there. The desire for him is there.

He turns my head by placing his fingers under my chin. "Look at me," he demands.

The sound of water surrounds us, and the steam from the warm water fogs up the glass.

My eyes finally look up at his and begin to sting from the tears that are building up.

"I did it for you, Gia." My brows pinch in confusion. "My father thought I was Drav."

I shake my head in denial. "There is no way. How?"

"We have perfected it through the years; we did it for our mother when he wanted to hurt her, and now we are doing it for you. We've had a lot of practice since we were kids. Drav kept quiet so he wouldn't notice. He wanted to use him to hurt you. If you notice, he addressed Drav like he was me. He said that he loved me more than my mother. My mother favored Drav, and he favored me because I always protected my older brother. I—we did it for you. We knew that it would hurt you if your husband took pleasure from another woman. I put myself out there for you. When she asked me if I was the older twin, I nodded yes. She mistook me for Drav."

"But you liked it."

While his other hand continued to hold on to my chin, his fingers pushed my hair away from my face. I avert my eyes so he can't see the hurt I'm feeling. "I didn't come, did I?"

No, I shake my head. He didn't, but it hurt to watch. It hurt to see and to hear.

"We did that to hurt you the first time, and we both regret it. We tried to get over you. I tried it, and it didn't work. I haven't fucked anyone since you."

My eyes meet his as I listen. I'm trying to understand him. His reasons.

"It hurt me," I whisper.

He leans in close and places a soft kiss on my forehead. His words and breath welcome on my skin. The drops of water slide over my face and neck.

"If you only knew how much it hurts me that I can't marry you. I want you so badly that I'd gladly live in my brother's shadow if it meant I could have you in any way. I'll sacrifice myself so that you never have to look at the man you marry and know that he slept with another person while being with you as your husband. He won't allow it, and neither will I. I'll be the sacrifice for your happiness."

Tears escape down my cheeks like carved words on wood—his words, words that etch themselves into the depths of my soul.

I sniff and close my eyes. How do you give yourself to two men who are identical twin brothers without cheating on them?

"Don't cry, our little Raven. If he gets your heart, I want your soul, and your body is our playground. You're perfect." He steps back and looks down with a side grin. "Let's get you out of these wet clothes so we can clean that bitch off me."

I open my eyes and feel his hands lift my torn shirt over my head, then my bra, letting it drop in a wet heap on the tile floor. He helps me with my shoes, socks, pants, and finally, my panties.

His eyes smolder when I'm completely naked. My nipples harden under his gaze when the water sluices down my body. The backs of his hands slide down my chest over my nipples, causing them to strain into two stiff peaks.

"I can't wait to see your beautiful breasts full of milk nursing our children and feeding them the way we feed you." His fingers slide down my torso to the apex between my thighs, igniting me from within. "I'm not going to be the one to give you the vanilla sex you read about in a love story. I'm going to be the lover that fucks you hard and fast." I'm about to mewl when his finger grazes my clit. "I'm going to rip your clothes, make you sore, and fuck you so hard and so good in every hole my cock can fit in." He leans back and whispers against my lips. "And you're going to like it."

Fuck. I shamelessly want him. My body needs him. It needs them both. His lips brush against mine, and he pushes me up against the tiles. He pushes the soap dispenser and takes my hand, sliding the soap between our hands and making suds. I look down between us, and his hard cock is aimed at my belly. His fingers are entwined with mine, and the smell of body wash is the same one his twin uses.

He places our hands over his cock and strokes his shaft from base to tip, washing himself. He steps back so the water can rinse him off. He raises our hands under the spray, and the soap slides down my arms, raising goose bumps over my skin. He places more soap on his hands and bathes me thoroughly, and I return the favor.

My hands slide over taught skin just like his twin brother, yet inside, he's so different. Different in a way that is forbidden. He is like a dark secret—something no one knows about. My own personal release. My hands slide over his chest, feeling it rise and fall like he is about to snap. His cock sticking out painfully hard against my stomach. My head angles up toward his gaze, his nostrils flare slightly, and he snaps on a growl.

He pushes me up against the tiled wall and lifts my thighs over his hips, grazing his teeth over my neck, knowing that he will leave marks.

"I'm going to take you hard," he growls.

"Yes," I moan. "Please."

I can't think of anything else at this moment except for him being inside me, filling me, and reminding me why I want him. I want him to take the pain away from me, of seeing someone else's mouth on him. I know it's selfish, but my grasp on what is right and wrong is blurring. These are my boys, and I'll give them all of me.

He slides his cock inside to the hilt, and I gape at how big he is. "Fuck. Yes!"

He pumps into me hard and fast without stopping. "You're mine. You're his, but you're mine."

He continues his assault on my pussy, which is deliciously unforgiving. I slide up against the tiles with each thrust he gives me. A demon who is nothing but pure evil and desire. My arms are wrapped around his neck while he presses his face into mine, placing his kiss on mine and biting my bottom lip until it bleeds.

"Bleed for me. Come for me. Milk me. You're perfect, my little Raven."

"I'll bleed for you. I'll come for you as long as you're inside of me. Filling me," I say, as my pussy spasms on his cock, coming for him. My breasts bounce with each thrust until he arches his neck and stills, spilling inside me as he comes on a roar.

The sound of water hitting tile is mixed with my rapid heartbeat as we both come down from that place. A forbidden place where there is only room for feeling what the body can take, and the memories of that place are the notes left on your skin.

CHAPTER FORTY
JESS

"PLEASE!" he pleads like the piece of shit he is.

It didn't take long to track down the jerk from the café. I didn't want to involve the others so they could tip Warren off.

"Tell me. Why?" I say it through clenched teeth.

"He threatened me. H-he said he would kill me and my family. He knows where they live. He knows everything. Please, it hurts. Take me down," he begs through each measured breath of agony.

"Are you sure this is a good idea?" Father Jacobs asks, taking a deep breath as his forehead drips with sweat. He's been sweating profusely since I barged in, barking orders to set up the church.

"Shut the fuck up and do as you're told," I snarl.

I glance up and see the barista from the coffee shop loll his head to the side. I nailed him to a wooden cross like a sacrifice, rope around his neck, waist, and thighs. I had the fake priest cover the statues behind him with a black backdrop with a giant wooden cross in front and the pussy I nailed against it. Candles are lit to give the massive area light, closing the church for three days. The glow reflecting off the stained-glass windows illuminates the messengers of God like judges, watching me torture the sinner for his sins—an eye for an eye and all of that.

I glance up with the hammer in one hand and the concrete nails in the other.

"Who is he?"

"Christ." He closes his eyes. "Warren. His name is Warren. He wanted me to poison her. That is all I know. He told me her name and came into the coffee shop as soon as she arrived."

"How did he know she was there, and how do you know her?"

"He texted me. He told me her name; that is all I know. He

made me do it. He said no one would find out because she was considered Prey, and he assured me it was all part of the Order. I did what I was told."

That motherfucker is dead. There was no such meeting about Gianna. Something isn't adding up. There is something bigger at play here. They are trying to eliminate our power and control by making us weak.

"You were told to kill an innocent woman. She almost died," I roar.

I grip the hammer and drop the nails on the floor, leaving just one in my hand. I move to where his feet are and place one foot over the other.

"Please! No!"

I place the sharp tip of the big nail and hit the nail in the head, causing him to scream like a person being mutilated. Blood begins to ooze like the blood on the airport bathroom floor from my baby dying in his mother's womb.

"She was pregnant!" I scream. "Pregnant!"

I spit at him while watching him suffer. This is nothing compared to what I'm going to do to that piece-of-shit Warren. There is nothing no one can do that will save him from my wrath and from his fate.

Jacobs comes up behind me. "I'm sorry, Dravin."

But there are no words that can describe the carnage I want to inflict on him. Our pain. My pain. The pain of losing our baby. The agony of almost losing her in the hospital. I lost my mother. I failed her, but I will not lose Gianna. They will have to get through me and my brother to get to her. Warren understands that killing her is a way to destroy the Bedford legacy. He wanted her for himself, but all he did was fuck himself. He knew. He knew she was pregnant.

I hang my head and close my eyes because all I see is red. Death and destruction are all I can think about. Leaving Gia in that house is a risk, but my twin brother would never allow anything to happen to her. What he did saved me from my father and his manipulation to hurt Gia for changing her mind about marrying me when she found out about Draven and that we were twins.

Once he had sex with her, I couldn't tell her. I wanted to, but I couldn't tell her. My father advised against it until she fell pregnant. She was untouched and perfect. I desired her as if she were my next breath. I'll always want her.

Draven sacrificed himself like he has always done for me, but I know he didn't do it for me. He did it for Gianna, so my father couldn't hurt her because I knew my brother was in love with my future wife.

He might not know it, but I do. He only sacrifices for the things and people he loves. He will gladly be the villain in her eyes as long as she sees me as the god in hers. It's the only way he can ensure she doesn't suffer the fate of death by her own hand, like our mother. It was the only way she knew to end her suffering.

I look up and meet the eyes of a dead man hanging from the cross.

"Please," he whispers. "Take me down. Please, God. It hurts."

I chuckle and laugh maniacally. "Pretty, pretty, pretty, pleee-assse," I mock him, tilting my head to the side. "If you play in hell, you get fucked over by the devil. God has no room here. He checked out a long time ago." I look up at the old cathedral-style ceiling and then down at the pathetic piece of shit nailed to the cross.

"Oh my god! It hurts." He continues to scream.

I look over at Jacobs. "Gag him. Shut him up."

He nods with a look of fear. He hasn't seen the dark games we play. My brother is a little more sinister when he commits his sins. He lets them pray before he kills them. I… don't.

Jacobs is getting the ladder, making clinking sounds as he places it to safely climb up to reach Timothy's face. I look up while I watch Timothy cry, not feeling an ounce of sympathy or empathy. He didn't feel that way when he tried to kill the mother of my child, causing her to miscarry.

I slide my phone out and call Draven, listening to the phone ring and waiting for him to answer.

"Hello."

"We have a problem."

"Tell me, and whatever you do, make it quick. She's wondering where you are and why you didn't say anything to her when you left."

"I'll be right over, but I can't stay long. Call the others. There are people within the Order who want to destroy us. Only the ones we have on the Consortium are to be trusted. She was right; it was Warren, but he isn't working alone."

"I'll make the call."

"Do it. I'll be there in fifteen minutes."

I hang up and look at Jacob's stricken face when he sees that I'm leaving him.

"Don't look at me like that. I need you to babysit for a while."

"W-what do you mean? You can't possibly expect me to stay with him like this. Do what you and your brother normally do: chop him up and bury him somewhere."

"No. You stay and watch him." I look up before I turn to leave. "I have a purpose for him, and it's not that," I tell him, heading to the side door and hearing Timothy's muffled screams as I take out my vape pen for a smoke.

"You're crazier than he is. You know that, right?" Jacobs says.

I turn around before leaving through the door. "No, I'm insane."

CHAPTER FORTY ONE
Gia

"THIS IS THE KITCHEN," Draven says, showing me the massive kitchen with dark wood cabinets and black-and-white marble counters. A window leads to the backyard, and I wonder what it looks like.

"It's beautiful."

"I'm glad you like it. We always have five members on staff. The butler and doorman are Norman, Sasha is the cook, Nikolai is the head groundskeeper, our driver, whom you have seen many times, is Germain, and there are two housekeepers, Miss Jean and her daughter Pricilla."

"Who was the woman in the office yesterday?"

He walks to the island and leans his forearms on the marble, with the massive centerpiece, which has black feathers glued to it like those on a masquerade mask. I want to know because I refuse to have her around me.

"Just a woman my father entertains. He prefers Pricilla."

"And you?"

His eyes smolder when he raises them to me while I lean my back near the kitchen sink. "I prefer you."

"You hardly know me."

"I know enough. I know a lot of things about you."

"Like?" I ask, intrigued.

How would he know me? I've never gone out with him knowing who he is. I know Dravin on a deeper level. Our long talks before and after sex, his letters. He's met my parents, but Draven hasn't.

"I know you prefer red roses to black. I know you like to talk to my mother, whom you think is actually buried in the empty grave."

My eyes flick to his. "What?"

"I'm afraid so. You have been talking to an empty grave. It is why he told you not to visit the grave. It is why you see that there are no flowers left there."

"Then where is she?" I gulp. "Buried, I mean."

I have been talking to an empty grave like a lunatic. I want to kill Dravin. He could have said something. I know it was my fault for assuming, but it's a grave with her name on it, like a normal person. I asked him before, and he said yes.

"We had her cremated. The necklace he gave you when you thought it was me—her ashes are inside the crow. She is with you and will help you see the light in your moment of darkness. You carried a part of her inside you. It is only right you carry a part of her with you, always and forever."

A tear slides down my cheek when I look down at the necklace, sliding my fingers over the crow. He walks over, wipes my tear away with his thumb, and slides it between his lips.

"Don't cry. We hate to see you cry. To see you cry is like watching our hearts bleed out. We need to stop it, or we end up dying. It's like hearing my soul cry out in pain, and your tears are the fire burning it to ashes." He places his finger over my chest where my heart beats and his eyes follow the movement of his finger as he talks. "They say there are only two halves to a heart, but ours isn't like that. Ours has three parts, like the pieces of a magnet coming together. See, we are your two halves, one on the left and one on the right. When you first draw it on paper, it starts in the middle. The beginning of the left and right always unite us in the center. Without you, we are never whole. With you, we are complete. The center is you and will always be you. "

He speaks like his brother is always with him and part of his thought process. Two souls linked to each other are trying to find their heaven. I'm their heaven and their salvation from the hell they live in.

I look up to find him watching me. "Where's your necklace?"

He raises his hands and removes a chain I've never seen before, one with a wolf and the raven from the necklace I gave Dravin that night at the cemetery. It's longer and hangs like a *T* at my navel. The crow and the raven meet in the center, near my heart, when he places it gently around my neck.

"I have been meaning to give it to you, but I never found the right moment."

"Thank you," I whisper. "It's beautiful."

"There is nothing more beautiful in my life than you. You're everything to me, Gianna. Did you think it was only Drav with you? I've watched you. We watch you. We talk about you and how much we want you in our lives. You don't have to love me, Gianna, or feel guilty for loving me less. I'll accept anything as long as it's from you."

I fan myself because I'm about to cry—not from sadness but from happiness at hearing his words.

"I want to get to know you. Both of you. I want you to meet my parents. I want you to meet my mother." I sniff. "Drav met them, and it's only right for you to meet them."

He smiles, and my heart melts. "We will meet them tomorrow. Call them, and we will have dinner. It can be their house or a restaurant. Whatever you want. Tell them whatever you want."

Shit. I have to think of something. I'll tell them the truth: he is a twin. What could go wrong?

CHAPTER FORTY TWO

DRAVIN

THE DOOR OPENS, and Norman, the doorman, nods his head in a silent greeting. "Dravin."

He knows I'm Dravin because my brother is inside with Gianna, and they usually call my brother, Mr. Bedford, to address us. Sasha, our cook, has been here since we were born and knew my mother very well. She is like a secret confidant. She can tell us apart, though she was sworn to secrecy by my mother so as not to let anyone know that she knows how. Especially my father.

I'm walking toward the staircase, but I can hear voices traveling from the kitchen, and one of them I know all too well. Her voice is like a sweet whisper in my dreams, singing to me like a lullaby full of promise in the darkness of sleep.

I walk through the dining room into the archway leading to the kitchen and see them together. I smile when he adjusts his necklace over her chest.

When she hears me enter, she gives me a sidelong glance. "Dravin."

My brother watches me and gives me a curt nod. He knows what I came for—my time with her. When I reach her, I slide my fingers over her throat, watching goose bumps rise on her skin in the soft light.

"Raven," I say softly.

Her eyes shift to Draven and back to me. Unsure. Torn.

I see it in her eyes. She is falling for my brother. It doesn't bother me because he deserves her. He deserves her love, and she deserves ours.

I slide the fluffy red robe down her shoulder so I can see her creamy breasts and puckered nipples harden against the cold air.

My tongue meets her flesh and flicks, twirls, and trails down until her nipple is in my mouth. Her gasp causes me to increase the suction and her robe to widen.

I grip her waist with both my hands, carrying her to the island, pushing her thighs wider so I can see her wet pussy drip for me. I look down at her swollen lips. My brother fucked her hard.

Her pussy is pink, wet, and swollen. My head turns to the right. "Damn, brother, you took her hard."

His eyes flick toward her. "She can handle it. Right, baby?"

She leans back, placing her palms behind her to arch her back. "Are you ready for me, baby?"

Her long hair slides over the marble counter like silk. She opens her legs wider, and I nudge my head toward my brother. "Get me some ice."

Gia quirks her brow, but I don't tell her what it's for. She knows I'll never do anything to hurt her. My brother opens the built-in fridge, grabs the ice cubes, and puts them in a glass. He walks over and clinks the glass on the counter.

"Do you trust me?" I ask her.

She slants her head, licking her lips with her tongue. "What do you think?"

I smile at her sassy mouth and look at her pussy dripping on the counter. "I think you want me inside you." I grab an ice cube with my fingers. The cold is freezing my skin as I place the tip on her nipple.

She gasps. "Dravin."

I slide it in a circular motion over each nipple. Her breaths come out slowly and evenly. She's trying not to shrink away. I lean in close and take one breast in my mouth while my brother takes the other wet nipple, warming her back up. I slide the cube down to her pussy lips and circle it at her entrance.

She moans. "Yes! Fuck, that feels so good."

I don't want anyone getting off on her moans, especially Norman. Releasing her nipple, I take out my phone and link it to the speaker in the kitchen, connecting with two distinct beeps. Marilyn Manson's "Sweet Dreams" begins to play softly.

"I told you, baby. Your body is our playground," Draven says.

We lick every inch of her, feasting on her tits, her pretty stomach, and her swollen pussy. I suck the inside of her left thigh while my brother takes the other. We take turns in rhythm, sucking after every melted cube of ice to ensure she doesn't feel a sting.

I slide my cock out of my jeans, fisting it in my hand. My brother removes the centerpiece and climbs over the counter, turning his head to watch her from above.

Her eyes flick to me, and I climb on top of the counter, taking the glass with me while my brother slides her down the smooth marble. Her robe is entirely open, exposing her flushed, naked skin.

Taking a cube, I slide it inside her hot cunt as "Beautiful People" by Marilyn Manson plays. I slide my cock inside her with a groan after the ice cube melts from the heat of her pussy.

My brother kneels and slides his cock out of his sweats. Her pretty lips open, and he slides his cock inside her wet mouth. I grip her thighs over my waist and take her soft and deep, being careful not to hurt her.

She pops my brother's cock out. "Faster, please," she purrs.

I bite my bottom lip and take her hard and fast, pumping into her.

She moans on my brother's cock as he fucks her mouth, placing his thumb on a cut on her lip. Fuck, he took her hard. I think we've corrupted our little Raven.

My brother holds her neck gently while he grunts. I pump into her, watching her pretty tits bounce.

"She's beautiful," I say quietly.

"Yes, she is," Draven says, watching her like she is a fragile piece of glass.

Her eyes are filled with tears as she takes him deep, relaxing her throat. My balls tingle when I'm close, and her pussy clenches my dick. "Fuck, she's tight," I say with a grunt.

"Everything about her is tight," Draven says.

She responds with her fingers playing with her nipples, her legs open wider for me so I can come inside her. I place my thumb on her clit and her fingers meet mine while we both play with her clit.

She moans when she comes with her mouth full of cock. My brother's cum spills down her chin like overflowing milk in a cup as she tries to swallow it all. Her pussy squeezes my cock as she comes, arching her back, and I groan, coming inside her, holding her thighs in place as my body slams into her until I'm spent.

I slide my cock out of her swollen pussy. Her tongue licks her lips and slides down her chin, licking my brother's cum. Her legs are wide open. Her pussy is a mess.

"You're a beautiful mess, Gia." I circle her clit softly, and she mewls. "Our beautiful mess."

CHAPTER FORTY THREE
JESS

AFTER GETTING to the dorm last night from the bar, I was ashamed of myself. Of how easily I lose my head when Reid is around. I can't help the way he makes me feel. It's like he tests my limits every time without taking it too far, but I think I'm past a point of no return. I've reached the point where I don't care and will take pleasure in being offered my two hot as fuck guys who are fucking insane. The things they have me do, no fantasy will be left unexplored. There will be no secret bucket list when it comes to sex with those two. The only problem is that I get the feeling Reid is more possessive than he lets on.

My phone lights up from a text notification. Gia is with her twin duo, probably holed up at the Gothic mansion. When I get out of bed to finish my class assignment, I notice a text from Michael. I have him saved under Fucking Loser.

> Fucking Loser: I'm parked on the curb by the main entrance. Meet me there. You have five minutes. Don't be late. Ticktock.

I close my eyes. He's here. He knew where to find me, but he did warn me he would find me when he wanted his dick sucked. My fingers shake when I close my notebook.

"Fuck," I mutter. Every time I do this, I fall deeper into the rabbit hole.

It's a good thing Gia is not here, so I don't have to explain. I look at the corkboard on the wall near my old desk and see the hundred-dollar bill from last time. How many will I have to collect to remind me what he thinks I'm worth?

I make my way to the main entrance, making sure no one is

following me. The sun has set, setting off a twilight in the sky of different hues. The trees sway and groan as the lights on campus become brighter as the sun disappears beyond the horizon. It's like darkness is falling, and the demons of the night have come out to play. The light disappears so the demons can collect and feed off the less fortunate.

I see his Mustang idling at the curb like it's a death sentence. I shiver under my winter coat. My boots are hitting the concrete pathway as I reach the passenger door, pulling the handle like a finger on the trigger.

The scent of leather mixed with Michael's cologne makes me want to puke. The bile that rises in my throat almost has me turning my head and emptying my stomach, but I take a deep breath and slide into the seat.

I close the door, and the car lurches forward at a fast speed, pinning me to the seat. My hand grips the door. "Did you have to do that?"

He grips the steering wheel and changes the gear down to third. "Put your seat belt on," he says.

I grip the seat belt and pull it across my body, hear it click, and glare at him. "What is your problem? Why are you here?"

His features are tight. His teeth are clenched, and I don't know why he is angry, but he's scaring me. It is a stupid question to ask him. I know why he is here, and it's not to talk about my mother's job performance.

He glances at me briefly as he winds down the road, finally slowing down to the forty-five miles per hour speed limit. "You know why I'm here. I'm here for you."

"I get that, but you can't just show up whenever you want. I don't live by myself, and for someone that doesn't like to be seen with trailer trash—"

"Who do you live with?"

"None of your business."

He grips the steering wheel, and I'm cursing myself for telling him that I live with someone else. I look out the window, watching the sun finally set.

"Tell me, or I'll find out my way."

"Why do you care?"

"I asked you a question. Who is he?"

He? He thinks I live with a guy.

I turn my head and snort. "I live in the female dorm. Why would you think I live with a guy, and more importantly, why are we having this conversation? You want to use my mother to blackmail me so you can fuck me? Fine. I will lie there so you can fulfill your sick little fantasy and slide me a hundred-dollar bill for my trouble, like that is going to make me feel any better for being a whore. Now, take me wherever it is you're taking me, and let's get it over with."

I hate him, and I hate myself for agreeing to do this, but every time I call my mom to check in with her, she sounds so happy, and he is keeping his end of what was promised. He made sure she got her bonus and the best shifts while giving her a raise.

After driving for nearly twenty minutes out of town, he stops at a hotel.

I raise a brow. "A hotel?"

"What's wrong with a hotel?"

I take a deep breath. "You know, for someone who has a problem with a girl who lives in a trailer, you've got no problem being seen with me."

"Don't get your hopes up. It's too fucking cold to take you into a parking lot, and my car isn't exactly comfortable. I can't take that cunt on top of my hood like last time, can I?" He pulls the parking brake when he pulls into the couples-only type of hotel. "I'm doing this for me and for the sake of not freezing my balls off."

"Gee, lucky me."

"Trust me. You are lucky. It could be worse. A whole lot worse, Jesse."

I hate that he calls me by my full name. It's like a pain in my ears to hear it coming from him. He loves to annoy me, and all I can think about is the hot shower and the scrubbing I'll have to endure after he is finished with me.

He gets up, and I make no move to open my door. I'm dreading his touch and the things he wants to do to me. I close my eyes for a few seconds, hating myself a little more, but I won't cry. I have to be strong for my mother.

Apart from Gia, she is the only person who cares about me. I can't tell anyone what I need to do to help my mother. She looked exhausted when I saw her on winter break.

If I dropped out, I'd be working a low-paying job back home or, worse, be preyed upon by Michael. This is only temporary. I have six months until I graduate, and I can start looking. I wish I could find a job between classes and send the money home, but knowing my mother, she wouldn't take the money. Her pride as a single mother won't allow it. She loves to tell people I was accepted to a fancy, elite college.

If she only knew that the fancy elite college is dark and evil. The church is just a front for what truly goes on in Kenyan—the parties and the mind games. Kenyan college students are the children of the people who control the major corporations—the corporations that control the economy. Those are the real players. They use people for their own gain and cover up the mess they create in their wake.

My problems back home and living in a trailer are nothing compared to the havoc the Order can create. I just have to find my way out of this maze unscathed. I'll have battle scars from what I have to endure, but I have a goal, and that is to use my affiliations from attending Kenyan, shut the fuck up, and turn my head the other way to provide a better life for me and my mother.

The door opens, and I look at my tormentor. If he sees the hate aimed at him through my eyes, he doesn't say anything about it. His eyes skim my pants slowly until they reach my eyes.

I step out of the car, and he pulls me up until my face is level with his chest. He looks down at me, and for one second, I remember when I thought he was the most attractive person I had ever laid eyes on. That crush in high school I had dreamed of doing everything with.

My first date, a kiss, lunch at school at the popular kids' table, and the guy I wanted to spend my first time with. Then, that memory goes up in smoke, and it's replaced with the night he spiked my drink and raped me with his friends.

My eyes sting from the memory, like a window looking into a past nightmare. That memory creeps into my mind when I least expect it to, and then I ask myself, *Why did I have to go to the party? Why didn't I just say no? Why did I ever think I stood a chance, knowing what everyone thought of me?* A poor girl living in a trailer with a single mother and a pipe dream.

"I think tonight is the night I make you come. You have never come for me, Jesse."

I harden my jaw and lift my eyes to his face, a face that belongs to the demon in my nightmare, the face I try to forget, and the scent of him I try to scrub off my skin. If you ever asked me if I hated anyone, I would say Michael.

"This isn't about me, it's only about what your twisted mind wants."

He pushes me hard against the car, and I remind myself that I have to play along. How will I get off when he is on top of me?

"Let's get inside before we freeze out here. We'll talk about it when I warm you up."

I wait for him to move toward the hotel's entrance, not wanting to be near him more than I have to, dreading the things he wants to do to me. He doesn't hurt me, but it is worse when he thinks I like the things that he does to me. In his mind, he thinks I like it. He thinks I want him. If he only knew the truth.

He pays the clerk for the room, and I stay silent, looking at the cream-colored walls and fake plants. This definitely is not like the hotel that Reid owns with its luxury carpets, bellman, impressive entrance with valet, and even the elevator he fucked me into was better than this place, but at least it's not a roach motel.

We make our way to room 504, and he unlocks the door. It doesn't have electronic key cards, but for a girl like me and where I was raised, this is better than my own room in the trailer. The difference is that I had happy times there with my mother growing up. It didn't matter if we were in a one-room shack; it was home as long as we were together.

When he opens the door to the room, at least it isn't cold, but he turns on the heater. When he flicks the lights on, my heart drops. There are mirrors everywhere around the bed. On the ceiling, the back wall, and the sides, there is even a heart-shaped Jacuzzi to the right.

"Really?" I ask.

He turns his head, removes his corduroy jacket, and begins to remove his sweater. I want to keep my jacket on for longer if I can before I strip my clothes off for this asshole.

A smirk plays on his lips, and all I can think about is punching him, but I can't; he will make me pay somehow.

"Come here, Jesse."

"Don't say my name."

"I'll keep saying it while I'm pumping my cock inside you until you come. Stop being a bitch and get over here."

I ball my hands into fists and walk closer. He removes my jacket over my shoulder roughly, and I flinch. "Don't make this harder than what it really is. I promise to make it good for you."

I raise my chin, but the expression across his face doesn't sit well with me. "Why are you doing this to me, Michael? Don't you have a girlfriend? You're a good-looking guy. You have money and could get any girl you want."

He laughs and pulls me to the bed, so I plop on top of it. I turn my head and lie there motionless as he takes my clothes off. Once my shoes and thick socks are off, he slides my bra off and leaves me in just my panties.

I raise my hands to cover my breasts. "No, no, no. Don't cover up, Jesse. I want to see you, all of you."

I close my eyes, thinking of anything but being here. On this mattress, in this pink room, with its unforgiving mirror and matching dreadful carpet. He wants me to see it. He wants me to remember him while he fucks me. I hate him even more.

"I had a girlfriend," he says, kissing my skin, and it's like a burn with every kiss of his dry lips. "But I couldn't keep fucking her while thinking of you."

What the hell? He's sick. There is no other way to describe him. Michael is sick. Infatuated with... me.

"I had to let her go. A girl can only take so much when her boyfriend keeps calling her another girl's name. Do you know how hard it is to not want you, Jesse?" He slides his hand down and cups my mound, and I cringe. "To want the girl who lives in a trailer so bad but can't risk being seen with her in town because his parents will never approve. The town would never approve of me choosing you, Jesse. Do you know how they made fun of me back in high school because I said you were pretty? I had to show them that I didn't. I had to lie. I had to do what I had to in a way that I could have you."

Bastard. He could have left me alone. He didn't have to treat me like that. He didn't have to drug me and rape me. His fingers grip my face hard, and pain radiates from my jaw.

"You're hurting me, Michael. Please."

"Then look at me when I talk to you," he snaps. My eyes open, and I look into his smoldering eyes full of hunger. "Good girl. Now open your legs and let me see. I want to taste you, Jesse. I want you to come on my tongue."

He slides down the bed, releasing his hold on my jaw, and places his face between my thighs. He slides his finger over my panties near my slit and makes me squirm.

"Don't resist me, Jesse."

I'm trying, but everywhere I turn my head, there is a mirror, and I can see myself practically naked in a cheesy lover's hotel suite with a blond head belonging to the man I hate. He raises his head, and his light eyes watch me.

"I want you to look up at the mirror on the ceiling so you can watch how I make you come."

I try to blink back the tears when he slides my panties off and begins to eat me out.

"Mmm. You taste so good, Jesse," he rasps.

My body biologically responds to the stimulation. I could kick him and scream, but it would make things worse for me and my mom. I have no control. He knows me. He knows my weakness is my mother. He knows what to do to get me in this position.

He slides his tongue inside me, and I close my eyes, refusing to look at what he is doing to me. I'm losing myself while he groans against my pussy. He slides two fingers inside me as deep as he can go while sucking my clit. My body shamelessly betrays what my mind wants and responds to the stimulation.

Needles prick my throat, and I tell myself it doesn't mean anything, but that is a lie. When you tell yourself something doesn't mean anything, it just means it does.

He grips my hips hard as my pussy gets wet, and I tell myself it's just me in the room and this is all a dream. I don't imagine it's Michael but someone else so that I can get through it. After a minute, my pussy comes, and I hate myself. I hate the way it responds to him. I turn my head and shut my eyes so the tears don't leak out and make it worse if he sees me cry.

When he licks me clean, I hear the rip of the condom wrapper, and I know it's just going to get worse, but this I can fake. This is the part where I have to act. I have to be the actress. When I look down, his condom-clad cock is near my entrance, and his lips, which I once found so appealing, are glistening.

He hovers over me, his palm flat on the flimsy pink comforter with ugly graphics, and slowly guides his cock inside me. He doesn't take me hard like he usually does but patiently waits.

His lips are inches from my ear, and I can smell myself on his chin. "Look up, Jesse."

I open my eyes and hate the sight of him between my thighs. My chest wants to cave in when he goes slow, like he is making love to me. His breath is on my skin, and that is when I give up. This is when I stop caring, and maybe it's a good thing to not care. That way, I don't need anyone else to erase the memory. One person treating me this way and not caring is better than hoping one will care for me. Maybe. Someday.

"I'm in love with you, Jesse."

"This isn't love, Michael. You know that, right?"

He pumps into me faster and rasps against the skin of my neck. "It is to me. I love you, Jesse. This is me loving you. I'm sorry, but it's all I can give you."

It's all I'm worth, a secret dirty fuck, but I don't tell him that. The irony of it all is that my high school crush raped me, blackmailed me, and now says he loves me. I let him fuck me and place the memory among all the other ones I have that I hate, becoming what I hate the most.

CHAPTER FORTY FOUR
JESS

"CAN I walk you to your dorm?" Michael asks.

I shake my head. "No, that's okay. It's a short walk from here, and you won't be able to get into the building," I lie as I open the door.

Before I step out of his car, he grips my wrist firmly, causing me to whip my head around. "I love you, Jesse. I'll see you when I can, okay?"

My eyes watch him like a psychopath. He reminds me of the face Jeffrey Dahmer puts on when he talks about his victims. His gaze is maniacal, as if he knows exactly how everything will turn out. I'm the victim on the outside, even if, on the inside, I refuse to be.

I just don't have control over what happens to my body anymore, and that's the saddest thing, to lose control of yourself. He claims to love me, but when he takes me or fucks me, it's like walking on a bed of nails. That's not love. My body can't fight him anymore. My soul is falling, afraid to let go.

I hate you. I tell him inside my head. *I'd rather die than ever have a man like you love me.* I can't say the words because it's too late; I've found my fate. The pain all over my body reminding me. I nod, slide out of the car, and close the door, watching his hand grip the shifter, hoping he leaves. I'm hoping I never see him again.

When I turn to walk toward the female dorm building, limping, he slides the window down and calls out, "I forgot to give you something, Jess."

I turn around, and he reaches the edge of the window; I hope it will close on his fingers with that hundred-dollar bill. His signature of what I'm worth every time he comes for me. My pride won't let my feet move, but he releases his hold, and it floats away to the concrete, and he takes off, peeling out onto the street into the dead of the night, hoping he disappears. For the first time in my life, I wish death on someone.

The smell of a strawberry mixed with marijuana hits my senses. "Who the fuck was that asshole?"

In the dark, by the wall of the side building leading to the quad, Reid is leaning against the wall with one leg bent, taking a hit from his vape pen. He pushes himself forward and walks toward me with a look of fury in his expression.

"Huh?"

My body feels dirty and unclean. I feel numb, and I don't care what he thinks. I won't try to erase the memories of the way he used my body. Reid bends down, picks up the hundred-dollar bill, and holds it up like a dirty rat.

"One hundred dollars."

I turn around, not caring about anything more, especially what he thinks of me. He has already expressed his feelings or thoughts about me. I'm a whore. Tears that I have held back silently slide down my cheeks as I pick up my pace, limping as fast as I can to go to my room, where I can take a shower and scrub.

"Where do you think you're going?" He catches up right beside me.

"I don't want to talk, Reid. Go home."

CHAPTER FORTY FIVE
REID

HE GRIPS MY WRIST, and I inhale from the pain. It hurts because it's red and sore. Michael held my wrists so tight because I couldn't come for him with the chains.

I thought he was taking me slowly, but I was wrong. It got longer and harder as the night progressed. He got frustrated when my body could no longer respond biologically. His words lure you in, and then the mask falls, and you see the true monster that's inside. The leather straps and the bindings I have never endured before on my skin were too much. It was all too much, too fast.

"Please let go of me. You're hurting me."

He looks down, slides his phone out, and presses the flashlight. The light reveals the red marks on my wrists.

"That motherfucker! You let that piece of shit do this to you?!" he roars.

I flinch and turn away. "It's not your problem. Please, just leave me alone."

I try to back away, but his lips turn into a frown. "No. I'm taking you with me, and you tell me where to go. You tell me who and what, Jess. He's dead. Do you hear me?"

My body begins to shake. "I-I need a shower. P-please."

It's all I can think about. My body feels sore, and my core aches. Reid's arms wrap around me, and my knees buckle. "Shit, Jess. I got it. I'll take care of you. I promise, Jess. Please, don't. No," he pleads. "Jess!"

My brain goes into a fog. There is a terrible ringing in my ears, and everything goes dark.

CHAPTER FORTY SIX

Gia

I HEAR a noise coming from inside the room, and when my eyes flutter open, I wince at the light filtering through the vast window to the right of the room from the curtains being drawn by an older lady. She must be the housekeeper. I must have fallen into a deep sleep after Dravin showered with me and placed me on Draven's bed.

I'm wondering why I'm in this massive room, which has black antique furnishings and blood-red curtains. When the older woman turns around, I grip the black satin sheet and raise it to my neck for modesty.

"Good morning, Gia. I'm the head housekeeper, Miss Jean."

"Good morning."

"Mr. Bedford is waiting for you downstairs for breakfast at the dining table. All your clothes and everything you need will be in the walk-in closet through those wood doors." She points to two massive double doors with brass gargoyles in the center. "I hope you don't mind. I have taken the liberty of picking something so you could have an idea of what he expects you to wear."

Great, I don't get to dress myself either. I have new clothes and a new room.

"How medieval," I blurt, my cheeks going red.

I hope I didn't sound like a bitch.

"It's all right. The late Mrs. Bedford felt the same way, but you'll get used to it. All your clothes and whatever else you need will be provided for you. Of course, you can pick and choose, but I must warn you. It's either black, red, white, or lace." She gives me a wink. "One thing the Bedford men have is, good taste in everything. You will not have a problem showing off your assets. They enjoy seeing how beautiful the lady of the house is and have no issues with showing her off."

It's fine for me to walk around half-naked. Not that I'm planning to, but that's what she's getting at. I'm about to ask her about the room and who it belongs to, but she beats me to it.

"This was Anastasia's room." She clears her throat, and her brown eyes turn glassy. "Excuse me. Mrs. Bedford's bedroom. Dravin has asked that all his things be moved to the closet from his old room for when you come to stay with us. His father sleeps in another room by his office in the east wing. He prefers his privacy."

She moves to open the doors and freshen the room. As it shines on the dark wood furnishings, the sunlight creates a sense of clarity. The bed is massive and looks custom-made for a king. There is an oversized nightstand on each side with white-and-gray marble tops. The walls have dark wood paneling that matches the dark wood floor. I look up, and a massive crystal chandelier is above the bed. The crystals glitter in the light like tiny mirrors.

"Thank you."

"My pleasure. If you need anything, all our direct numbers are programmed on your phone."

I give her a grin when she turns and heads to the door. "Thank you, Miss Jean."

"Of course, Gia."

She closes the door, and I hear the slight creak and a thud from the antique knob turning.

My gaze darts around the vast space, taking in the aromas of rich wood and bergamot. The scent of the twins. It's amazing how two men are so alike in many ways, but as I'm sucked into their world, they allow me to see, touch, and feel them. They are different and feel things differently. Drav is more emotional, feeling things on a deeper level than his twin brother. Draven is not colder, but harder. He sees things in a practical way. Maybe it is why he is more accepting of his future. He risks himself for the people that he values the most. I notice a piece of paper and my heart skips a beat. It's a letter but from Draven.

Gia,

There are so many stories of happily ever afters—plenty of books written about them. You probably have a favorite. Mine would be the one I want to create with you, the love story you can't find on paper, in a poem, or in a book. It's the one no one could ever find because this one is ours.

Love,

Draven

Tears flow down my cheeks at his beautiful words. The books he must have read in his room.

I don't want to keep him waiting, so I freshen up in the shower while keeping a wary eye on the marble bathtub. I can't help but wonder whether she committed suicide there. At the point at which she made the decision to give up, due to the fact that I now know it was how she ended her life, I won't ever use the bathtub when the twins are around. I would never, ever bring up the painful memories of how their mother died in front of them.

Thinking how horrible that must have been, I'm happy that I will get to see my parents today. Even if they are divorced and my father lives with another woman, I want to look past the hurt and pain my father has caused and my mother's decision to not fight and accept another woman coming between them. She knew that she was breaking up a marriage and that I would be affected in some way, but that didn't stop her. She did what she felt was right for her, and so did my father.

I press the electronic button that turns off the water from the shower and open the glass door, stepping out onto the plush white bath rug, my toes sinking into the luxury carpet. When I step on the tiles to make sure my feet don't slip, I notice the tiles in the bathroom are warm and not cold like I'm used to back home. The luxuries that money can buy are paid for by the souls of the departed. Nothing in life is free, even if you think you got away with it.

I make my way out of the massive bathroom with matching vanities fit for a queen to the right, where the double doors have the gargoyles in the center, watching everything that goes on in this house. I grip the antique brass handle, turn the handle, and pull.

I gasp when the door opens and enter the massive walk-in closet. Just like Miss Jean indicated, there is a hanger with a tiny black lace minidress and a matching silk robe. Not what I expected, but the housekeeper did warn me, and I guess their mother did the same. I touch the necklace hanging from my throat and close my eyes, saying a little prayer for the woman who was gone too soon.

I tie the red sash at my waist and slip into the soft house slippers, with a red mink tickling my toes. I make my way down the hallway toward the stairs. My hand slides down the railing, and my eyes fall on Norman. He looks up at me and nods in silent greeting, and I'm thankful for the robe concealing my body from prying eyes like the staff in the house.

I walk past the living room and pause when I see Draven seated at the head of the table with a red rose in his hand. Flutters form in my stomach when I watch him look at the soft petals like they hold the secrets to his desires. When he notices me, his face brightens. His gaze slowly travels from my feet to my face. He smiles, and I swear my heart skips a beat for a second. Gorgeous. He is utterly gorgeous. He isn't wearing a shirt, and all his muscles are on display like a god seated on a throne.

"Sleep well, gorgeous?"

"Yes, but why did you move me to the room?"

He slides the chair back, and I pinch my brows when I notice there aren't any plates or breakfast served. I point toward the massive table for fifteen. "Where's breakfast? Do you want me to make you something?"

He chuckles and shakes his head. "No, you don't have to cook unless you want to, and to answer your question, I didn't move you to the main bedroom, Drav did."

"Oh," I say, pursing my lips.

Well, that explains why I ended up in bed.

"He's away, taking care of some things. He left early this morning. He will meet us there. After I eat, I'll feed you, and we can get ready to head out. The plane will be ready within the hour for Wisconsin."

I step closer, and he holds his hand out for me, and I take it. He places a kiss on my hand, his lips feeling like soft petals over my skin. His dark hair is falling forward over his brow. The wolf and the raven tattoo are calling out to me from his skin like a three-dimensional mural. I love that they placed the tattoos in such a way that I can tell them apart. They are identical, but I can see through the placement of the tattoos that, if you look really closely, there is a glimpse of a difference in their features. Tattoos can hide things in their bodies, such as birthmarks and minor differences. I researched how it is possible that they look so alike and are identical, and any differences they have, they have mastered the art of looking like each other while hiding it. The Crow is Dravin, and the Wolf is Draven.

He placed the petals from the rose on my skin like the satin already on my skin.

"So, what are you going to eat?"

He gives me a grin and watches a rose petal fall. "You."

CHAPTER FORTY SEVEN
DRAVEN

"WELCOME," Mr. Taylor says when he opens the door to me and Gia.

"Thank you for having us, sir. It is a pleasure meeting you."

He looks at me like I'm fucked in the head, but he doesn't know that I'm a twin. None of them do. I'm dressed to impress. Gia filled me in on the details of what happened when she was here for Thanksgiving with Dravin. I almost showed up to switch with my brother before she knew there were two different men who were interested in her but didn't want to risk it, and Dravin was serious about her.

Their house is a typical modest home. White railings and the white door that most homes have made it seem like a heart-warming family lives there with their two kids and Labrador retriever they call Ben. But I know the truth. This is her father's house, which he shares with his former mistress, Carolyn. No small children and no dog. A house full of hypocrisy.

"I was afraid you all weren't going to make it. Gianna's mother is waiting in the living room."

"My apologies. We had a long breakfast."

Gia's eyes widen, and a cute blush creeps up her cheeks. "Right, baby? It was good, wasn't it?"

Her father swallows, but I think he caught on that I wasn't talking about the eggs or the coffee. He has the same dark features as her hair and eyes, but her other features must belong to her mother.

Her mother is looking at me with a reserved expression, and I remember the hospital. She must feel like we abandoned Gia. We weren't there like we should have been, but that all changed when we almost lost her. My brother and I weren't thinking. We didn't anticipate a threat so severe that it would endanger Gianna in that way.

"Hello, Laurie," I greet her.

Another knock sounds at the door, and Carolyn, her father's girlfriend, watches me with appreciation. I expected it. Laurie glares at her, but Carolyn smiles like she isn't caught. Gia stiffens, and I murmur into her hair while inhaling her flowery scent.

"We'll handle it," I tell her.

The sound of clearing throats and holy shit from her father at the front door has me smiling like the Grinch who stole Christmas.

When Laurie glances behind me, her mouth slacks open. She points behind me at my brother. I turn around and watch as my brother kisses Gia in a sweltering kiss. The silence that falls in the room is almost comical.

My father stands while her father closes the door. "Father." I nod, and he smiles like the devil was just granted permission to enter.

"So, you're twins," Carolyn says, stating the obvious.

The clanking of glasses and utensils scrape the plates at the dinner table. Carolyn insisted on catering a meal because, you know, she is a coldhearted bitch that hates to cook and is fucking her boss behind her father's back. Colin. The same one she tried to put on Gia to hide it. She's a real piece of work, but she's just fucked with what's mine. Now we need order.

"That's right," I answer, eyeing my brother across from me. Gia is seated between me and my father, with Dravin directly across from her. My father hasn't returned to the table, so I can look directly at the home-wrecker. She wreaks havoc on Gia's, and I'll annihilate hers.

"The same name spelled differently. That's..." Carolyn trails off.

"Perfect for Gia. She can't ever forget our names."

"Excuse me?" her father asks, perplexed, his fork in midair crossing his features. The room fell silent.

"Are you trying to say both of you are fucking my daughter?"

My father returns with a flustered Laurie following behind him.

"Excuse me," Laurie says, taking the glass of water off the table and downing it in one go.

"Yeah," Dravin answers.

"Gianna!" her father bellows. "Are you insane?"

"Wow," Carolyn says, staring at her plate with a nervous laugh.

"Laurie, did you know?" her father asks, but she is silent.

"You are all sick, twisted individuals, and I'll not allow you to corrupt my daughter with your filth."

"Dad, I'm a grown woman, and you are the last person to tell me anything," she quips.

"Are we, Mr. Taylor?" I ask, quirking a brow at him.

My father laughs like a puppet master ready to make the puppets dance on their strings. He throws the napkin over his plate. "Touching, Mr. Taylor, but you should be more concerned about what happens in your home than what happens between your daughter's legs; her legs are the ones you shouldn't be concerned about. See, as a rich and powerful man who has raised very rich and powerful sons, I have a few things at my disposal, such as power, connection, wisdom, and a big cock with a big set of balls."

He gets up and buttons the top button on his immaculate black suit jacket. "Your daughter has made a very good decision; she is set for life, and she will produce heirs for the Bedford name, and yes, I meant plural, from whichever son can get my grandson into her belly first. She will marry one, and her lover will be his twin brother. On the other hand, you are no different, fucking a woman while married, then divorcing your wife, breaking your home, and driving your daughter away so that you can act like this." He leans forward and places his hand on the table so his eyes are level with her father's hard glare. "This is for the soap dish I broke while I was fucking your ex-wife Laurie in the bathroom while she milked my cock."

Carolyn gasps, and Gia's head snaps to her mother's flaming red cheeks. I stand up, sliding my hand and tugging on Gia to get her to stand. "We're leaving," I say.

"Good idea," her father snaps. "And take that whore with you."

"How dare you," Laurie seethes, getting up from the table and throwing her napkin.

"Don't call my mother a whore," Gia snarls.

Her father raises his hands. "I'm sorry, Gianna."

Dravin lowers his voice. "Your girlfriend Carolyn is fucking her boss Colin behind your back." He opens his jacket and slides an envelope with pictures of them fucking on the table. "Have a great rest of your day."

"You bitch!" Gianna's father bellows at Carolyn. He lifts the table, flipping it over in a fit of rage.

Fuck with what's mine, and I'll destroy it. I'll lift the world and drop it on their fucking heads.

CHAPTER FORTY EIGHT
GIA

"WHY ARE we going to the church?" I ask.

We're driving toward the school, and it's already nightfall. I'm seated across from the twins, but they are silent since the showdown with my parents at dinner involving my mother and their father. I wonder if Dravin planned it that way, instead of him wanting to meet my parents.

"You'll see," Dravin says. "Just remember, I love you, Gia. Everything we do has a purpose. What happened at your father's house was for you and your mother's benefit."

"My mother?"

"Since the hospital, your mother and my father have been in contact with each other, but that is the first time my father and your mother had sex. I think he planned it that way."

"Why?"

"Because it's what my father wanted. Don't worry, we won't hurt your parents, but Carolyn is a two-faced bitch that needed to be outed that way."

I agree with him on that. The look on my mother's face when Mr. Bedford threw the money for the soap dish on the table was priceless. I bet she couldn't get that satisfaction anywhere. I never thought my mother would be that promiscuous. Good for her.

The driver pulls up to the gated cemetery and opens the rear passenger door. We arrived from Wisconsin three hours ago, and they brought me here. They didn't tell me why we were coming to the church, but I'm curious. Is it a meeting with the Order that I've been mandated to attend?

"Is this a meeting with the Order?" I ask when the door closes behind Dravin.

"No," Dravin says. "We've created a society besides the Order in case there's an attempt to disrupt or annihilate the legacy built by our founding fathers. It is known as the Consortium."

Draven knocks on the door, and it opens; once inside, people wearing black leather plague bird masks with black robes simultaneously turn their heads in our direction. I notice they have white crosses marked on their foreheads with what seems to be ashes, and under the cross, it reads *Sinner*.

When I walk inside behind the twins, my first reaction is to turn my nose up at the putrid smell of a rotting corpse. "Oh, dear God," I say, placing a hand over my mouth.

"Welcome to the Consortium, my love," Dravin says.

WANT A SNEAK PEEK AT HE LOVES ME NOT

PREORDER ON MY WEBSITE FOR THE EBOOK OR PRINT BEFORE IT HITS RETAILERS.

https://carmenrosales.com/shop/

Forbidden love never felt so right...

Rubi Ray struggles to keep her home-life a secret--even from her best friend and soulmate, Ky Reeves. When the two met as children, social and financial differences couldn't deter their friendship and devotion to one another. But Rubi will not dare admit that her family refuses to accept Ky as her "pretty little rich boy" friend--let alone her boyfriend. Day in and day out, she endures the pain and abuse her stepfather inflicts upon her for just one more moment with Ky.

But all good things must come to an end...

When Ky receives a message that Rubi is gone, his anger and abandonment threaten to destroy him. After all of their time together, he deserves more than just a note with a silly symbol of their friendship. Now, it's up to Ky to pick up the pieces of his shattered heart. Was their relationship a simple game of "He loves me; He loves me not?"

HE LOVES ME NOT
SNEAK PEEK CHAPTER

Dear Ky,

I'm sorry. I have to go away and can't see you anymore. It is not your fault. It is mine. I miss you. I hope you get this. You were the best friend ever. I hope to see you some day.

Oh. I forgot super man is better than batman. Pizza hut sucks. The big flat pizza is better.
    Love
    Rubi

I re-read the letter over and over without tearing it. I've balled it up a couple of times and thrown across the room but always pick it up and flatten the lined school paper. It was the last letter that she wrote me before she disappeared, and I never saw her again. I went to the tree house I built with a sheet I took from the hallway linen closet every other day hoping she would show up but all she left me was a letter under a rick with a dried-out flower with a last petal. I kept in a Ziplock bag hidden in one of my favorite comic books featuring Batman. I take it every time I have the same reoc-curring dream I have of her but in the dream she isn't ten years old but the same age as I am. I can't see her face, but I can hear her say my name. When I hear it, I wake up like I'm drowning, and I'm in need of oxygen. The sweat drips over my body like I was bathing in a pool.

I hear a tap on my door as my best friend Chris pushes it opening further.

"Give me a minute."

"Let's go dude. My father's going to go ape shit if I'm late to school," he says.

Chris needs me to give him a ride until his car is out of the shop. He got into a fender bender on the way to school and he's getting it fixed.

I look up raising an eyebrow. "I'll be right out."

He knows the look I give all my friends. The *don't fuck with me drop it* look. I know I have a short temper and I hate giving him attitude, but I also hate repeating myself. My temper started flaring after that day. The day she left me with a sorry letter and wilted flower like that was enough.

I wait until he leaves before folding the old notebook paper and the Ziplock bag away containing the dried flower inside the comic book and place it under my mattress.

Swiping my keys and wallet from my nightstand, I stand and grab the strap of my gym bag and head outside remembering the line that has been plaguing me for the last seven years. *It is not your fault. It is mine. I miss you.*

For years I hoped to see her again. To tell her how I felt as a kid, but I never got the chance. How quickly she could just forget about me only leaving a stupid letter with no real reason.

For the whole year, three times a week we would meet in the woods where her town ended and mine began. We talked about everything a ten-year-old could talk about. It was right behind my father's estate.

My mother left me and my dad abandoning us for another life after my tenth birthday.

It had been raining for a while, and the sky was dark and overcast, and I could still recall the distinct odor of fertilizer mingled with the damp grass. My father standing in the entryway of the mahogany-colored front door, wiping away the tears that were streaming down my face and I knew in that moment; she was never coming back. I would never see her again. I would never smell her lovely perfume and her home-cooked meals would never be mine again.

She stooped until our eye levels were aligned. I would never forget what she said that day. Lips painted mauve as she said, *"it is not your fault sweetheart. It's mine. You're better off with your dad and don't give him a hard time."*

I hiccupped wiping my face not understanding the reason why she was leaving. "Are you coming back? I promise to be good, mommy. I promise," I pleaded.

She gave me the impression that I was bothering her by shaking her head and then straightening while exhaling a breath. She looked up at my father standing behind me with a glare. *"Get him inside Richard. You're making me look bad."*

I turn my body at the waist to look at my father hoping he would tell her not to leave. Not to leave me. I watch him but all he does is nudge his head for me to get inside.

When I turn back to see my mother one last time, she was gone in the awaiting car. She left me. She was gone.

I followed my father inside the massive house devastated. He gave me a stern, emotionless stare before pushing the door shut behind me with the knocker's distinctive thud.

He reached out and put his hand on my shoulder, gazing at my face as he said, *"Don't ever trust a woman with your heart. They will take advantage and then they will abandon you like you meant nothing. Always, remember that."*

After Rubi left her letter, I knew what my father meant was true. I would never forget the way she left me. The way Rubi abandoned me just like my mother.

How quickly they leave by choice because you didn't matter enough. Their promises broken—only to be rewarded with blinding hate. Whatever they left, is just a reminder of how much you meant to them. A reminder of what happens when you go soft.

"Are you going to put the top down?" Chris asks, as he slides in the passenger seat of my matte black BMW M8 convertible.

I place my gym bag in the back leather seat and slip inside the driver's side at the same time shutting the door and press the ignition button with my foot on the brake starting the powerful car.

"Didn't you say you were going to be late and your father was going to go ape shit," I mock.

ABOUT THE AUTHOR

Carmen Rosales is a best-selling Dark Romance and Latinx author. She loves to write in different genres of Romance and erotic horror under her alter ego, Delilah Croww. Beyond her writing, Carmen is a devoted wife and mother who loves spending time with her loved ones. Join her VIP list at www.carmenrosales.com

Join her VIP list- www.carmenrosales.com

Carmen Rosales